T0116979

The Return of Marie Joelle

Christiane Angibeau-Thompson

iUniverse, Inc.
New York   Bloomington

iUniverse books may be ordered through booksellers or by contacting:

iUniverse
1663 Liberty Drive
Bloomington, IN 47403
www.iuniverse.com
1-800-Authors (1-800-288-4677)

ISBN: 978-1-4502-1469-8 (sc)
ISBN: 978-1-4502-1470-4 (hc)
ISBN: 978-1-4502-1471-1 (ebk)

Printed in the United States of America

iUniverse rev. date: 3/12/2010

To my beloved Grandparents and my beloved Pets

PART I

CHAPTER 1

"WHAT IS THE matter with you this afternoon, Clothilde?" asked Elise glancing at her wristwatch. "You seem to be in a strange mood. Since we have met, almost half an hour ago, you have only said a few words. Why are you so nervous and why do you repeatedly look over your shoulders? have you seen a ghost, or expect to see one at any moment?"

Clothilde started as if she had been suddenly disturbed from a state of deep reflection. She shook her head, cast a quick, uneasy glance at her surroundings and half focused, looked at Elise. She did not mean to be unmindful of her friend's company. However, all she could deal with at this moment, was to brood over the inner turbulence precipitated by a very unusual incident she had come upon earlier in the day. Relentlessly, her puzzled brain searched for answers through a maddening maze of contradictions, but all in vain.

Up to this disturbing experience, she had thought herself secured in a contented provincial way of life well planned, seemingly predictable and likely to provide her with a pleasant future sheltered from risky circumstances. Now, nothing made sense. On the verge of tears, she drew a heavy sigh, and with a quivering voice, she apologized.

"Forgive me Elise, it is not my intention to ignore you, but something has happened to me; something very bizarre."

"What happened? Please, tell me at once what this is all about," urged Elise, now unable to contain her mounting anxiety.

Clothilde growing more restless shifted her position to better face Elise.

"I don't know how to explain it. How can I tell you? How can I explain something I don't understand myself? It makes absolutely no sense," she replied irritated by her jumbled thinking.

Elise too pressed by impatience, overlooked her friend's reticence.

"What is it that you can't explain? Are you withholding some drastic news from me? When we spoke on the phone this morning, you were so elated at the thought to see Jean Luc again and to meet his American friend. What has changed since then? Please tell me. Does it concern Philippe? . . Is he. . ?"

"Everyone is fine," interrupted Clothilde nodding affirmatively to reassure Elise. "Please, don't worry yourself."

Clothilde Tremonges had just reached her twenty-third birthday last May. Elise Duchesne was not quite three months her junior. Their families belonging among the excellence of the provincial gentry, since generations past had bonded in a profound friendship. The two girls became aware of each other's existence on this planet when still in the cradle, while their mothers visited daily to share the joy of motherhood. Both being an only child, they were raised together like siblings. Pride in their lineage and the finest local traditions strongly influenced by their Catholic creed, had shaped their fundamental character. Even as they grew older, they remained inseparable. When in grammar school, they boarded at the same convent. Later on, they shared a small apartment while they pursued their education at the university. Clothilde earned a Bachelor degree in Art History; likewise, Elise graduated in Western Philosophy. However, it was from the library of her paternal grandfather who had been a professor of philosophy at the Sorbonne that Elise learned the most and progressively molded her own system of thought, which her more conservative friends often considered too avant-garde or even too uncanny.

Neither of the two girls could have possibly contemplated to part from one another and from their most cherished ancestral legacies. They had enjoyed traveling extensively over the European continent, yet, not once had they been tempted to move away from home. Because, Grolejac, their beloved village embedded in the heart of the magnificent Dordogne valley, in southwestern France, to them would forever seem the most beautiful place on earth.

They were lovely young women.

Clothilde was tall and svelte. Her thick chestnut hair reached down a little below shoulder level and framed her oval face delicately accentuated by high cheekbones. Her ivory-white skin enhanced the deep, velvety darkness of her intelligent eyes. Her mouth, softly delineated, integrated perfectly with all her features. Her entire persona embodied a flawless grace, which bore the stamp of good breeding.

By contrast, Elise was more cherub-like. The colors nature had bestowed upon her seemed to have been inspired by the palette of Fra Angelico. Her eyes appeared larger than they really were, due to the subjectivity conveyed by their blue, as if they had the capacity to absorb the infinity of the sky. She wore her flaxen blond hair short, in loose natural curls that bounced mischievously close to her pretty round face. She was slender, and about the same height as Clothilde. Her deportment could have been mistaken for a haughty pretense, but it was nothing other than the self-assurance of a young woman soundly in accord with herself.

While Clothilde was at the grip of her perplexing situation, she and Elise were sitting side by side on a stone bench, at the edge of a meadow fringing a pebble beach gently slanting towards the Dordogne. It was a Saturday afternoon on the fourteenth of July. They waited for Jean Luc Ganzac, Clothilde's first cousin; their mothers were sisters. To fulfill the requirements of his military obligation, Jean Luc had been assigned to the French Liaison at the American Air base of Dreux, in the Department of Eure-et-Loir, near Paris, when the American occupation was still maintained in France during the first years of the 1960s.

Late during the previous night, Jean Luc accompanied by a guest, had come home to spend a weekend leave. A few months before, he had befriended with Paul Earlston, who as a young psychiatrist at the base hospital, was also serving his country and those among his fellowmen distraught by homesickness. On his visit to Grolejac, Jean Luc eager to introduce Paul to his family had invited him along. But being an enthusiastic tiller of the soil, Jean Luc was much eager also to share with his friend, all the many reasons why he felt such a passionate love for his village and for the land of his patriarchal estate *la Madrigale,* because, Paul also had an ardent interest in farming and rural living.

Clothilde and Elise had decided to meet a little sooner than at the time Jean Luc and Paul were due to arrive. They had so much to discuss.

The museum of local history they were in the process of organizing needed their joined attention. Moreover, to consider those exciting new ideas concerning the reception for Clothilde's engagement to Phillippe was no less important. It had been planned to be given soon after Phillippe would return from Egypt, where since last May; he had gone in quest of data for his thesis in archaeology. However, as the day had unfolded, other preoccupations had intruded into Clothilde's mind.

Summer was then thriving in Grolejac. Under the warm weather, the river having fully recovered from a long winter ennui had lowered its water. Now, sparkling beaches of pearly white pebbles cheerfully meandered like a radiant smile amid luxuriant expanses of alluvial terrain and grandiose gorges. The summit of the highest ridges were flooded with sunshine and gloriously paraded ruin after ruin of majestic feudal fortresses, heroically standing near superb castles from a less remote period. Down the slopes, colorful medieval villages, ancient abbeys, churches and monasteries snuggled in the dense foliage. Only the nearby caves where prehistoric men had dwelt were well shielded against the sunlight, to protect their famous wall and ceiling paintings. While one beheld so many splendors, it did not take much effort to visualize the knights of the land, astride their valiant armored horses, as they dashed home with passion in their eyes, to relate the mad sagas of frenzied rivalries. Neither was it difficult to recreate in one's mind the flamboyant pageant of a seigniorial wedding. No doubt, at dawn, from the monks of long ago, one could have clearly heard the Gregorian chants rising in duets with the songs of the larks. If quite attentive, it would have been possible also, to shed a tear over the troubadour's lovesick laments, which seemed to still echo across the valley.

Facing Clothilde and Elise, at the opposite side of the river, high on a plateau, a late Renaissance chateau was only perceivable by its windows glittering through the foliage. Next to it, above the tallest trees, loomed the belfry of the twelfth century village church. Below, from a cluster of houses huddled by the waterfront, rose the gay voices and laughter of children playing in the streets. Small fishing barges anchored to stone blocks, lazily swayed in the current.

Clothilde and Elise avoided to look on their left further upstream, where the river narrowed into a strait called the *Chambre,* due to a forbidding hollowness in the rugged acclivity. Occasionally, their glance unwillingly strayed toward the calm, emerald green water, which below and in front of the overhanging boulders, deceitfully glistened like a polished mirror. Nevertheless, it ran deep and troubled over bottomless crevices in the rocks beneath. The treacherous undercurrents, gathering in lethal whirlpools, mercilessly snatched boats, canoes, swimmers and all. To Clothilde and Elise, this area now seemed like a sinister abyss stirring too many painful memories that would forever haunt their heart. It was there, that three years since, at the age of seventeen, Philippe's sister, Marie Joelle, had tragically lost her life.

On their right, a magnificent white bridge resting its weight upon Herculean piers, sent forth its slender yet robust upper structure soaring towards the infinite, with the gracefulness of a swan in flight. Then further downstream, the Dordogne flowed past the arches of a timeless Roman viaduct, and finally disappeared in the forest. However, before long, it would reflect again the picturesque towns, villages and enchanting landscapes bordering its waterway.

Inland, at close distance behind them, a clubhouse encircled by elms, birches and willows trees, provided refreshments in the afternoon. During the warm season, on weekends, young and not so young would come there to be entertained by concerts of popular music, which would keep many dancing merrily until all hours of the night. At the back was a tennis court, and beyond the farmland stretched far towards the horizon. The scents of cut grass, ripen fruits and fresh running water mingled in a rich pastoral fragrance.

Tourists from more northern countries always came here yearly to spend their summer vacations. Some returned more than once, renting cottages, villas or bungalows for several months. On this particular afternoon, throng and throng of people had joyfully flocked to the beaches. A Babel like cacophony of different languages rose in joyous clamor and then bounced all over the canyon. One could have thought that half the world had gathered there to celebrate with France the downfall of the Bastille. Explosions of energy radiated from everywhere. All along the river, the water splashed in iridescent crystal jets. Through their transparency, the dispersed light converted them into splattering rainbows that dissolved in shimmering vapor. Even the air had taken a dynamism of its own, as if all at once too electrified, it had imploded on itself. Myriads of released particles almost palpable like pulverized gems whirled toward the sky spanning the earth with a turquoise dome supported by the four horizons.

CHAPTER 2

"Yes, EVERYTHING IS fine," Clothilde, repeated. "Phillippe phoned last night after you left. He sounded as enthusiastic as ever concerning his work ... but there was something slightly different about him."

Not giving more details, Clothilde bent forward to pick up a pebble from the ground and in a frustrated gesture; she hurled it toward the beach. Elise watched it bounce to a stop and then turned a curious gaze toward Clothilde.

"What do you mean by different?"

"Oh, he seemed somewhat vague or even elusive at times and occasionally there would be awkward silences. I can't be specific."

"Is that what's bothering you?" Elise asked with a concerned expression.

Clothilde took a moment to think before answering.

"Not really. Anyway, it might just be my imagination ... and all is well with Jean Luc. He and his friend have arrived safely, as I have already told you."

Apparently satisfied to have put Elise at ease, Clothilde ventured in no further explanation. Her eyes followed a flock of birds flying aloft toward the hilltop, and then she again withdrew behind a somber mutism.

She was sincere when she apologized for her unsociable attitude. All the same, it did not prevent her from slipping into another refusal to communicate. She could not help it though. At this point, her ability for logical reasoning was severely impaired. She felt helplessly immobilized, like raging water trapped behind an insurmountable dam.

Too many others, what Clothilde had confronted might have passed as an unusual incident, a bit peculiar perhaps, but nothing to obsess about. However, due to her nature, Clothilde could not welcome it so lightheartedly. She was still the fixed sum of an upbringing rigorously structured upon valued traditions and principles she had until then unconditionally accepted. Most of them had turned into deeply engrained convictions, which gave her a sense of security and permanence. She had never questioned whether they would be applicable to the intrinsic demands necessary for the realization of her separate selfhood. As a result, she found herself thrust into an inward schism, which totally rocked her emotional and spiritual equilibrium. She was unprepared to grasp that she had begun an inevitable process of individuation into her very own destined uniqueness, quickened by new inputs, new dimensions, and a complexity of mysterious but fascinating forces, she yet rejected. Indeed, how could she understand all of this, when having to contend with so much antagonism between her reason and her emotions? Moreover, she had been intolerably impatient to confide in Elise, who had not been available. Well, Elise was beside her now, why then was she incapable to utter a single word? How could she unravel the least thread of sense out of all this?

At this point Elise chose not to press matters further, thus allowing her friend more time to reflect and she hoped, soon recover from her unusual state of mind. In an effort to dispel her insufferable apprehension, she got up to take a walk along the beach. For the first time she felt alienated from Clothilde. Had an uncanny and silent rift maliciously crept between them? Lost in thought, she had carelessly drifted all the way to the *Chambre*. Memories of Marie joelle gushed to her mind. Tears blurred her vision. "What was this all about? Was fate once again knocking at Clothilde's door, at their door? For what affected one affected the other. Was life cautioning "wake up both of you! wake up! look me in the face, because I have no intention of sparing either one of you the full portion of your due misery!" At once, Elise repelled a gloomy presentiment and hurried back to Clothilde. Without saying a word, she had barely brushed against the bench, when inexplicably and at long last Clothilde broke the silence.

"I……..Well….I…..I am ashamed of myself," she announced pitiably, with her eyes fixed upon the grass spreading in front of her.

"What?" cried Elise, astonished by such an unexpected statement.

Clothilde automatically stole a rapid glance right and left, lest they had attracted the attention of an indiscreet ear.

"Hush!" she promptly interjected, bidding Elise to calm down.

"My dear friend, of what are you so badly ashamed?" Elise asked in a lower tone of voice.

"I believe I carry within me the seeds of an adulteress," Clothilde confessed in a whisper, as she leaned toward Elise who drew back a little while frowning with stupefaction.

Clothilde once again tossed around a nervous glance. Confident that no one had violated her privacy; she sighed into a more relaxed posture and gave Elise a rueful smile.

"I came across someone this morning. I came across a young man. I don't know who he is. I have never spoken with him. I have never seen him before."

Clothilde paused. She needed to gather all her courage.

"Yes, go on," directed Elise.

Clothilde abashed by what she was about to openly admit, gazed at the ground spreading in front of her.

"Ever since then, I can't get him out of my mind." so saying, she lowered her brow, then turned expectantly at Elise and waited as it were, for some kind of shocked response.

"This is what disturbs you so terribly?" asked Elise still perplexed, not convinced yet that only this could cause such a great deal of anguish.

"Yes!" stressed Clothilde, overtly implicating "isn't it enough?" Somehow, Elise's undisturbed reaction amazed her.

"Well, I never!" Elise could only exclaim when she discovered that no serious threat was hovering over their head. Elated by relief, an irrepressible joy lightened her spirit.

"Is he handsome?" she inquired in a playful manner. Not that she was amused by, or insensitive to Clothilde's feelings, but mainly, because of a desire to dissipate the tension, which had built up between them, and the need to vent her own inhibited uneasiness.

"Really Elise!" Clothilde protested while affecting a prim demeanor.

"Well is he?" insisted Elise, encouraged by a sudden sparkle in Clothilde's eyes.

"All right, yes he is a very handsome young man," conceded Clothilde as her facial expression softened. Appalled by her self-absorption, she was ready to comply with good grace.

"Do you wish to know him, are you attracted to him?" Elise went on good-humoredly.

"Why no! . . Well, yes … yes, I am intrigued … I should like to know more about him. Yes, in some way I am attracted to him. But no … no, it is not simply a physical attraction. There is something much deeper between us, much more disturbing. A feeling … Oh! How can I tell you?" Clothilde tentatively made the effort to clarify.

"Let me see," Elise resumed. "If I understand correctly, you declare that you don't know this person, this young man. You have never seen him before. You have never spoken with him, yet, you believe there is already a *deep something* between the two of you?"

Having summed up Clothilde's account of her adventure, needless to say, Elise observed instantly that a total absence of logical progression by which, usually consequences unfold from causes was evident. The order of things did not seem quite as it ought to be. That was of course, if considered from a mainstream point of view. She took a moment to examine further her thoughts.

"Yes, I know," said Clothilde, answering what she assumed to have guessed in the silence. "I know. Some people are declared deranged for much lesser reasons. However, this has instantly awakened a cluster of unconceivable emotions and Elise; I have no idea what to do with them."

"I think you have had an encounter with someone from your past." Elise stated, as though she had finally put the puzzle together and it all made sense.

What?" questioned Clothilde with a frown creased by more confusion.

"I mean, I think you have had an encounter with someone you knew in a past life. To me it is as simple as that." Elise rephrased to be specific.

"Elise, please, don't add more absurdity to a situation already insane enough as it is," Clothilde rejected categorically.

CHAPTER 3

CLOTHILDE STOOD UP, loosened her posture, and paced back and forth upon the grass. Although she had been sitting on that bench for only a little over an hour, it seemed she had been glued to it forever. She felt like an Etruscan statue stepping down from the lid of a sarcophagus. Elise rose also and looked at the tree under which they had enjoyed a pleasant shade. Due to the sun changing position, now the branches cast their shadow away from them.

"Let's take a walk," Clothilde proposed pointing to nowhere in particular. Their differences concerning each one's otherworldly convictions, as always when occasionally voiced, were soon forgotten. Again, Clothilde was eager to share with Elise, in far more details, how she met with this disturbing experience, whereas Elise was no less impatient to hear all about it.

They made a detour to the Club House for a glass of iced water. After they struggled their way out through a boisterous crowd and greeted a few friends passing them by, they immediately set foot in an alley of aspens, winding far off downstream along the riverbank.

"Now then, tell me please when, where, how all this happened?" Elise asked without delay as they began to leisurely stroll. I should like to know before Jean Luc and Paul arrive, for I couldn't bear much longer the torment of more suspense. Besides, my understanding might improve much for that.

Clothilde looked in the distance and drew a long sigh.

"This morning …" she attempted to explain, sending a sideway glance at Elise. "Well, this morning, after our phone conversation, I drove to Sarlat to pick up an ointment for grand papa's sprained wrist."

"Yes," said Elise, listening attentively.

As I walked out of the pharmacy, he, this young man walked in. We stopped and like if immobilized by an invisible force, we faced each other utterly baffled. I could not avoid noticing how handsome he was. Tall, I am sure above six feet, his brown hair was cut short but one could notice the suggestion of some waves by his temples. He had the deepest blue-green eyes. He somewhat reminded me of those Grecian shepherds depicted in the bucolic scenes from antiquity. You know what I mean?"

Elise nodded.

"After I regained some countenance, I still stood ther embarrassed, not knowing why this had happened. I perceived a similar awkwardness in him. He recovered his composure faster than I did, then he gave me a kind smile and went on his way. I remained behind blushing like a woman who had been publicly undressed. I then drifted aimlessly on the sidewalk. I was so disturbed by such a bizarre encounter, by my inconceivably odd response to it, and so confounded by the intense feelings it stirred in me, that I did not see what I was looking at. When I reached the public park, I found a quiet area, sat on the grass to consider and reconsider every minute detail I could possibly remember from this incredible episode. Although I had never seen him before, I had it seemed a certain unspecified remembrance of him, a peculiar impression that we already knew each other. Was it because of an association with someone else I have been acquainted with, but could not bring to mind? Was I dramatizing a simple incident out of proportions? But why did he react in the same manner as I did? Ah, Elise, so many questions leading to no answers!"

Clothilde slowed down her pace almost to a stop and faced Elise.

"Are you still with me?" she then asked, clearly coming out of her own separate world.

"Of course!" Elise reassured. She then checked her watch to verify if they had yet plenty of time available before the arrival of Jean Luc and Paul.

"Well after a while of vain pondering," Clothilde went on, as she moved forward, "I ordered myself to set aside my obstinate thoughts, so that I may reexamine them later on with a refreshed mind. Thereupon I got up, brushed the dry blades of grass from my clothes, and proceeded in direction of my car. Passing by the library, I decided to go inside. Elise, with what amazement I found him seated in the lobby, reading a magazine."

They had arrived almost to the end of the lane. Elise took hold of Clothilde's elbow and motioned her to turn around.

"He noticed me," Clothilde continued without interruption. "We exchanged a smile. Elise, his smile spoke a thousand words. I wish I knew what they said. I randomly pulled out any book at my reach and with a trembling hand checked it out. I didn't dare to look at him again. I flew by with my eyes fastened on the front door and hurried away."

Clothilde paused.

"And so, you never spoke with each other?" Elise inquired, wondering if Clothilde's saga had ended as such.

"No, but I drove home thinking of nothing else but him. When I arrived at the house, no one was there. Relieved to be alone, I lay on my bed, beset by puzzlements and completely exhausted. As I began to doze, waves of merging and dissolving appearances of this stranger passed through my mind then diffusely slipped away. I could grasp none of them. It was like trying to catch the depth of the ocean between my fingers."

Clothilde looked at Elise and shook her head.

"Elise, have you ever had ... ? Oh! My God! Look! Elise, look!" she abruptly exclaimed, as her eyes had drifted upon the colorful crowd.

"What is it?" Elise inquired. She scanned their vicinity, not knowing what to look for.

"Well, look!" Clothilde insisted, pointing towards the white bridge.

"Oh yes, there is Jean Luc! Let's hurry," urged Elise as she caught sight of Clothilde's tall, dark haired, charismatic cousin decisively advancing in their direction.

"Holy Virgin!" Cried out Clothilde squinting to better focus on who really was with Jean Luc. "Oh! Elise, look who is with him!"

"Who?" Elise asked, curiously staring also in direction of Jean Luc.

"The ... The stranger I came upon this morning ... the young man I ... "Oh dear God! He and Jean Luc seem to be together. They are walking side by side, talking to each other. I see no one else with Jean Luc."

Clothilde dumbfounded stared at her friend.

"Why are you so quiet, Elise? Say something. Are you thinking what I am thinking? Could it be ... ? Could it be that ... ?"

"Mother of Jesus! Clothilde exclaimed while trying to tame her excitement by taking several deep breaths.

She had not so earnestly invoked the Holy Virgin since her days in the convent, when she implored time to flee away so she could go home. She tapped her cheeks with the tip of her fingers to bring back some color. Was there still blood in her vein? She felt like it had all drained away.

Thank goodness! A friend accosted Jean Luc, and detain him for a short while. It allowed Clothilde to rally a certain calmness; but even so, not understanding why, she could not stop her heart either from sinking to the center of the earth's bosom or soaring high above in the ethers, wherever heaven was for her at that moment.

"What a strange coincidence!" she uttered without being much aware of what she was saying.

"This could not be a coincidence," stated Elise under a spell of amazement.

They quickly assumed an easy poise to welcome Jean Luc and Paul who were now approaching.

CHAPTER 4

"HELLO! HELLO! MY beautiful ones!" Jean Luc greeted, as they all blithely embraced. Paul was introduced in the midst of their emotional outburst. Once more, they embraced; they voiced their happiness to see each other again.

Clothilde having recognized Paul from afar, and Jean Luc's having been delayed by his acquaintances, had given her some time to regain a certain composure before their reunion. But when Paul caught unawares, found himself facing her, and furthermore learnt that she was Jean Luc's cousin, all his senses froze. His sanity faulted for an indefinable length of time, due to some uncanny defense mechanism mercifully providing him with a shrewd strategy to survive the shock. Although he showed no outward signs of astonishment, he maintained his self-possession with great difficulty. The cumulative singularities of this day, had already reached a level pervasive enough to drive any sound mind to the verge of madness. An avalanche of questions had begun to prove themselves inapplicable when seeking out rational answers. If it had not been for the sake of discretion, he would not have taken his eyes off her, so much he was eager to grasp a certain something; anything that might throw a light upon such a mystifying combination of circumstances.

All the while, Clothilde also abstained from the temptation to gaze at him beyond the dictate of good manners. Naturally, through a silent understanding, both sensed that each was conscious of what had previously happened between them at Sarlat. However, now and then, Paul's eyes irresistibly swept over her like a gentle touch stroking the outline of a delicate work of art.

She looked beautiful. She wore white shorts and a pale yellow sleeveless blouse, which heightened the healthy glow of her suntan. Her hair parted in the middle, fell naturally along her face.

"Who is she really this exquisite young woman?" he wondered.

Jean Luc had extensively and fondly spoken to him about her, however, Paul could have never imagined that if one day he should meet her, she would elicit so great a fascination to his soul.

"Who is she really? Who is she beyond all this? Why do I have that impossible impression to know her when I have just become acquainted with her?" he asked himself repeatedly. It seemed that in her presence, new inexplicable emotions flared to his awareness from an unknown depth, and inundated his heart with delight.

"Shall we all go and sit under this tree?" Jean Luc proposed as he pointed to an enormous weeping willow that invitingly spread its shade over a patch of soft grass. He then offered cold drinks. Everyone accepted readily and thereupon along with Paul, he went to order a tray of refreshments. Wordless, Clothilde and Elise moved under the tree while they interrogated each other's eyes. Both had the same recondite riddle on their mind: "what exactly is the significance of all this?"

"Who knows? Fate does not always make sense to our perception." Elise stated in reply to their unspoken question.

Clothilde gazed into the depth of space, into the unknown. She could not remember to have yet seen a summer sky so vast, so beautifully blue.

"What?" she asked oblivious to what Elise had just said.

Jean Luc and Paul returned. They all sat on the ground, forming a circle. They had not completely settled themselves with drink in hand, when at once Jean Luc opened the conversation.

"By the bye Clothilde, Grandmaman, Grandpapa and your mother came to the house this morning. They arrived just as Paul and I were about to leave for Sarlat to have my car checked, for last night a couple of miles before we reached home, the engine started to make a suspicious sound. Of course, we had the intention to make a detour on our way and give all of you a quick hug, however, they were ahead of us. They had the opportunity to be acquainted briefly with Paul. He kindly volunteered to take the car to a mechanic himself so I could spend some extra time with them. I am pleased to know that grandpapa's wrist is healing well. I expected to see you appear from somewhere, until I was told you had gone on some errands.

"Ah! This is why he was in Sarlat this morning!" Clothilde mused. She and Paul exchanged a flash glance noticeably allusive to their first encounter.

Jean Luc sitting on Clothilde's left gave a gentle pull at her hair.

"Have you good news from Phillippe, since I last spoke with you?"

Clothilde assumed a casual composure.

"Yes, very good. He phoned yesterday.

Jean Luc took Clothilde's left hand in both of his.

"So, is the merrymaking day still in September, no change?"

"Probably," replied Clothilde. She looked down at the trampled grass by her feet. Why was she afraid that she might blush?

"As I have told you already," Jean Luc reminded Paul, "my dear cousin here is quite near a serious commitment."

Every one had understood that Jean Luc had referred to the celebration of Clothilde's betrothal to Phillippe. As a result, Paul felt struck by a violent sensation, much like a darting fear. To master it, required a will power he was unaware to have within reserve.

"What had taken hold of him? Thank God again, it had been indiscernible by his company," he observed. He was a man who without boasting had always considered himself reasonably in control of his emotions. "What was this all about?" Luckily, he was able to feign and uphold a certain poise while congratulating Clothilde.

Elise aware of Clothilde's uneasiness and focus of immediate concern took it upon herself to direct the conversation toward other topics. The opportunity was as good as ever by drawing their attention to Paul.

"Well, now it is time we know more about you, Paul," she said gaily with the prettiest blue twinkle in her eyes. "But to begin, Clothilde and I wish to welcome you as our friend also."

"Thank you Elise for your graciousness and thank you Clothilde," he acknowledged with recovered ease.

Clothilde acquiesced amiably. She made a swift movement of her hand against the side of her face, like sweeping a strand of hair away from it. She was actually rallying all her self-assurance to challenge that untimely nervousness, which inhibited her from acting natural.

She wanted to be as comfortable with Paul as she would be in the company of any one else.

"You must be heartsick for your homeland, Paul," she ventured to ask with an ostensible poise that strove to regain her habitual social grace.

"Yes, at times, I have longed for home. However, I also feel very privileged to have been stationed in France. It is indeed a beautiful country, and I consider myself even more fortunate now from being so warmly received into your kind family."

Paul paused and directed a smile toward Jean Luc.

"I am very grateful to you."

Jean Luc nodded.

"It is my pleasure. You are very welcome my friend. I wish it would have been sooner."

Clothilde looked down to conceal an uncontrollable sadness, for Jean Luc had told her already that Paul's sojourn in France had now ended. Elise understood and again came to her rescue by taking on the conversation.

"Tell us please, about your life in the United States. Is it much different there than it is here? We have been acquainted with people of diverse nationalities and cultures, but we haven't yet met anyone from America."

It was with an engaging accent that Paul spoke fluent French. Upon Elise's request followed by a horde of questions, he began to relate that he was born and raised in Santa Barbara, California. He had neither brother nor sister. His father had taught mathematics at the University of California, until he lost his life in a private plane crash five years past. His mother, Isabelle owned a very chic fashion boutique on State Street. During World War II a German raid had slain her parents in Paris. A few years back she had inherited a farm in France, left to her by an uncle and an aunt. It was located near Chartres, in the Beauce region, and now in the care of dependable tenants.

From his father's ancestry, English, Irish and Dutch blood ran in his veins. His mother was authentically French and very Parisian. His father had met her when as a young man he was called on duty at the American embassy in Paris where she worked as well.

To satisfy Clothilde who inquired about Santa Barbara, Paul described briefly how the town elegantly unfolded its Spanish-style architecture and luxurious vegetation against a mountain slope bordering the beach, along the Pacific coast.

When Elise inquired if he intended to stay in the Air Force? Paul's answer was a categorical no. Yet he had not made any subsequent plans. It would all depend upon the options offered by his work, which at this point was also indefinite.

While Clothilde listened to him, she found herself swayed by his every word, by his every smile, by his every gesture.

She observed that the limpid transparency of his eyes revealed subtly a profound sensitivity, and his facial expressions suggested a centered, discerning intelligence. His voice was pleasantly masculine. There was something substantial about him; something genuine. She also perceived him as a very private man, reserved, sober in his taste and manners.

She was encircled by his presence.

As he spoke time stood still. The bustle of the crowd had become only a distant murmur. Driven by a surge of unutterable sentiments, she felt a strange desire to sit close to him and hold his hand. Simply hold his hand, that was all.

CHAPTER 5

AFTER A SHORT while, Paul concluded that he had sufficiently talked about himself. He had not much more to say anyway.

"I hope one day, I shall have the pleasure to welcome you on my side of the world," he said sincerely, as he brought to a close a brief version of his life story.

Everyone received his invitation with unrestrained exhilaration. Paul let his gaze glide over the vast surrounding view. In one deep breath it seemed, he absorbed the scents, the sounds, the color, and the scenery, which so gloriously offered themselves to all his senses.

"This is … truly beautiful," he stated while he once more appreciatively took a sweeping view of the landscape. "Jean Luc, I perfectly understand now, why you speak with such deep attachment about *"Your country"* as you call it."

Jean Luc beamed proudly as though he were the First Cause who had conceived such a magnificent creation.

Answering to his life call, Jean Luc had graduated as an engineer in agronomics. The termination of his military duty seemed like a mirage in the infinity of time. As a lover would long to entwine with his beloved, he yearned feverishly to reunite again with his patriarchal land. He hungered for the fragrance of its soil, for its bucolic rapture, for the throbbing of its womb to bring forth new births, for the harmonious merging between nature and species in the rhythm of life.

"Ah, and I still have almost three more years to suffer the anguish of exile," he bemoaned emphatically, in reply to Paul's comment. He tried to introduce a little humor by over dramatizing his lot. It was his way to sneer at the inevitable.

"Poor Jean Luc!" Elise whimpered by simulating an excess of empathy. They all joined her by looking at him with exaggerated commiseration.

"Moreover, to make matter worse," Jean Luc complained further with a heavy sigh of exasperation while he pointed at Elise. "This young lady here throws me in thousands of torments. I have eternally been in love with her, and have longed for her with a burning desire, ever since the moment I opened my eyes on this world. She persistently declines all my proposals of marriage. She is impossible!"

"Oh yes, I have heard about this!" Paul said, smiling at Elise.

Elise laughed heartily.

"Jean Luc! I was not born when you first opened your dazzling eyes."

Jean Luc expressed amusement at her teasing flattery.

"But I knew you would be. It had been seriously discussed by our souls before I returned on this earth, that I should wait for you," he reminded Elise by teasingly alluding to her concept of rebirth.

Elise feigned a moment of deep concentration, as if trying to retrieve a long forgotten memory.

"Now that you bring it to my mind, I thought that your voice sounded familiar when I first heard it."

Jean Luc tossed her an expression charged with simulated reprimand.

"Now, don't be sarcastic. Furthermore, Clothilde and I have always dreamed for a double wedding, if you do not wish to marry me for myself, at least consent to it to please Clothilde!"

"Jean Luc!" again exclaimed Elise, in the midst of joined laughter. "Your wit shall forever amaze me! Besides, you are much too handsome. I could not measure against the competition. By the way, has someone told you yet that your ardent paramour Therese has said "I do" last week to someone from Bordeaux? She cried all the way down the church aisle, calling your name."

Jean Luc chuckled.

"Oh, well, we were not intended to be together, I mean Therese and I. Undoubtedly I must have been spared to be available for you when in due time you will change your mind," he jested. An irresistible mischievous smile filtered through his facial expression, suggesting that he knew a certain secret all in his favor, but it had not yet been unsealed to Elise.

"Ah, who knows? We can't change what could not be otherwise, " Elise answered with good cheer. She pulled a handful of grass and scattered it back on the ground. She then unconsciously looked at Clothilde, and as if wanting to caution her that some unforeseen developments might be awaiting her, she added in an impulse, "Fate alone shall ultimately decide and quite often to achieve its own purpose, it artfully twists us into the most perplexing dilemmas."

"Yes indeed, I know what you mean," approved Jean Luc, "and lately I have had my share of those."

Paul had been pleasantly intrigued while listening to Elise's determinism in her playful interchange with Jean Luc. When it was brought to a close, Clothilde briefly moved her eyes in his direction and caught him looking at her. She was able to notice that he had yielded to a pensive mood. She immediately lowered her head and looked away pretending to be distracted by the frantic uproar of the swimmers and divers.

"Had the conversation reminded him of someone? perhaps of a beloved he has left behind in the United States, and like Jean Luc, he is not sure if his devotion is reciprocated?" she questioned.

This thought provoked a strange heaviness in her heart. She at once made the effort to suppress it. How could she accept a feeling that so threatened her integrity? Thank God, Jean Luc diverted her from these bothersome contemplations when he turned to her as though he suddenly wondered where she had been for the last hour or so.

"Clothilde, my darling, you are very quiet, do you miss Phillippe? Now cheer up! He will soon be back with us again."

She started from this unexpected concern.

"Oh, no … Well, yes … But … Oh, I … I was listening … I am fine."

"Good!" Jean Luc said enthusiastically. He laid his right arm around her shoulders.

"Now what else is happening besides Therese *"eloping"* to Bordeaux with her husband without my knowing?"

CHAPTER 6

On EACH OF his return home, Jean Luc always received a thoroughly detailed account of the events, which had developed in Grolejac during his absence. However, at his return inevitably, everyone had still a great amount to tell him about recent weddings, divorces, births and all kind of happenings in his family and in his friend's life; some of which even if imparted earlier on, were yet repeated with abundant details.

As Clothilde and Elise unfailingly related in a colorful chronicle the joys and sorrows of the villagers to Jean Luc, they assured themselves that they did not ostracize Paul like an outsider. Therefore, they tactfully drew him in the conversation, and soon he found himself quite fascinated.

Once everything about so and so, and how and when had been covered to their satisfaction, it was Paul who in turn became the object of their concern. Although Jean Luc had acquainted him to the area, they deemed it apropos that if in such a short visit, time regretfully did not allow him a thorough excursion of their region, they nevertheless would give him a verbal grand tour of the countless diversities of its historical magnificence. They proudly took him through the centuries, all the way back to their prehistoric ancestors. He marveled at the architecture of the different periods and delighted in the noble epics of chivalry along with the adventurous romance of the troubadours.

Clothilde could have gone on and on sharing with him her love and respect for such legacy; what in due course led Paul to ask questions pertinent to the museum Clothilde and Elise were setting in order. They readily gave him a notion of their desire to reawaken a cultural awareness and an appreciation of those rare treasures surrounding them and taken for granted by too many. For this purpose, Clothilde's family had put at their disposal her paternal grand parents'house, which dated from late seventeenth century. It offered the ideal locale, situated on a hilltop over looking the Dordogne. In fact, they could see it very clearly from where they sat. A well-documented collection of epochal artifacts ranging from the Stone Age to the Nazi invasion would display quite a succinct anthology, so to speak, of the history pertaining to the Period.

An audiovisual room would accommodate the projection of slides showing all the wonderwork of nature and man, which had flourished through the centuries. It would otherwise require an array of books to describe it fully and justly.

They also expressed to Paul, their wish to initiate a revival of the ancient songs and ballads together with a delightfully melodious dialect called the *"patois,"* still spoken by the oldest generations, but at great risk of being abandoned as antiquated.

Jean Luc emphasized that Clothilde and Elise having an adequate knowledge of other foreign languages besides English, would be a great asset to interact culturally with a broad variety of the yearly tourists.

The museum would include also an art gallery. There, the works of local artists along with reproductions of walls paintings from the prehistoric caves would be exhibited and sold.

"The entire project should be completed by the beginning of next April." Clothilde concluded looking at Jean Luc then at Paul, and so bringing that subject to an end.

Paul had been totally captivated by the sense of earnest dedication Clothilde and Elise conveyed about their work. He made haste to praise such a commendable enterprise.

With unconcealed sadness, he deplored that circumstances would prevent him from participating in the opening.

"What a pity!" promptly lamented Elise. "When must you return to the United States?"

"Next Friday," Paul replied, involuntarily glancing at Clothilde.

Instantly, Clothilde had the impression she had sunk into the darkest chasm.

"Next Friday! But, why are you leaving so soon, can't you stay a bit longer?" she exclaimed in an outburst of disappointment, before she realized she had overstated her concern. Jean Luc taken aback by her unseemly behavior, frowned with surprise. Shocked at herself she blushed, lowered her brow and diffidently withdrew into silence.

"Yes, next Friday," Paul restated. "I regret, we have met too late," he then said with a chagrined smile while looking sideways at Jean Luc. His gaze returned to Clothilde. He thought to have noticed that her face appeared paler than her normal coloring. However, he might have been mistaken; perhaps it was caused by the afternoon light casting a shadow upon her.

"Indeed we have met too late, but this is the only leave I was able to obtain, which at last gave me the privilege to invite Paul before his departure," rejoined Jean Luc, almost apologetically. "For all that however, I am still glad I could do so, even for only once."

"Thank you, Jean Luc," Paul acknowledged. "This will always be fondly remembered."

"Be that as it may," Jean Luc continued, "we must foster the hope, that in spite of all apparent obstacles, we will have the opportunity to cultivate our friendship with more than some occasional phone calls to merely give each other news of the different phases of our existence while we grow old and feeble."

"Meanwhile, let us take care of today," Elise decisively reminded everyone. She wanted to drive away the melancholy that suddenly had swept over them.

"All right," assented Jean Luc, with a more enthusiastic tone of voice "Indeed, today calls on us to be patriotic and participate in the nation festivities, but also it calls on us to celebrate the good fortune of our own amity and love. Therefore, I propose that later on this evening, we gather again here at the Clubhouse and be merry. What do you think, yes?

A collective "yes!" was the answer.

They stood up amazed that time had flown away so rapidly. The crowd had begun to disperse itself in different directions. Around the Club, waiters and waitresses were setting up tables for the night entertainments. The water of the Dordogne, now undisturbed, calmly ran its course, reflecting again the scenic beauty of its luxuriant valley bathed at this hour in a gold and amethyst glow. Already the sun, like a dying God, prepared to lie in his sumptuous sepulcher. His expiring breath veiled the western horizon under a shroud spun in delicate tints of orange, pink and violet hues.

At this moment, Clothilde felt less restrained by unsettled feelings. It was not because the dimmest light had pierced into the enigmas which consumed her. It was rather, as if she had reached a certain toleration of the unexplainable. Even though this day had been extremely wearisome, something seemed strangely right about it.

"Clothilde, we will pick you up at eight o'clock, prompt! Then you Elise, at eight thirty," Jean Luc coordinated efficiently, while they walked to their respective car.

Paul and Clothilde exchanged a glance. Although both tried their best to conceal it, a silent anticipation to see each other again was subtly obvious in their eyes. Then they parted.

CHAPTER 7

WHEN CLOTHILDE WALKED into the kitchen, Madeleine beamed with a smile. Promptly, she freed her hands from gathering glasses on a tray, and kissed her granddaughter.

"Hello darling, you are just in time for dinner. Actually, you are a little early, it is not quite ready yet."

Clothilde cast a look around the room.

"Where is Maman?" she asked as if Suzanne was supposed to be in the kitchen also.

"She was not needed here, so she went to work a bit in the garden; now she is in her bedroom getting dressed for the evening."

"Oh," Clothilde voiced, absentmindedly."

"Grandpapa is attending to Canon d'Or," went on Madeleine, as she anticipated the next question.

Clothilde gazed outside the kitchen window in direction of the pasture.

"Yes," she uttered remorsefully, "I went by the stable and saw Grandpapa there." She felt neglectful of her favorite responsibility, for it was with a vigilant devotion that every day she unfailingly took care of Canon d'Or, her beloved horse. Today though, she felt like such a disappointment in so many areas of her life.

Clothilde helped her grandmother to set the table.

"How was your afternoon? Madeleine inquired. We went to *la*

28

Madrigale this morning; we could not wait to see Jean Luc. We then briefly met Paul. He seems like a very nice young man."

Madeleine laughed at her rather banal comment describing the first impression she received from Paul.

"Well, he must be quite special since he is a friend of Jean Luc," she attempted to repair, by being a little more specific. "After you left for Sarlat, Berthe Lespargue phoned to invite us for lunch together with a few other friends; you know how good she is at deciding something wonderful on the spur of the moment. We had no other particular plan in mind, so we went, and as always it was very enjoyable."

"Is dinner ready?" Emile's jovial voice resounded, as he opened the front door.

"Yes, it is," Madeleine hastened to reply. "Come along everybody, and I shall serve it at once.

Clothilde greeted and embraced her mother who appeared at the same time Emile walked in the doorway.

They all gathered around the dining room table.

In these old, solidly united families, the evening meal was always observed like a religious ritual. At that time, everyone's undertakings and daily activities were discussed. Thereupon, if needed, the elders gave their wisest advices to respectful young ears. Reminiscences, dreams, sadness and joys were also caringly shared.

"Jean Luc and Paul will meet me here at about eight o'clock, we will then pick up Elise and return to the Club. A great deal is going on by the Dordogne tonight for everyone to enjoy, will you come along with us? Please come along with us," bade Clothilde after Madeleine had said the Grace.

"Not this year, darling," her mother declined, "the Tournais will be here later on. Elise, Jean Luc and Phillippe's parents will join us too. We intend to watch the firework from the terrace, and have our own private party."

"That sounds like fun too, conceded Clothilde. "I will miss dancing with you, Grandpapa. Do you remember last year, you waltzed me out of breath?"

Emile beamed from the delight his granddaughter never ceased to be.

"I'll make it up to you and waltz you breathless again at your engagement party. I promise."

"You promise? All right," she consented.

Clothilde was not hungry. She ate the most she could only out of consideration. Her excess of impatience turned the least act of swallowing into the most uncomfortable effort.

"I should get ready. May I be excused?" she finally asked, unable to contain much longer an irrepressible need to be in motion as if it would accelerate time into a faster rate. She only had a little over an hour before she would see Paul again, but it seemed so far off into eternity. To be in his presence had suddenly grown into an impossible urge she was utterly helpless to overcome.

"Go ahead dear. Go and make yourself all beautiful," Madeleine encouraged.

"That should be easy," interceded Emile, beholding Clothilde with tenderness.

She smiled at her grandfather to thank him for the compliment and hesitantly darted a look about the table as she rose.

"The dishes?" she questioned apologetically. Although she knew she would be exempt from her contribution to clear the dining room and kitchen after dinner, she wanted to show that she didn't consider it her due to avoid her part of the task.

"Will you please go on and not worry about washing dishes!" insisted her mother. We will take care of it."

"Thank you." Clothilde accepted without hesitation.

They enveloped her with an adoring smile, while she distributed a round of kisses before leaving the dining room.

Since the German had killed her father at the front, during World War II, Clothilde then three years old and her mother Suzanne had moved in with her maternal grandparents, Emile and Madeleine Augelier.

They lived in a house, which for three centuries at least, had been passed on to the descendants of the same lineage all the way down to Emile.

Long ago, it was consistent with traditions for several generations including the servants, to cohabit comfortably and happily in those large ancestral homes. Essentially, they were designed for that purpose. Nursing facilities or day nurseries would have been frowned upon, as an unfortunate alternative for the care of the elderly and the young. The welfare of each and all was the concern of everyone. This was a sound way of life, which sealed the family bonds.

The style of Emile's ancestral house was unique with its many characteristics and charms. It was a robust piece of masonry constructed with huge blocks of cut stones that had the texture and brilliance of blond granite. They were extracted from a quarry on the property. The estate had been named: *"La Brisante"*

A very distinctive feature unduplicated anywhere else in the county, was a magnificent terrace, which flanked the right wing on the east side. It had been built with tons upon tons of soil encased in a thick wall. The ground was paved with octagonal tiles of flat slate. A large frieze, in high relief, hemmed the upper part and continued along the front facade of the house.

Within the enclosure of the terrace, at the right corner, a centenarian acacia had grown luxuriantly. In spring, its branches toppled under the weight of blue flowers that dangled in opulent clusters and pervaded the air with their sweet fragrance. Along the inner walls, where a narrow border of soil had been left bare for ornamental gardening, rosebushes mingled their blossoms in a vivid range of yellow, purple, red, white and all the delicate nuances of pink. Their beauty and their scent made one feel glad to be born on this planet.

From the main road, a winding causeway ran across an orchard and led to an oval front lawn divided by a cobblestones path. On each side, flowerbeds, from the first buds of the spring daffodils to the last chrysanthenum of autumn constantly changed their brilliant display of variegated hues, depending upon the blooms of the seasons.

Behind the terrace, a rugged hilltop covered with moss, verbena and ivy abounded with dwarf oaks trees and hawthorn where joyful birds fluttered about in carefree warbling.

On the left behind the house, green hills unfurling like sheets of silk billowed by a sudden gust of wind, undulated down toward a meadow. There, a pasture enclosed by a wooden fence was the territory of a flamboyant Arab-Morgan Palomino; a dearly loved family horse. At the age of eighteen, he was still admiringly endowed with the spirited disposition of youth, and frolicked about as sprightly as a saucy yearling. Oh! But when he stood placidly still while the locks of his silvery mane formed a shimmering halo around his gentle brow, then one had truly the vision of an angel who stirred and humbled one's soul. Canon d'Or was his name, because of his golden coat.

CHAPTER 8

The AGELESS GRANDFATHER clock stood commanding in the entrance hall of *la Brisante*. Like a mummified patriarch whose heart was still beating, it unremittingly reminded the living that the hours forever flee in the irretrievable past. It had just rung eight o'clock in the evening, when Jean Luc accompanied by Paul stopped his D.S. 19, in the front driveway.

The dramatic beauty of the house immediately captivated Paul. For a brief instant the dim thought that there was something familiar about it sprang up in his mind; but at once his blurred recollection vanished, leaving behind a vague sense of longing. Certainly, this was the first time he had ever seen this place! But didn't he experience a similar elusive impression when he acquainted himself with the area this morning?

At the sound of their car, Suzanne followed by Emile and Madeleine hurried outside to warmly receive them.

Clothilde stayed behind in the dining room to prepare an assortment of *digestifs* on a teacart.

As they all entered the vestibule, she heard Paul's voice. A sudden wave of ineffable joy invaded her so profoundly that she felt lightheaded.

"Hello Clothilde!" he said simply, gazing at her as she walked toward them.

He felt overwhelmed by an incomprehensible sentiment of tenderness.

"Hello Paul!" she responded glad that at the same time Jean Luc gave her a hug, for she still was a little giddy.

She wore a turquoise dress, which softly followed the contours of her slender figure. A fine gold chain adorned her neckline. As in the afternoon, her hair fell in its natural flow. Everything about her was unaffectedly graceful. Paul noticed that no doubt she had inherited her beauty from both her mother and her grandmother.

After entering a front hall, they came into a long corridor stretching to an oak staircase that spiraled to the second floor.

Madeleine graciously invited them to the parlor through the first door on the right. In comparison to the other rooms of the house, it was relatively small. However, once inside, one had instantly the illusion of ethereal spaciousness. The walls and the high beamed ceiling were tinted by a wash with only a suggestion of lavender mixed with the white paint. Delicate aquarelles hanged against the walls in a well-displayed arrangement. A Persian rug of muted colors covered the middle area of the wood floor that had the luster of furbished copper. At the center was a low table upon which a sparkling crystal vase overflowed with freshly cut fragrant roses. A Victorian settee and two matching armchairs upholstered in hazy mauve damask sprinkled with a print of white forget-me-not were conveniently placed around it. An ancient upright piano stood along the opposite side; an aura of nostalgia for the songs of yesteryears hovered over its engraved rosewood.

A fireplace faced the entrance door. The white marble of the mantle piece was so intricately etched; it resembled fine embroidery appliqued to the wall. The mantle ledge supported a bronze statue of the Roman goddess Diane the huntress reclining upon a pedestal enfolded by twigs, and stags in repose.

Antique wall tables, Queen Anne chairs and consoles furnished the rest of the room. Here and there, lamps, vases and decorative objects of Sevres or Limoges porcelain exuded delicate nuances and highlights that sealed the exquisite ambiance of the room.

"You have a beautiful home," Paul felt compelled to express. For who could walk into a place like this and stand there, showing only a casual indifference to the host.

"Thank you," accepted Madeleine. "We are very attached to this house. It has been in my husband's family for centuries. It seems to evoke memories of times and ancestors we have never known but yet are dear to us, even though they are of long gone eras.

Paul smiled and nodded, then his gaze paused on the piano. In an unexpected flight of fancy he vividly envisioned Clothilde sitting there. Softly she hummed along while playing one of those beautiful French ballads longing for a lost love. It was winter. Tall dancing flames flared up in the hearth, casting gleams of amber upon her white chiffon gown and along her chestnut hair flowing down to her waist. Outside the window a thick fleece of snow spread a polar-bound stillness throughout a landscape bathed in frosted moon rays. It was incredibly real.

"Well," he thought, "this place certainly stimulates the imagination!"

Emile, who had poured drinks in dainty glasses according to each one's taste, passed them around on a tray. He was a handsome seventy-year-old man with a dignified bearing and a long grey moustache that turned up at each end.

Paul was asked a few informal questions such as if he enjoyed his stay in France or if the military life suited him and of course, how he must miss his family and his country. Everyone communicated his or her regrets about not having met him sooner. Suzanne expressed her gratitude of knowing that "their" Jean Luc while away from home had been in such good company until then. Madeleine inquired if they were both well treated and decently fed. In an impulse, she took her grandson's face between her hands and kissed him as if he were a toddler.

"This is the way things are done here, Paul," Jean Luc managed to mutter while still in his grandmother's grasp.

Paul tossed him an amused smile and quickly returned his full attention to Emile. They were having a one on one conversation, tightening as it were, the Franco American Alliance. Soon Paul understood he was in the presence of a noble soul.

Without questioning why she felt so strongly about it, Clothilde was absolutely ecstatic as she watched her grandfather and Paul connect so cordially. They gave the impression that they would have liked to talk for hours on. However, Emile knew that now was not the time to engage Paul in extensive discourses and in so doing detain his grand children and their friends from their nocturnal diversion; therefore, he diplomatically broke off everyone's chatter.

"Yes, Jean Luc," said Emile considerately, as if his grandson had voiced what was on his mind. "Yes, you go on young ones, go and glean the happy memories of youth; they are the buttresses that strengthen the spirit against the damages of time."

"My husband is an untiring *"poete-philosophe"* Madeleine informed humorously.

Truly charmed by Emile, Paul smiled.

With a swift movement of his right arm, Emile prompted everyone toward the front door. Madeleine and Suzanne followed.

"Now Jean Luc darling, we will have an early family dinner here tomorrow. "We will serve aperitif at six and dinner at seven," please be in time!" reminded Madeleine, as they all stepped outside.

"Yes Grandmaman, we will be on time and we will look forward to it, I assure you!" Jean Luc responded jubilantly.

Standing in the front garden while immersed in the fragrance exhaled by the flowers in full blooms, they went through their *aurevoirs*.

"God, I love them!" Jean Luc mumbled while walking away with a heart bursting from the deep affection he felt for Suzanne and his grandparents.

"So do I," wholeheartedly joined in Clothilde.

"Jean Luc and Clothilde have grown into so beautiful and fine young people, and so is our dear Elise," sighed Emile standing on the front steps of the house and staring at the trail of dust left behind by Jean Luc's car as it disappeared beyond the orchard.

Suzanne noticed a teardrop whirling down his left cheek. She gently caught it with her thumb.

"Pap?"

"Yes!"

"Have I ever told you how thankful I am to have you for a father?"

"Oh, you might have, once or twice if I recall correctly."

Madeleine smiled.

"Your father is a sentimental one, isn't he? Well, that is only one reason among countless others, why I fell in love with him."

Emile's eyes beamed with contentment.

"Shall we have another glass of this delicious Chartreuse?" He proposed taking his wife and his daughter by the hand to lead them back into the parlor.

"This American friend of Jean Luc ... Paul, I mean," Emile added with a serious expression, as though giving much attention to what was on his mind. "he is very nice and well mannered; a real gentleman. I like him."

"Yes, I like him also," Suzanne, rejoined approvingly.

"Absolutely charming," assented Madeleine. At the sound of a car parking in the driveway she walked to the window. Their first guests had arrived.

CHAPTER 9

As AGREED, AT eight thirty Elise was ready to meet again with her friends. A short but warm-hearted visit at her house, gave Paul time to be acquainted with her parents, Bernard and Melanie who were also on the point of leaving to spend a few hours at *la Brisante*. Then, they all proceeded toward their respective destination for the evening.

Jean Luc rode leisurely, allowing the bucolic charm of the surrounding to be conducive to a carefree mood.

A sheet of violet haze floating over the hills then settling in a shimmery mist over the haystacks scattered over the meadows, announced the approaching twilight and perhaps even a few drops of rain. Yet, broad sweeps of fertile land patched with blond wheat fields, pastures, orchards and vineyards were all in a stir with hardy farmers bustling about. They harvested their fruits and vegetables, they loaded their trucks with bails of alfalfa, they gleaned wheat behind the reapers, they sang and whistled. Some waved cheerfully at the cars passing by. The drivers would then blow their horns to acknowledge their friendliness.

"Why was it that she felt so shamelessly elated, whereas to befit circumstances everything should have appeared forlorn without Phillippe?" Clothilde asked herself. She tried to dismiss any further questioning lest a repressed guilt should flare up with revenge and shatter that fragile state of bliss. She immediately forced her attention to focus away from any inextricable brooding, and simply delight in the moment. As she gazed toward the horizon, she was amazed when she caught sight of the sudden change, which had taken place since she last glimpsed at the sky, just a short while ago.

"Oh, have you noticed how dark clouds have gathered over the forest? It looks quite stormy." she spontaneously pointed out.

"Hmm!" I am afraid we might get wet, Jean Luc observed as he knitted his brow to examine the weather condition. Paul, I have already told you about our thunderstorms during the months of July and August, we …"

"Ah! Please let's not talk about this," Elise hurried to interrupt, apprehending that Jean Luc might unintentionally bring sinister reminiscences of the wicked storm, which had caused Marie Joelle to drown. "Please! No storm tonight!"

"Well, all right," accommodated Jean Luc.

Having so settled the issue, they went on talking about this and that, with apparently no other concerns than keeping Paul agreeably entertained.

While they crossed over the white bridge, they could view the multitude below swarming like bees along the ground bordering the water. The air throbbed with cheerful sounds. The voices of a baritone and a soprano accompanied by a guitarist and a trumpeter rose in a duo as they captivated the crowd with ancient French romances and the favorite songs of the time.

The only available parking place they were able to find was in an area further up the grassland. Preceded and followed by a horde of people, they were obliged to go afoot for quite a way through one of the many paths descending to the river shore. They had just begun to take a few steps when a flute stroke the first notes of a beautiful old French song called: *Le temps des cerises. (The cherries harvest)* To which the generations of their great grandparents and grandparents had waltzed in their youth.

This delightful song told of *an undying love that had blossomed at the time of the cherry harvest, and had left on its wake an inconsolable wounded heart.*

Clothilde and Paul walked abreast. The melody, the words, the magical ambiance that surrounded her together with the intense pleasure of being close to him, aroused in Clothilde an unprecedented transport of rapture, she could never have thought of being capable to attain.

Paul himself was suddenly overcome by an impression of vulnerability elicited it seemed from a certain sensitivity to Clothilde's mood. She looked up at him, he glimpsed back at her. A subtle expression seeping through their glances briefly conveyed as it were, a tacit disclosure of each other's feelings. She had an odd sense that suddenly she had become transparent and had laid bare to Paul the very core of her soul. Embarrassed, she wished she could instantly have become as invisible as the music that soared in the air.

With both hands tucked in his pant pockets and noticeably engaged in thought, Paul followed the path. He was soon distracted by Jean Luc and Elise who rejoined them after a temporary separation caused by the disordered flow of the crowd or the greetings of some acquaintances.

They soon reached the Clubhouse where Jean Luc was again accosted by friends who wished to welcome his return home. While eager young men flocked to greet Clothilde and Elise, several young women intrigued by Paul's presence and allured by his good look, flirtatiously asked to be introduced to him.

"Please! God do not allow any of them to attract his interest!" Clothilde silently besought. She was astonished at whatever motivated her to do so.

One of the waiters they knew well accommodated everyone by connecting two large tables, so they could all stay together outside in front of the river. Clothilde sat on the right of Jean Luc, Elise was seated next to her at the left of Paul then the rest of the company gathered around them.

"Garçon!" Jean Luc summoned. "Champagne if you please!"

Champagne was brought and served.

With a festive spirit they lifted their glass to each other's happiness and soon a sparkle fluttered through their eyes as they mingled enjoyably.

The music filled the valley with the most enthralling melodies. Elise was solicited to dance by one of their friends, whereupon, Jean Luc excused himself, rose from his chair and took Clothilde's arm.

"Come my cousin. Since grandpapa is not here to whirl you around, do me the honor to waltz with me," he courteously bade, with a nuance of jocosity that was entirely his own. Clothilde accepted good-humoredly. By then the bubbly elixir seemed to have wonderfully revived her self-possession. Paul's pensive gaze followed them to the dance floor, which was packed right away.

"Can you waltz Paul?" encingly asked Helene, one of the young ladies who previously had been most anxious to meet him and now was part of their group.

"Certainly I can waltz," he answered, amused by Helen's eloquent hint at an invitation. "My mother is French," he added, as if this explained why he could waltz. "Would you care to …?"

"Yes I would, thank you," she hastened to accept before he had time to say another word. She spiraled about her chair then rushed to offer him her hand.

As Clothilde spun in Jean Luc's arms, she noticed them among the dancers, which caused her to miss a few steps and almost lose her balance. Disconcerted, she nonetheless was able to swiftly fall back into the rhythm. She needed another glass of champagne and why not? It was the fourteenth of July, an acceptable reason to feel a little hazy, she rationalized. Well aware of the true reason why she could use a second drink, she instantly rejected to pronounce mentally the word "Jealousy." It was too suggestive of a debasing sentiment she did not care to own. Truthfully, she was growing quite annoyed with her obsessive reactions to Paul. It was like having to contend with an intrusive second personality she disapproved of, but could not overcome. What possessed her to be so besotted by a complete stranger she had just been acquainted with, while being in love with a man she had known since childhood; and a wonderful very special man for all that? No doubt she had lost her wit. How would she ever recover from this lunacy? she relapsed into questioning.

They had not yet reached their table when everybody stood in silent awe at the outset of the glorious firework that blazed into the last oozing glimmer of the waning twilight. One could have thought that Paradise had opened its gates to dazzle the mortals with visions of the celestial gardens come in full bloom, while it showered the river with myriads of fallen petals. The ecstatic crowd, mesmerized, reverently responded in waves of mounting and fading outcries to each multicolored explosion. Then it all ended. The obscurity at first appeared darker in contrast with the outbursts of resplendent light, but it soon dissolved into the cerulean translucence of a still early summer night.

Now everyone was ready to give free reins to a festive mood. People sang and cheered inside and outside the Clubhouse. On the riverbanks and the beaches, the music seemed to gush out from the sky like a cascade of exquisite melodies. Well, of course joy triumphed and echoed all about the dale and the highland; they were celebrating their basic human rights to "Liberty, Equality and Brotherhood!"

Clothilde observed and admired with great relief that Paul thank Heaven showed no inclination toward any flighty romantic interlude. Definitively, he was not responsive to Helene's inviting glances or any one else's flirtatious expedients. By then Clothilde had deemed herself quite relaxed. Why then was she so nervous when he asked her to dance, and why was it all in vain when her heart constantly tried to resist from being swept off so sinfully but so rhapsodically when she was close to him? If only she had known what supreme effort Paul withstood to preserve his poise and conceal the incredible rapture, which flooded his soul when they danced together. He then held her in his arms so delicately, almost timidly, as if afraid to tarnish the exquisite aura which glowed around her. And if she seemed irresistibly alluring, he realized it was not prompted by any shallow intent to charm, but purely in complete spontaneous innocence; for he knew without a doubt that she was a well-bred, young lady. Likewise, he would have never allowed any faux pas to suggest the least indiscretion toward her. In all appearance, it simply seemed that they were taking pleasure in a friendly social interaction with each other and their company.

However, if by virtue of their honorable principles, they were reluctant to approve of their innermost feelings, behind this shield of lighthearted diversion Clothilde relished in every minute that brought her near Paul, while he wished this night could be eternal. For if their heads did not yet, could not yet dare to recognize it, already in their hearts, a faint voice defiant of reason, whispered. It was too subtle to understand clearly what it said. Nevertheless, it was real and it yearned to be heard.

CHAPTER 10

THE CLOCK OF the church belfry drizzled a silvery chime over the valley plunged in darkness, and then rang eleven times. The air had turned increasingly sultry. Above the forest, the wan moon was no more than a smear of light barely perceivable in the thick gloom of space. It seemed sunken and stranded in a lagoon of molten lead, while scattered white clouds wandered from its trail, like sheep straying from their shepherd. The starless sky hung so heavily, one could fear it might cave in and topple at any moment. A few sporadic streaks of lightening beamed across the horizon. Given that a good lapse of time passed before the thunder followed each flash of light led to suppose that the turbulence was a good way off and might fade far into the distance. All the same, a storm was looming. The local people and the habitual tourists who consistently returned each year were well accustomed to this kind of erratic midsummer weather, therefore without much abating the festivities went on.

"Should we leave now?" Jean Luc inquired out of consideration, while he escorted Elise back to their table after a dance.

She looked at him, undisturbed,

"Leave, why?"

"Jean Luc swept a broad gesture across the sky.

"Have you seen what's simmering up there?"

"Are you all ready to go home?" inquired Elise as she regained her seat, ignoring to answer jean Luc.

In complete agreement, "no" was the answer.

Clothilde impulsively smiled at Paul. She was happy to notice he wished to stay.

"Well then, we should move inside at once, otherwise we risk to get considerably wet. Moreover, as you can see, the Clubhouse is getting crammed, if we don't find some chairs now we might have to stand up on our feet the rest of the night," Jean Luc pointed out.

They went in and conveniently found a place by the window, which opened upon the Dordogne. The waiters being extremely busy, Jean Luc and his friends took it upon themselves to again join a few tables to preserve their group together.

"We should phone home to reassure everyone we are safely sheltered inside until the storm has passed," Clothilde thoughtfully suggested.

"Yes, I'll do that," Jean Luc approved decisively, and at once he tried to find his way to a phone.

Paul courteously offered a chair to Clothilde who stood by him. He sat beside her.

Within the next hour, already the storm raged over their head. The frantic multitude had deserted the river shores to seek shelter. The electricity was cut off. In a regular and swift tempo, the lightening pierced the darkness, flooded the landscape with a metallic glare that cast fantastic and mysterious shades. Then the thunder roared. A sudden outpour of rain pounded the ground, clanked against the walls and the glass panes, like swords striking bronze shields in a tempestuous battle. Meanwhile a gusty wind rallied to lash across the gorge, bending, tossing, twisting trees, grass, reeds and flowers. The tall, lean aspens curved their tops and writhed like possessed question marks. Torn leaves and twigs whirled up and away. The water of the Dordogne riddled as if assailed by a hail of bullets.

At the Clubhouse, the music having been intentionally subdued, had tamed the crowd into slow motion. Immersed in the surrealistic glow of the candlelight, a few couples danced nonchalantly, the rest of the people idled away the storm in carefree conversations, or they simply stood there transfixed while gazing at nature's awesome supremacy.

Paul casually sat with his arms crossed loosely against his chest. He appeared to be in a contemplative mood.

During an interlude of half an hour or so, the storm had slightly decreased its momentum when in a swift fury the lightening and the thunder redoubled their discharge, causing outcries of amazement rather than panic. Promptly, all eyes were set on the outside. Clothilde in an unlikely impulse drew closer to Paul and leaned her head against him, while laying her left hand on his arm. At first, he was surprised and did not dare to move. Then he turned to her and without hesitation, as if in the most normal reassuring gesture, he responded by taking her hand in his. He retained it gently but soon released it as she pulled away absolutely confounded.

From the flickering candlelight, dark shadows fluttered over her face; however, he could perceive her embarrassment and immediately wished to put her at ease.

"Are you feeling well, Clothilde? Perhaps you are a little afraid?" he asked in a low, concerned tone of voice.

"Paul!" she could barely utter. "I am sorry. I ... I am extremely sorry ... I didn't mean ... I shouldn't ..."

"It's all right, I understand perfectly ..."

"Oh! I should not have," she interrupted. "I was not scared, I am so used to this kind of weather ... well, I suppose I was a little frightened," she finally pretended to admit for a way out of her mortifying predicament. She quickly checked around to assure herself that no one had taken notice of what she had just done or said. She could have cried. At a glance Paul discerned across her face the affliction she tried to conceal. He was left deep in thought. What was this mysterious, this "very special something" she had about her? And even though it had lasted only a brief moment, how could he possibly ignore to recognize that when their hands touched he had been swept by a sensation of ineffable bliss.

Soon the storm vanished as speedily as it had exploded. Before long the heavy rain was absorbed by the parched soil, leaving behind no more than a film of glistening dew over the battered grass. The limpid and serene beauty, which now emanated from the Dordogne was only disturbed by a few trouts that darted to the surface like the glittering spears of under water warriors.

It was two o'clock in the morning when they went home.

Paul drifted into sleep finding it impossible to avert his thoughts from Clothilde. She, seized by an insufferable agitation could not find rest. Indeed, how could she calm down, when exhilaration enwrapped her, obsession infuriated her, amazement dazzled her, guilt from what she felt and what she was supposed to feel crushed her. She finally dozed off a few minutes after the Grandfather clock had rung five o'clock A.M.

She dreamt that: *"Once the storm had receded Paul invited her to take a walk along the riverside. They had advanced only a short distance on the footpath edging the water, when Paul laid his left arm around her shoulders and directly asked,*

"What happened to Marie Joelle?"

"She drowned, and was found not far from here, under the Chambre," replied *Clothilde pointing upstream.*

"The Chambre?" questioned Paul.

"Yes, this grotto over there in the large rock hanging above the Dordogne is called the Chambre, because it is very deep and hollow. It is one of the caves where our ancestors the "Cavemen" lived during the Old Stone Age."

"Oh, yes ... yes ... a prehistoric cave," Paul acknowledged quite casually.

"Something really extraordinary happened late in the afternoon after Marie Joelle's fatal accident," pursued Clothilde. "Her mother, Veronique, being still in shock, was seated by her bedroom window. She was staring at the outdoors as though under a spell, when suddenly she heard Marie Joelle say in a very clear voice: "Don't cry mother, I shall soon return.""

"How anxiously then, Veronique must be waiting for her daughter's return!" Paul exclaimed.

Totally undisturbed by Paul's comments, Clothilde for an indefinable length of time walked silently by his side until they reached an arbor formed by a cluster of trees intertwining their branches. They stopped abruptly at the sound of an infant prattling in the rushes nearby.

"Oh, look!" they both cried out in wonderment as they laid their eyes upon a little girl dressed in pink, all alone among tall reeds. Although she was still a baby, she was able to speak and walk. Undaunted, she said "hello!" Then she rose and hurried toward them pleading

"Oh, take me with you!"

"What's your name?" Paul asked most gently.

"As you wish to call me," she answered in a gay tone of voice.

Paul gathered her up in his arms and turned to Clothilde.

"She shall be ours!" he stated resolutely.

Upon awakening, Clothilde had some difficulty discerning whether this had actually happened or if it had only been a dream. How so clear, so real it all seemed!

CHAPTER 11

CLOHILDE LAY ON her bed completely still. She did not dare to stir a finger, lest she would disturb the recollection of her dream as she tried to reconstruct it detail by detail on a screen spread out in front of her mind's eyes. Hypnotized by her own thoughts, she was beginning to slip into a slumberous haze when a knock on the back door of the kitchen awoke her. She feared she had overslept and leaped out of bed, but when she realized that not much time had elapsed since she last looked at the clock she heaved a sigh of relief. Leaning over the ledge of her open window, she saw Suzanne accompanied by Andrea, a neighbor, as they entered the paved path leading to the pasture.

"People were up and about facing a brand-new day, energetically and purposefully. Why was she still in her bedroom, absorbed by shallow preoccupations, dwelling on dreams that made no sense?" Clothilde asked herself with self-reproach.

She grabbed a pair of blue jeans and a blouse from her wardrobe. Mainly through the motion of habit without giving attention to what she was doing she dressed herself, and carelessly gathered her hair into a ponytail. She then went to the kitchen.

"Oh, hello darling, why are you up so early?" inquired Suzanne when she walked back in the house and found her daughter setting a kettle on the stove to boil water for tea.

"What would Maman think if I should tell her I dreamt that Paul and I were picking up babies stranded on the bank of the Dordogne, in the middle of the night?" Clothilde wondered as her dream partly flashed back through her memory. Quickly she drove such an insane notion away and gave her mother an affectionate hug.

"I have the same question for you Maman. You ought to be enjoying a late sleep, for you too were up until very late last night with the festivities."

"Andrea stopped by, so I hurried down to answer the door hoping no one else had been disturbed. She brought us these. They are freshly laid by her hens," Suzanne indicated as she held out to Clothilde a basket filled with beautiful amber eggs.

"Well, Maman it seems you and I are up for the same reason. I was awakened by Andrea also, when she knocked on the back door."

Suzanne put coffee and water in the percolator then turned it on.

"I am sorry darling. You should feel tired having had so little sleep. Why don't you go and rest a bit longer before Mass? We have a busy day ahead of us," Suzanne advised as she carefully put the eggs in a bowl and stored them in the refrigerator. "Oh, I fed Canon d'Or while I was out. He is quite happy eating so you have no immediate need to give him additional attention at this moment."

As Clothilde thanked her, Suzanne noticed a trace of sadness briefly passing across her daughter's face. "Poor child! No doubt she misses Phillippe in the midst of all this merriment," she silently bemoaned. But her spirit was promptly cheered at the anticipation that Phillippe would be back home in just a few days and Clothilde finally would enjoy the everlasting happiness that was due to her. Therefore, she avoided any comment, which could have elicited a gloomy mood.

Clothilde reached for two cups and saucers from a tall pine hutch.

"Anyway, it is time I put an end to idling and make myself useful, for I am ashamed to admit, yesterday I have been very neglectful of my duties," she said in answer to her mother's suggestion for additional rest.

Suzanne removed a strand of hair away from the side of Clothilde's face.

"You do plenty of your share around here Darling, so don't worry yourself if you take time to enjoy some well deserved diversions befitting your own age. Now then tell me, did you have fun last night?"

"Yes, we had a lot of fun in spite of the storm. Was your evening quite pleasant also Maman? I hope Jean Luc's phone call put your mind at ease."

"Well, although this storm was magnificent, it was a bit of a nuisance for a while and we were relieved to know you had found shelter in the Clubhouse. But otherwise yes, we spent a very pleasant evening. We watched the fireworks from the terrace. It was quite a spectacle."

"Absolutely beautiful! How late did your company stay Maman? asked Clothilde. They sat snuggly at the kitchen table to savor their first cup of steaming hot tea and coffee.

"Almost everybody had left by eleven o'clock," Suzanne answered. "However, Philippe's parents stayed a little longer and just the four of us took the time to enjoy a visit." There was a silence. "They absolutely adore you, Clothilde dear." Suzanne then said looking at her daughter with such tenderness it could have inspired the most touching painting about motherly love.

Clothilde only sighed; her face took a grave expression.

Suzanne added an extra half spoon of sugar to her coffee.

"They both can't wait to see you and Phillippe exchange vows at the altar and have you for a daughter."

"I hope to fulfill well, at least some of their expectations."

"No doubt, you will darling. Simply by being yourself should be quite sufficient to make any one happy."

Clothilde gazed at Suzanne through a pensive affectionate smile."

"Thank you Maman."

"Ah, with what glow in her eyes, Veronique told me that her grandmother Manouche's diamond ring has been polished and is now ready for her son to slide it around your finger on the day of your betrothal. You bring so much comfort in her life."

From across the kitchen window Suzanne watched a cluster of white clouds as they changed form and gently dissolved away in space. When she looked back at her daughter, a sparkling smile in her eyes conveyed that an amusing but fond thought had just crossed her mind.

Without having any idea why, Clothilde found herself smiling also. She looked inquisitively at her mother who was pouring herself a fresh cup of coffee.

"I was just thinking," said Suzanne.

"I already guessed that," Clothilde acknowledged good-naturedly.

"I was just thinking about last night," pursued Suzanne. "After a coupe or two of champagne our dear Veronique began to reminisce about Philippe's childhood. She brought back to my memory a particular afternoon during summer, when Phillippe was no taller then three apples stacked on top of one another so to speak. Veronique and I had just played ball with him, here on the front lawn. Due to the intense heat we interrupted our game to take some refreshment under the sycamore. As we sat idly chatting, his mother asked him, "Phillippe, what do you want to be when you grow up?" At once he forthrightly answered," *"a priest, I want to be a priest, like I used to be."*

"Like you used to be! When ever were you a priest?" asked Veronique laughing."

"A long time ago!" he exclaimed staring at us indignantly as if we were two simpletons deprived of the faculty to remember."

"Yes," joined in Clothilde. Now I vaguely recall to have heard about this story. Didn't he also play at saying mass and such?"

"Indeed, yes and he was quite good at it. The most extraordinary thing was when on more than one occasion he was found in his bedroom where he had withdrawn to simulate a priest piously offering mass in the exact sequence and details of the Catholic rituals. He used his little desk for an altar. Even now and then some words, although unintelligibly mumbled had a Latin sound. It was truly remarkable considering he was so tiny. Evidently, when in church with his mother he had observed and registered all this. He showed an impressive ability to memorize, for being such a small child. However, after he had turned six or seven years old, strangely he had forgotten all about it."

Clothilde carelessly pushed her empty cup aside.

"Would his parents have encouraged it, had he persisted in that direction?"

"I don't see why not, what ever makes Phillippe happy is always what they wish for him." Suzanne paused for a moment to think further. "Well so much for priesthood! Look at him now, smitten with love for you!" she pointed out lightheartedly. Her face was radiant with delight as candid visions of Clothilde's future happiness dazzled her imagination. No doubt at this instant, she thought her daughter's earthly bliss was entirely achievable and exactly as she had projected it for her.

"I am so glad you have … Clothilde are you listening?" Suzanne asked abruptly.

"Why, yes Maman, certainly I am listening," Clothilde stressed, taken aback by the unexpected question.

However, Suzanne's guess that her daughter had somehow drifted into reverie was not far from being accurate, for despite her good intent to remain fully involved in the current discourse Clothilde's thoughts had begun to irresistibly stray into recollections of the most intriguing last twenty-four hours.

Suzanne smiled.

"Oh, all right dear, it just looked as if your attention was preoccupied by something or other, although I would not be surprised if it were with so much to think about."

The ongoing conversation was further interrupted by the sound of light footsteps that seemed to only brush against the rug spread out over the wood floor in the hallway. Knowing it was her grandmother, Clothilde spontaneously motioned to go and meet her. She had barely time to rise from her chair when Madeleine walked into the kitchen with extended arms towards her daughter and granddaughter to embrace them.

"There you are, welcome to a new day!" Madeleine greeted. She then made a swift gesture toward the open window. "What a beautiful morning! There is not a cloud in the sky and everything is refreshed by the rain; thank goodness the storm did not cause too much damage."

Clothilde drew a chair away from the table and placed it next to hers.

Grandmaman please come and sit, but first I need another hug from you to make my day a special one."

"I will be delighted to oblige you my angel." Madeleine held Clothilde in her arms for a moment then released her.

"Did you have a grand time last night?"

"It was great."

"Good, very good!"

"Please Grandmaman, come and sit." Clothilde invited Madeleine again. "I'll bring you a cup of coffee."

"Where is Papa?" inquired Suzanne as she stood up to kiss her mother.

"He is still in bed," Madeleine replied with a tender smile. "He is all lazily nestled in his pillows, watching the morning news. I should join him there for coffee."

"Let me prepare it for you then," offered Clothilde.

"Thank you so much darling."

Madeleine went back to her bedroom carrying two cups of coffee set upon a tray covered by a lace doily.

Suzanne looked at the wall clock.

"Oh! It is getting late!" she exclaimed. "We must at once put an end to our idling or we will be late for mass!"

Thereupon, they both hurried in direction of the dining room to prepare the table for breakfast.

As soon as Clothilde drew the drapes from the windows facing east, streams of morning sunrays drenched the room with a golden brightness, and precipitated brilliant splashes of light on all the polished surfaces. A rich moss green was the dominant tone of this large room. It enhanced beautifully the vibrant burnt sienna of the antique and rustic furniture of different french periods. Some were as ancient as the house itself if not older.

From the center of the high ceiling, a colorful enamel chandelier with floral designs in cloisonne on white ground hung above a massive carved oak table.

"I meant to ask you, did Paul enjoy himself also?" Suzanne inquired. She unfolded a crisp white tablecloth, while Clothilde took four flowered Limoges plates out of the china cabinet.

"I should think so, maman."

"He seems so reserved. How did he survive our french exuberance so notably displayed on the fourteenth of July? Although I imagine, the fourth of July must cause as much excitement in his country?" Suzanne continued questioning.

Clothilde fetched the silverware from the top draw of a long buffet and laid it neatly by each one's place setting.

"He took part in the celebration as enthusiastically as we all did. Our group inevitably discussed the topic of the French Revolution; he joined in the conversation with much knowledge about it. I was surprised."

Suzanne rolled up four linen napkins that matched the tablecloth, and then inserted each one in a silver napkin ring etched with their respective names.

"His mother is from Paris, right? I remember Jean Luc telling me so about her. He also mentioned that she still has a piece of property somewhere near Chartres. No doubt she must have kindled in her son the curiosity to learn about his french heritage.

"I am sure she has," Clothilde conceded distractedly.

On a china platter, Suzanne grouped a butter dish with little glass bowls filled with various homemade jams.

"Did he dance?" she asked brightly.

An amused expression crossed Clothilde's face as she heaped fresh harvested fruits in a crystal compotier.

"Yes, he danced quite often, actually. He made it a point to let us know that his Parisian mother had taught him how to waltz."

Clothilde paused for a moment as though having been distracted; she needed a moment to think over what she wanted to say next.

"He noticeably spoke of his mother with great fondness and deference, giving the impression to be profoundly attached to her," she then stated.

"How very dear of him," Suzanne acknowledged and she emphasized playfully, "Paul is a very engaging young man, I should think many young ladies have wished for a dance in his arms."

Clothilde afraid of blushing at the thought of her own delight when she danced with Paul turned away from her mother and fumbled in the silverware draw.

With a nod of satisfaction, Suzanne took a survey of the table to make sure that nothing had been neglected.

"I am glad Jean Luc has invited him into our family. What a pity he has completed his sojourn in France. But who knows? Perhaps a kind providence shall bring him back to us again."

Clothilde had removed a vase of flowers from the middle of the table and had put it aside on a teacart. She transferred it back to its initial place. A sad and pensive expression weighed upon her face while she lowered her brow to conceal teary eyes. Her mother did not notice it, she was busy at the sideboard, filling a food warmer with crisp, butter crescents.

"There, all set!" Suzanne sighed once this last task was completed. "We should yet have plenty of time to dress for mass before breakfast, come along darling."

Clothilde walked to the window and pretended to smooth down the creases along the folds of the curtains.

"Yes Maman, I'll be coming promptly," she responded with affected gaiety in her voice while avoiding looking at her mother. But first, she would go to the pasture and tell Canon d"Or how troubled her heart was.

CHAPTER 12

When Clothilde and her family entered the church to attend the Grand Mass of eleven A.M., it was still early enough to find a vacant pew in the front rows of the transept, close to the chancel, where Elise already sat. Clothilde had just risen from a kneeling position to pray, and was settling down on her bench with missal in hands, waiting for the Mass to begin when Jean Luc and his own family arrived. Paul accompanied them more by politeness and respect for their religious observance than because of devotion to the practice of Catholicism and the customs attached to it. He had been raised in that faith, but with the passing of years a more personal interpretation of religion had altered his beliefs to a broader philosophical view of Christianity not structured and restricted by the definitions set by an institution.

He immediately recognized Clothilde ahead of him at the opposite side of the nave. His gaze rested on her for a moment. He thought she looked adorably dashing in her two-piece summer suit of white raw silk and her navy blue boater teasingly tilted toward the right side of her head. She wore accessories of the same blue. Her hair was pulled back in a French braid that elegantly molded her graceful nape.

She wished to know if Paul would attend Mass also, and even though an obstinate curiosity tortured her thoughts, she did not dare to look if he was among the new arrivals as they gradually filled the church near and far behind her. Oh, it seemed to take an eternity for the service to begin. Everything was so oppressively hushed except for the resounding clank of shoes on the cobbled stone floor and the pounding of her heart against her chest. Finally, driven by an excess of eagerness to know if he was in the church, she cast a swift glance over her left shoulder, and as she saw him sitting next to Jean Luc her dream of the previous night instantly gushed to her mind. She blushed from shame, feeling like an impostor who driven as it were by inappropriate desires, had fantasized to associate herself intimately with him. To mask her uneasiness she opened her prayer book and pretended to be duly exalted by spiritual inspiration. Soon, she would be severely frowned at, if she continued to behave so unfocused. She even tried to pray; but she tiresomely repeated the same litany as a result of straying from her intended prayer and having to start all over again.

At last, the priest vested in his white sacerdotal alb and chasuble, escorted by four acolytes, proceeded from the sacristy to the choir while reverently carrying the Eucharist. They gathered around the altar and the service began.

The first part of the ceremony held Paul's visual interest, but after a brief lapse of time, he allowed his attention to be swayed by the wondrous beauty of this little medieval church, where for centuries the reflection of heaven had fired up the villagers to exercise good will.

The rugged cold smell of the old stone floor and walls, the lingering trails of incense, the scent of melted wax from the votive candles and the fragrance of all imaginable flowers evoked in him what seemed to be some vague sensory impressions of which he had no precise recollection. He admired the magnificence of the stained glass windows portraying scenes from the Bible, while through their pure transparency the intercepted sunrays strewed sheaves of brilliant colors and draped with a chatoyant glaze the statue of Saints in their niche. A special vaulted recess was given to Saint Francis of Assisi who was gently whispering to a dove perched on his right hand raised in front of his chest.

In the left wing of the transept, a small chapel dedicated to the Virgin Mary holding the infant Jesus in her arms, was filled with glorious roses. One almost expected the flowers to extol suddenly the Holy mother and Child with glorious hymns rising to Heaven in clouds of perfume.

Along the walls, the Stations of the Cross depicted in high relief, poignantly epitomized the torment of the Christ being mercilessly driven to the Calvary. Paul's serene facial expression suddenly turned somber. He saddened as he began to reflect upon this unblemished sacrificial life. How it has been so ruthlessly violated by being used as a psychological contrivance to dominate and exploit the masses.

In the meantime, along with the congregation, Clothilde went through the motion of kneeling, sitting, standing, consistent with the traditional rituals of the Mass but not exactly aware of what she was observing. In truth, she had not listened to the least word pronounced in the sermon given by Father Baptist Vernier, the parish priest; nor had she paid heed to any part of the ceremony, which seemed interminable.

She was thinking about Paul.

How could she disregard the extraordinary affect he had on her? How could she fill her mind with holy thoughts when he was only a few meters behind her? How could she find peace when she suffered so much remorse yet drew such infinite pleasure from what gave rise to it?

In a moment of frustration, she wished that for some urgent reason (but not any drastic one, she specified,) Paul and Jean Luc would at once be called back to duty. She then condemned her willful, self-centered thinking. Dismayed, she ordered her chaotic brain to be still for a while. She needed to collect her thoughts and call upon God to grant her understanding. She really was in dire need of some enlightenment. She intensely appealed, then for a moment quietly listened. Not even the slightest clue was revealed to her. Out of patience to wait much longer for Divine Illumination, she endeavored to initiate a more aggressive, down-to-earth approach from a different perspective. For instance, if she were to advise a friend in a similar predicament what would she encourage? Well, she would counsel her to promptly dispel the obsession that is consuming her, to cease her futile struggle and to regain her self-possession. In other words, she would urge her friend to do away with her neuroses and resume her life as it was a few hours since. Indeed, all this sounded very wise, however it was a waste of time to consider any of it. Hadn't she tried to apply those remedies to herself but all in vain? "How could any normal human being remain so stoically objective amid this earth shattering madness?" she protested inwardly heaving a long sigh. "Oh, why can't I simply think of how much in love I am with Phillippe and of all the marvelous plans we have made for our future together like I am supposed to do? Why is this so difficult to take hold of my full attention? God forbid that I should ever bring any disgrace or deceptive follies between us!" she sorrily admonished herself as the priest announced that the Mass had ended and earnestly conferred blessings upon his flock. Thereupon the congregation began to slowly flow toward the west portal.

When Clothilde walked down the nave and passed by Paul, he was still seated. His head was turned away from her as he listened to Jean Luc who whispered something. She caught sight of his chestnut hair, which handsomely glistened under the sunbeams pouring through the stained glass. She could have slapped herself for having been tempted to run her fingers over the softness of it. Furtively, she pressed her way out.

CHAPTER 13

AS WAS THE custom after Mass, people took time to spend a few moments on the church lawn for the mere pleasure to socialize and perhaps even to indulge in a bit of harmless gossip. There, they leisurely interacted, asking news of each other, of their families or simply give way to trivial chats while the very young paid their respect to so and so of more advanced years. Invariably, Father Vernier could be seen among them like a good shepherd attending to his fold. He projected a striking presence with his white long beard and the grand bearing of his tall, robust stature clad in the black cassock worn by ecclesiastics. Thick, snowy eyebrows heightened the transparency of his intelligent blue eyes unfaded by the years but quite the contrary embellished by the gentle glow reflecting an inexhaustibly generous heart.

Elise had often pointed how Father Vernier with his breviary in hands, dallying in the midst of his followers within the church precinct, portrayed quite a colorful incarnate rendition of old Plato from Raphael's painting: *School of Athens*.

Because of her inner discord Clothilde on that Sunday morning felt oddly severed from the outside world. Distractedly, she stayed by her mother and grandmother's side while feigning attentiveness to their conversation with friends. She made a supreme effort not to look for Paul, but her eyes were less wise than her intent and they yielded to temptation. When she saw him, he and her grandfather were side by side while they faced the church entrance. They were observing the sculpture of the tympanum above the west portal. Clearly, Emile was explaining something that seemed to hold intensely Paul's interest. She quickly turned her eyes away from them and looked around wondering where in the world Elise was? Ah! There she was, further on the left in company of her elderly aunt. As Clothilde considered joining them, her gaze came upon Father Vernier crossing the lawn in her direction. Her face beamed with a smile and as if suddenly set free from a straight jacket, she sprang forward to meet him on his way.

"Here is my dear girl! And how are you today?" he greeted cheerfully taking her hands in both of his.

"Very well Father and how … ?"

"Ah, I am fine! Just fine!" he hurried to inform letting go of her hands. "The Good Lord takes great care of me. He keeps me fit so I can do His work. I am glad to see that Jean Luc is back with us for a couple of days, he looks well. A short while ago I had the opportunity to meet his friend Paul who seems to be a fine young man also. Have you good news from Phillippe?"

"Very good. He always asks about you Father. You are his hero.

Father Vernier laughed heartily.

"Well, next time you speak with him along with my fondest regards, please tell him to hurry back. He is missed and much needed here."

"I shall not forget."

"And how is the museum progressing? At the end of summer I should have some free time at my disposal; if I can be of any use it would be my pleasure to lend you a hand."

Father Vernier was a scholar.

"I thank you very much Father, your good advices and knowledge would be greatly appreciated," Clothilde accepted amiably.

He made a slight movement indicating he should move along.

"Well my dear, I must now take leave until we meet again at dinner tonight."

"Oh yes! It will be so wonderful to have you with us." Clothilde exclaimed joyfully in spite of her troubled state of mind. "It has been so long since you have spent time at our house, you are always so very busy."

"Indeed I am, but it is good. There is no such thing as working too much when one loves what one does."

Father Vernier remained silent for a brief moment. She thought to have read a question in his eyes and almost waited for it, but he simply said.

"Until later then, good bye Clothilde, go in peace and do well with your day."

She stared down at her shoes like a guilty little girl caught in wrongdoing. She raised her head again and made an effort to smile.

"Thank you Father. I shall try my best"

"That is really all what is required of us."

Father Vernier looked at Clothilde with as much love in his heart as a father could possibly hold for his own daughter. Thereupon, he turned about and walked toward Madeleine and Suzanne.

The affection was mutual. Clothilde loved Father Vernier. Being considered a dear friend held in very high esteem, he was always warmly received in her family circle. He had baptized her. He had taught her catechism in preparation for her first communion and her confirmation. Soon he should also have the joy to unite her and Phillippe in the sacrament of holy matrimony.

As she watched him walk away, she caught sight of Jean Luc hugging Madeleine; Paul stood next to him, talking to Suzanne. Clothilde sensed Paul was desirous to come and talk to her but was detained. She felt like a bird on a branch, undecided about which way to fly. She would have loved to join them and wish good morning to Jean Luc and Paul, like she ought to, but she willed her feet along the slated path that led to Elise. She had only taken a few steps when unexpectedly Jean Luc appeared behind her and gave a little tug to the rim of her hat, causing it to tilt backward. She sprang sideway in surprise.

Jan Luc broke into laughter.

"Sorry, I didn't mean to …"

"Jean Luc!" Clothilde cried out, also amused. She readjusted her hat back in place and lightly smacked his hand while looking passed him to check if he was alone. He was.

"Jean Luc! what are you doing?"

"I had in mind to ask you the same question. What has become of your social manners, not even a hello this morning?"

"Why yes! … I meant … I was going to … but first I wanted to say a few words to Elise's aunt before she went home. I see her so rarely."

"All right, you are excused," Jean Luc said indulgently. "You look cute in that hat," he teased affectionately. "Paul and I must leave now; actually we are late," he then informed looking at his watch.

"Leave?" she asked seized by a twinge of panic, afraid that what she had wished for was about to happen.

"Yes, Paul and I are invited at the Tournai's for a game of tennis and then for brunch."

Clothilde sighed with relief.

"See you at dinner," he said dashing off. "I shall give Paul your …"

Jean Luc was already too far, she didn't hear the rest of what he said. Shortly after, she watched him and Paul drive away and felt so discontented with herself because of her devious behavior. What had she turned into?

Elise and her aunt were no longer in view.

"Are you ready to go home?" asked Madeleine as Clothilde walked back to join her and Suzanne. "I must get to work; I could not bear to prepare dinner in haste and not measure to Jean Luc's expectations." A hint of pleasantry was in her voice but pride twinkled in her eyes.

"And furthermore, it is no less important that you should excel in your cream puffs for Father Vernier, or else he might ban you from the church for a while if not excommunicate you altogether," added Suzanne.

Madeleine laughed goodheartedly.

Upon this cheerful note they parted from their friends.

CHAPTER 14

"Are you in dreamland Clothilde?" I don't see a drop of oil pouring out of the bottle. At this rate, I may whip the eggs until the end of time and still get nowhere."

Clothilde darted a puzzled look at Madeleine when realizing she had slipped into her own world and had neglected to give full attention to what she was expected to do.

"I am sorry Grandmaman, apparently I have been distracted for a minute," she apologized as she redirected her concentration appropriately.

"There, you have it right again. Let the oil flow like a tiny thread, just like so," Madeleine instructed Clothilde. Thereupon they both resumed their teamwork in the busy kitchen of *la Brisante.*

They were preparing a mayonnaise for an aioli to be served with a cold salmon trout as an entrée; one of Jean Luc's favorite dishes.

Madeleine energetically whisked the egg yolks with the oil.

"Oh, I understand darling," she went on after having fallen back into the mechanism of her task, "I can very well understand that on such a beautiful Sunday afternoon you should have your thoughts upon other matters than on some boring domestic chores with your grandmother. While a young lady waits for her fiancé to be, as you are, she should be in the midst of nature surrounded by birds and flowers and butterflies while writing poems about all her dreams and desires."

Clothilde laughed.

"Grandmaman! You are truly a born romantic; the soul of a troubadour from among our ancestors must still be echoing through your own."

Madeleine amused, shook her head.

"Well, let me tell you, when I waited for your grandfather to return home from his military duty, in spring and summer I spent quite a few hours upon the hills behind our house or in my bedroom during the frosty winter evenings, letting my heart speak through my pen while I was lost in endless reveries."

"Did you really Grandmaman?"

"Oh yes! It was wonderful. Many, many times my dearest mother had to call me back to the mundane realities of the day."

"How lovely!"

"Well darling, it is the birthright of youth to construct beautiful dreams upon the many hopes offered by a life yet unlived."

"To be with you Grandmaman, even when attending to the least menial task, is certainly among the true joys life can ever offer me."

Tears welled up in Madeleine's eyes.

"Clothilde my girl, you are such a blessed joy!"

But far from having yielded to fantasies, Clothilde was given to pangs of anxiety and contradictions. She dreaded how she would conduct herself in the presence of Paul while concealing her inward feud, whereas she wished the clock would shrink time so that her desire to see him again should be promptly satisfied.

She was tempted to confide in her grandmother who by a sensible explanation, would probably draw some logic out of so much incongruities, as she usually did out of the most absurd situations.

"Grandmaman?"

"Yes darling?"

Clothilde remained mute.

Madeleine briefly glanced at her.

Yes Clothilde, were you about to ask me something?" she inquired, while transferring the blond sauce from a plastic bowl into a pretty porcelain dish.

"No, not really. It was just … oh, it was nothing," Clothilde replied in a casual tone of voice, which pretended to suggest that what she wanted to say was insignificant.

"Oh, all right darling," Madeleine said agreeably, although she sensed a certain restlessness in her grand daughter. "Well, I think this is done," she next concluded. "Yes, it looks just perfect. You see how it easily separates from the spoon without leaving the slightest smear? that is precisely the way a successful mayonnaise should be. Now I shall start immediately with the cream puffs."

"Good afternoon ladies!" greeted Elise as her crystalline voice rippled throughout the kitchen. While being affectionately welcome, she appraised the delicious food scattered all over the table and counter tops.

"I came to lend you a hand, if you have any use for it."

She did not wait for an answer but directly went to fetch an apron from the top drawer of a chiseled pine hutch and walked to the sink.

"I'll wash the bowls and the utensils as you use them, it will keep things tidy," she energetically proposed, unbidden.

Amused by Elise spontaneous good will Madeleine proceeded to gather flour, butter and eggs for her next recipe.

"A marvelous idea sweetheart! Thank you."

"Clothilde dear, would you mind chopping this parsley over here in the green bowl; I shall mix it with garlic to season the mushrooms." Suzanne requested while she opened a few jars of preserved boletus, agarics and chanterelles harvested from the rich moist soil of their woodland.

Elise put clean dishes in the cupboard and glanced sideways in direction of the table upon which Suzanne had just begun to slice a couple of plump dark truffles exuding the most exquisite aroma.

"Hmm! It smells so luscious!" Elise cheerfully exclaimed. "Indeed, this evening, Paul will be regally feasted upon our local culinary delicacies!"

"It is intended as such. We plan to lure him into coming back to visit us, if only for the food," Madeleine pointed out lightheartedly.

Elise wearing an air eloquent with implication, looked at Clothilde.

"I believe he may wish to be back for many other reasons, even though, rest assured, the food is not to be underestimated for its enticing merits."

At the thought she might never see Paul again, Clothilde sank into despair and had the impression that the floor had vanished into a void beneath her feet. She squeezed her eyelids tightly closed to stop her tears from flowing over and turned toward the sink where she went to wash her hands.

Madeleine glanced at her and pensively churned a custard in a pan on top of the stove.

"We have been acquainted with him just a few hours ago and already we feel like he is part of the family," she then voiced. "Isn't it strange how certain people are drawn to each other by some mysterious affinities, even upon their very first encounter?"

Clothilde listened to her grandmother while she let the water rinse her hand longer than necessary.

"Yes," she mused. "Yes, this is exactly how I feel concerning Paul; exactly. I have the impression to know him already. Does it mean I am disloyal to Phillippe?" she argued mentally. She shut the water off with a brisk gesture. "But all the same, there is something else, something beyond … "

Clothilde, would you please whip the fresh cream for me?" requested Madeleine as she poured the custard into an earthenware container. "I shall put this aside to chill then we will blend it together."

Suzanne who had concocted a vinaigrette for the salad, set apart the oil and vinegar bottles upon the shelves and gave a pleased look around her.

"We have done well. Thank you for your help, Elise."

Clothilde wrapped her arms around her mother's shoulders.

"Elise and I will finish cleaning up the kitchen. You and Grandmaman should take time to relax a bit with Grandpapa who will be back in a minute from his game of boules. Elise will you please help me lay the table, also?"

"Yes, of course, I gladly will, but before I need to go home and dress suitably for dinner."

Glancing at her own clothes, Clothilde laughed.

"And I should do so as well." She shifted her eyes toward the pasture. "However, not until I have given due attention to Canon d'Or. He must be well awake from his afternoon nap and wonder if we have moved away. Although after lunch I saw grandpapa leaning on the fence while he whispered to him, but that was very long ago in Canon d"Or's concept of time. Do we set the table in the garden?"

Subsequently to Clothilde's question, Suzanne sought advice from her mother.

"What do you think Maman?"

"I think it is a grand idea, the weather is so lovely, no doubt every one is likely to enjoy the outdoors," replied Madeleine.

Clothilde went to change clothes, her mother and grandmother as suggested took a moment of respite and sat on the back patio to enjoy a cup of freshly brewed coffee Elise had prepared for them.

Soon, Emile was back from his Sunday afternoon game of boules; an ancient and popular sport of the region. Upon arriving, Madeleine instructed him to go in the front garden, and under the widely spread branches of the old Sycamore join two long folding tables to comfortably accommodate the number of guests expected for that evening.

CHAPTER 15

DURING THE WARM season, people of the south
of France enjoyed dining in their garden. Clothide's suggestion to
entertain the guests amid the luxuriant sylvan setting of *la Brisante* was
an excellent choice. It was a delightful midsummer day that provided
the ideal weather for such an enjoyment. The westward sun trailed
streams of golden mist in the air suffused by the prevailing fragrances
of roses, carnations and lavender while the lethargic echoes of nature
weary from the heat hushed the countryside into a serene mood.

Elise returned dressed in a pale blue silk ensemble. Clothilde
reappeared into a cool sea green cotton dress that Madeleine had
crocheted. It was lined with satin of the same color, which subtly
shimmered through the patterns formed by the needlework. The
loveliness of the two young women enhanced the beauty of the
landscape as they bustled about in the front garden, and left on their
trail subtle hints of Christian Dior's perfume.

They were setting the dinner table.

"Let's first bring out all what we need and gather it over here,"
proposed Elise, pointing to a round wicker table with a glass top, always
kept on the front patio.

"A good idea," Clothilde consented.

They went back and forth with trays heaped with glasses, silverware,
tablecloths and napkins.

For the occasion Elise chose to take out the Limoges dinner service bordered by a pattern of pink and mauve flowers. Clothilde selected the etched blue crystal glasses that would sparkle in the sunlight like sapphire chalices.

In the nearby trees and brambles, the birds joyfully fluttered from twig to twig, for they had soon guessed that surely some kind of feast was on the agenda at *la Brisante*. The topic of their conversation focused exclusively upon the many delicious crumbs they hoped would fall on the ground. Whereas in the thick foliage of the acacia shading the terrace, myriads of cicadas disturbed from their daily siesta began to fill frantically the air with their trilled chanting.

Elise went into the kitchen to wash her hands soiled from dusting the chairs. Clothilde sat on a bench to pause for a minute and glanced at the house where the dearest to her heart were gathered. She also gave a tender look toward the pasture. Then she thought with joy that Phillippe would be coming home in a few days. She had no need to fantasize about those wonderful hopes from a life unlived, as had mentioned her grand mother only a few moments ago. Didn't she already hold it all in the palm of her hands? Why then, in a matter of a few hours, had she allowed inexplicable intrusions to throw everything into complete disarray?"

When Elise came back she found Clothilde sternly polishing the plates while piling them up on the dinner table. At once Elise helped her.

"I need a psychiatrist," Clothilde voiced bluntly.

Elise taken by surprise at the unexpected statement, stood still for a second, stared at her friend and faster than she could think asked playfully, "in what way?"

Clothilde frowned, hesitated for a second and then looked askance at Elise.

"What?"

As the ambiguity of the double meaning insinuated by Elise was implicitly elucidated they both gave way to laughter. However, soon Clothilde deliberately took on a reproachful look rendered all the more severe by her long eye lashes drawing a dark shadow over her eyes.

"You are odious!" she exclaimed.

"I know," Elise agreed.

Cothilde smiled and assumed a more relaxed stance.

"I am just frustrated … with myself, that is."

Elise sighed.

"I understand." There was a silence. "I have come to think of only one explanation for all what's happening" Elise resumed " but given that you would categorically dismiss it, I simply withhold to express my opinion."

"Would you be alluding to your reincarnation and …?"

"Yes," Elise hastened to reply assertively.

Clothilde grasped a cloth to buff up the silverware and shook her head in a sign of rejection.

"Please Elise! Your speculations are much too far fetched to be acceptable to me. You are well aware of that."

Elise held each glass against the light to verify if they were clear of fingerprint or dust.

"Ah, because my assumptions are not agreeable to you, doesn't nullify their possibility," she stated, ignoring Clothilde's protest.

Clothilde made a hand gesture expressing refutation.

"Your system only justifies a fixated attachment to the physical aspect of life on this earth. It perpetuates a worldly bondage from which at long last one erroneously refuses to detach. Furthermore …"

"This is not true," interrupted Elise.

"It makes absolutely no sense," pursued Clothilde. "I have much difficulty accepting how a stranger such as Paul for instance, would suddenly pop up in my life, just like that!" she emphasized what she intended to convey by snapping her fingers. "And moreover, purposefully come from a different world so we could specifically cross each other's path. Then as we meet, I would very casually be driven to ask *Well hello there! Excuse me, but don't I know you? I have a notion that from a remote stratum buried deep in my subconscious, I have met you somewhere and apparently we have to bring an old disagreement between us to an end. Do you remember me? My name is so and so. I am awfully curious to know why my thoughts and my emotions are stirred into sheer havoc as a result of simply having looked at you?*"

Elise expressed amusement at Clothilde's caricatured interpretation of two souls who consistent with the principle of rebirth come together again on this earth and experience a certain attraction, which will be defined by the nature of their previous relationship in a former life.

"You know it is not quite as such."

Broodingly, Clothilde ran the palm of her hand over the white tablecloth that glistened under the late afternoon sunlight as if it had been sprinkled with powdered mother of pearl.

Elise positioned the chairs around the table, sat in one of them and followed Clothilde's hand movement.

"Love has no frontier, and presumably the soul has no concept of distance. The reason for such a reunion is to bring back together two or more entities as often as necessary, so they confront issues left unresolved between them during a former life. It is said that the participants being fully cognizant of this fundamental necessity before their rebirth, in mutual agreement ask for this encounter.

"How long does that go on?" Clothilde asked without bothering to conceal the sarcasm in her voice.

"Until we have paid the bills claiming our due for our wrong doings. Until we have purged our sins and have reached the zenith of purity worthy of God's realm. Then we will no longer have need for this dense earthly condition, unless to serve some noble cause like the Saints do."

"Clothilde threw up her arms in exasperation.

"On what grounds can you so determine the certainty of all this? How do you know if it is supported by any truth? All what you are telling me is nothing other than utter conjecture based upon an antediluvian ideology."

Elise laughed.

"My dear, every facet of our existence meets with uncertainties. It is foolish to repudiate what we consider improbable, for it may give way to some very exciting enlightenment. If we avoided the risk of assumptions that might lead to explore the unknown and possible discoveries, our world would be an unthinkable pool of stagnant ignorance. I do not assert an absolute truth; neither do I reject its possibility. Little children are known to remember clearly their past lives. Verifications have confirmed their memory to be accurate. I think that when Phillippe was a little boy and stated to his mother, *"I was a priest before,"* might not be just a child giving in to some fantasy."

What? … What are you talking about?" Clothilde questioned as a chill passed through her. "Are you telling me that Phillippe was remembering having been a priest in a previous life on this earth?"

"It's possible," Elise maintained.

Cothilde imploringly stared at the sky, clearly asking Heaven for help. All this sounded so "heathenish." It made her feel queasy.

"Please Elise, I don't care to go on deliberating on that subject. The entire day has caused enough uneasy feelings without adding more to it."

"All right," Elise complied in good humor.

Clothilde's face cheered up when her attention suddenly shifted to Madeleine opening the front door and then stepping outside. She and Elise hurried toward her.

"Oh! How beautiful! The color arrangement is ravishing! Madeleine exclaimed when laying eyes on the table. She then looked up at the acacia.

" Oh, my! the cicadas are of a merry spirit this afternoon!" She gaily observed.

At the sight of her grandmother's pleasure, Clothilde's mood was immediately lifted.

"The table is all set, Grandmaman, well almost, except for candles and flowers."

"I'll get the candles for you, what color?" offered Madeleine briskly going back in direction of the house.

"White will be just fine," replied Clothilde in accord with Elise's assenting nod.

"Come along Elise," Clothilde beckoned having forgotten all about their disagreement. "Shall we go and gather a pretty bunch of flowers?" she proposed pointing to the violet Venetian vase standing empty between two crystal candle holders at the center of the table.

Together they walked into a path leading to a cluster of rose bushes.

CHAPTER 16

JEAN LUC'S MOTHER, Justine, stroked the front door bell of *la Brisante,* with her index finger, as if brushing a speck of dust away from it, then not waiting for someone to answer she instantly walked inside leaving the door ajar for Charles, her husband who was behind by a few steps.

"Anybody home?" she called out and peeked into the parlor where she saw no one. Clothilde met them half way down the hall.

"Oh, hello Aunt Justine and Uncle Charles! she greeted. Since they were close enough to each other, she gave a hug to both of them at once with her eyes fixed on the entrance. A twinge darted through her heart while she apprehensively expected Jean Luc and Paul to follow. The door stayed shut. Immediately, they went to the kitchen where the rest of the family was keeping good company to Suzanne and Madeleine who were giving a last touch to their superb culinary creations. Emile was there as well, not that he was of great help . He mostly sampled a taste of this and a sip of that, dispensing his opinion on the flavor. But Madeleine enjoyed having him around, although sometimes she really had to gently slap his forearm and order him to keep his hands "off the pots."

"Come in, come in! Make yourself at home!" he invited as Justine and Charles entered the kitchen. He rose from his chair that was a bit set back in front of the window. For the last hour or so, he had prudently been sitting there out of Madeleine's way. He looked past their shoulders with the anticipation also that Jean Luc and Paul would enter next.

"Well, where are the handsome fellows?" he soon inquired keeping his gaze fixed on the doorway.

"Here is one of them!" boasted Jean Luc's father, Charles, as he puffed his chest like a wooing peacock.

"I realize that and indeed I am dazzled, but I mean the other two," Emile acknowledged good-naturedly while he cleared his throat. Casually he motioned toward Clothilde and laid both hands on her shoulders. She had been sitting quietly on a bench alongside the huge oak table; and speechless from curiosity waited for the answer to the question she ached to ask herself.

"They should be here soon, by their own independent mean. They mentioned something about a flower shop in Sarlat," informed Charles with an air of affected nonchalance, ostensibly pretending to cover up a little secret he had in part given away deliberately. "They intended to drive there earlier after lunch, when the sprinklers in the orchard broke," he then explained. "Since I found no plumber available without delay, I came to the decision to turn off the main water valve and wait until Monday to have it mended. However, Jean Luc insisted upon fixing it himself and Paul seemed very much in favor of taking the task in hands as well. So both relentlessly dug the ground. Weltered in mud up to their knees and elbows for a couple of hours, they seemed to enjoy every minute of it. The repair was as efficiently executed as if handled by a team of the best professionals. Paul's competence in this kind of labor was truly impressive."

"Did they put it back together?" inquired Clothilde in a spontaneous outburst of candid admiration that everyone easily shared with her.

"They did," answered Charles with the tone of a proud father.

"Paul is such a dear!" added Justine as she made a tour of the kitchen counters. "Oh, everything looks so exquisite! Jean Luc will be in heaven!" she voiced suddenly sidetracked by the colorful display of tempting food. She then whirled toward the ice chest that Charles had carried over and had placed by the sink.

"Here are the hazel nut ice cream and fruit salad I prepared this morning," she indicated while storing them respectively in the freezer and the refrigerator.

"Thank you so much. These are always welcome at our dinner

parties," acquiesced Madeleine as she listened to the clock ringing five times.

"Oh my! It is much too late now for us to stay in here and continue to chat like if we had settled in the most elegant drawing room. Our guests will soon arrive, we cannot keep on receiving in the kitchen among saucepans!" she declared with a suppressed laugh. "Is everything ready in the parlor, Emile? "I mean all what is needed for the *aperitifs*? Oh, here, take those nuts and olives there also, everyone will enjoy nibbling at them while sipping on their drink," Madeleine requested further.

"Yes, my dear. Well, it seems that some of us have been unceremoniously dismissed from here," responded Emile with feigned meekness, but with a tender look. Charles, come along! Indeed, it is not too early to quench our thirst with a few drops of whiskey on ice, is it? Ladies," he invited as he slightly bowed, "would any of you care to join us? We will be in the parlor eager to again enjoy your gracious company."

Justine put her arms around her father's shoulders and rose on her toes to kiss him on his left temple.

"What a fantastic idea Papa! you have the gift to always come up with some excellent suggestions at the most opportune moments."

"Certainly you have that incredible talent!" reinforced Suzanne, who then turned to her mother.

"Dinner is all ready Maman, so come also, let's go and freshen up and then take a moment to relax and enjoy a cocktail."

Madeleine stroked her chin with the fingertips of her right hand. For a second she considered Suzanne's request.

"All right," she then accepted, and decisively unfastened her apron string.

Suzanne looked at Clothilde and Elise with the overt expression: "will you join us also?"

Clothilde did not need to be begged, for the expectation of Paul's arrival caused an irrepressible anxiety difficult to overcome. Yes! A chilled Martini chatoyant like liquid amber over sparkling crushed ice, indeed sounded very, very nice.

As soon as everyone had entered the parlor, Emile walked to the window and gazed outside watching for Jean Luc's car to appear on the orchard road. The air sparkled over the landscape stretching far off until the green mass of the forest had engulfed the distance. The cows and the horses out of their stables, wandered away from the tree arbors where they had found shelter against the afternoon sun. they placidly grazed about the pastures and seemed in perfect accord with their existence. Sheep and goats rambled in the meadows, followed by their frolicking young. In the midst of them, a few farmers yet at work in the fields, completed a sublime statement of the indivisible merging of nature and life into a harmonious relationship.

"We ought to sit in the garden, the weather is glorious." Emile encouraged as he leaned over the windowsill and took a long, deep breath. They all went to sit in wicker chairs gathered on the front patio.

Clothilde welcomed her grandfather's suggestion, for truly the walls of that room seemed ready to close on her. Her nervousness being so oppressive, she was in need of fresh air. Socially refined by habit, she delicately sipped her drink, but honestly, she wished she could gulp it down all at once. The soothing effect of alcohol, might bless her with the inner calm she so desperately sought.

CHAPTER 17

As THEY ALL began to chat, Emile felt the urge to move after having idled too long in the kitchen. He stood up, quietly scanned the surroundings and then motioned in direction of the steps leading up to the terrace. He had in mind to gather a few small folding tables, which had been left there the previous night after being used by the company. He came to realize that if scattered around the garden they should be a useful means for the guests to free their hands of empty glasses. When he reached the upper level towering over a vast panorama, he took a moment to contemplate the beauty of the landscape dramatically immersed in the golden glow of the declining sun. Even though through the years he had watched every conceivable hour of the four seasons pass over *la Brisante*, each time yet, when his gaze wandered over his beloved land, he was swept over by new enchantments to behold.

From below, Madeleine noticed that her husband was detained from their group by clearly having strayed into a reflective mood, as he enjoyed doing from time to time. She went up the terrace to join him.

"You seem lost in reverie my dear," she observed and understood why as she glanced over the magnificent view.

"Ah! I came to pick up these, and indeed I have let myself drift into a flight of fancy," Emile conceded while pointing at the tables. "Ah," he went on looking again at the lands and driven back to the course of his thoughts. "It seems it was only yesterday that you and I walked in those meadows with so much sunshine in our heart. It seems only like yesterday that our daughters and our grand children filled the countryside with their carefree laughter, while Canon d'Or still being a little colt cavorted so endearingly around them. We all thought our youth was everlasting."

Emile stood silent staring at the distance.

"How elusive everything is!" he then said as if thinking aloud. "When we are young, life ahead of us seems like an expansible universe. A universe with golden suns and silvery moons amid an infinity of glittering hopes, and bulging with illusions. Then, when it is all behind us, it amounts to no more than a shrunken star where all our dreams lay buried." Turning to Madeleine, he then considered, "what's all this really about? There again, the more I think about it the more I come to wonder if Elise's concept of our existence through the cycle of rebirth could be the answer to this riddle after all? Sometimes she sounds so convincing. Her system of beliefs certainly imparts some sense of purpose to our journey on this earth. Don't you think so?"

"Well yes, you know that I too often ponder upon such notion. It gives one plenty to think about," acquiesced Madeleine, while gently laying her hand on Emile's left elbow.

"Ah, He alone has the answer," sighed Emile, while raising both arms toward the heavens. He then shook his head, looked at Madeleine and with a teasing smile, feigned an overstated self command as if to offset his indulgence in an excess of sentimentality.

"Now come along Madeleine!" he beckoned taking her hand in his. "Will you please stop standing there and encourage my jabber when our guests are about to arrive. Have I not told you I only came here to fetch those tables?"

"Oh, of course dear, of course!" my deepest apologies for having distracted you. How very inconsiderate of me," went along Madeleine with an amused expression in her eyes. She looked over in direction of the main road and noticed Jean Luc's car. "Oh! Here are the boys!" she abruptly announced. Forgetting all about the tables she and Emile hastened down to join everyone rushing toward the driveway.

Clothilde thought luck was in her star. Deeming herself unnoticed, she sprang from her chair and leaped over the stairs like a nimble dear. She tossed a nervous glance around, then entered the parlor. There, she furtively grasped a bottle, any bottle at her reach and administered herself a copious dose of whatever was inside it, which happened to be brandy. But Elise nonplussed by the unforeseen behavior of her friend, had soon followed her steps. Approaching the door she caught her in the very act and grinned with tight lips in an attempt to suppress an outburst of laughter that might have drawn the attention of anyone near by. She leaned against the doorjamb.

"Really! Is this necessary? My dear friend, what are you trying to escape? What are you running away from, yourself?" she reprimanded.

Clothilde wiped her mouth with the back of one hand and raised the other to signal that she was not disposed to hear an admonition. She gave a little nudge to Elise's elbow.

"Come! I'll be just fine."

They both walked outside with a composed appearance somewhat exaggerated by Clothilde who a bit light headed, feared to reel out in front of family and guests. At once, she was seized by the incredible desire to rush toward Paul and welcome him in an embrace as he and Jean Luc alighted from the car.

After the greetings, Jean Luc walked to Emile and presented him with a smartly wrapped package containing a bottle of Calvados, a famous brandy extracted from pressed apples after their juice has been drawn for cider. It bears the name of the department of Calvados, a region north west of Paris where it is traditionally distilled. Jean Luc obtained it home made from a military comrade. It was always a much-praised gift to offer his father and his grandfather when coming on leave.

Paul rested his gaze on Clothilde for an instant.

"Good evening," he said with a slight nod as he approached her with a smile.

"Good evening, Paul," she acknowledged. Offering her hand to his she stoically preserved a calm countenance. He excused himself, went back to the car and returned with a lovely but unpretentious assortment of orchids. In an easy bearing, he carried it to Madeleine and Suzanne who at that moment stood side by side.

"I have heard, you are very fond of these, it is the least I can do to express my gratitude for your kindness," he said presenting the bouquet with perfect simplicity. Since circumstances did not allow Paul to return the invitation, he had asked Jean Luc what would be apropos to offer the hostesses Madeleine and Suzanne for their thoughtful consideration. Jean Luc positively informed him that he could never go wrong by way of orchids; his grandmother and his aunt having a consummate passion for those flowers.

"How lovely!" exclaimed Suzanne, deeply touched by such delicate gesture.

For a moment Madeleine was wordless, she then took a long sigh and looked at him.

"Oh! Paul, you really should not have! Oh! How magnificent they are!" She raised both arms to reach his face. He bent forward to allow her to take his head between her hands and to kiss him gently on the right cheek. She carefully took the orchids with as much wonder and tenderness in her eyes as though she was receiving a kitten. She motioned toward the dinner table and then went back on her steps.

"I would like them to be in front of our eyes during dinner, but it is not a wise idea, the sunrays are still strong enough to damage those fragile petals," she said looking at them caringly. "Shall we keep them in the parlor, Suzanne?"

"An excellent suggestion Maman, they can be admired by everyone there also," agreed Suzanne whose pleasure was greater still from seeing her mother so overjoyed.

"If a man knew how irresistibly masculine and appealing he is when he shows his gentle side, the world would turn so much smoother," Elise whispered to Clothilde who meanwhile had been transformed into a drooling bundle of mush.

Paul's equanimity, his sober dignity, his total lack of affectation moved her so profoundly, that she could have quite easily fallen in love with him at this instant if circumstances had been different, of course. Her attention temporarily shifted to the cheery appearance of Father Vernier followed by Veronique and Frederick.

Elise's mother and father, Melanie and Bernard, regretfully were unable to partake in this family reunion, due to a previous engagement elsewhere.

After having served a scotch to Paul and a Pernod to Father Vernier, Jean Luc poured himself a gin and tonic. Madeleine and Suzanne excused themselves to go back into the kitchen.

Even with the help of her self-prescribed tranquilizer, Clothilde never reached the level of relaxation she had hoped to attain. She tried to apply the suggestions she had considered in church and pretended to be the friend she advised. Well, theoretically all those marvelous ideas appeared like an effective recourse if proposed to someone else. However when making an effort to abide by them, she found herself so entangled into a web of mental acrobatics that not even an entire regiment of Spartans could have kept up with it and neither could she. When Paul looked at her, or she happened to glance at him, a horde of emotions stirred in her like frenzied butterflies caught in a net.

Ever since the first time Paul had laid his eyes on Clothilde, she had been on his mind as well. Possibly, he was in a lesser emotional dualism than she experienced, in the sense that he did not carry the extent of guilt, which burdened her. Having no commitment to a romantic relationship he was accountable to himself only. But all the same, he had his own butterflies to tame from being so uncommonly captivated by a young woman he had barely met; a woman who was not free and who belonged to the family where he had been most generously invited. Certainly, it would not have been in this setting that he would have sought an amorous escapade. Anyway, he had no propensity for that kind of frivolous entertainment. The very thought of it appalled him. Therefore, because of his inappropriate sentiments he found himself seized by pangs of despair at the conclusive recognition that there was nothing to foresee and hope from this unfathomable adventure.

CHAPTER 18

AMID SMILES AND laughter, the company began to mingle in amiable conversations. Clothilde stood next to Justine and Frederick who discussed the brilliant colors and poetic style of Marc Chagall's painting. She really took no notice of what they were saying. Her concentration was deflected by Paul, toward whom now and again she darted a few surreptitious glimpses while Father Vernier and he were becoming acquainted. Jean Luc joined them at the same time Madeleine came outside to spend a brief moment with the guests. After she and Father Vernier had exchanged a few words, Madeleine apologized for having to return into the house. The good Abbe excused himself also and escorted her back to the front door. Jean Luc guessed Paul had taken notice that Madeleine at times, addressed Father Vernier by his first name whereas everyone else always referred to him as "Father."

"Let me tell you a secret even so it is known over the entire county," Jean Luc felt compelled to share with Paul, while his gaze affectionately followed his grandmother and Father Vernier walk away together. "Once upon a time when still in high school, this holy man and this beautiful lady had very tender feelings for each other; but one day, God came along, my grandfather came along, and so they were driven asunder to live happily ever after."

Paul fascinated by the story, spontaneously turned his attention in their direction, and then gently smiled as one would at the narrative of a charming idyll. Thereupon Father Vernier returned to resume his conversation with Paul. Jean Luc seeing a vacant chair next to Clothilde, politely distanced himself and went to sit opposite her with a scrutinizing frown.

"Why are you so silent and aloof this evening? Is everything all right Clothilde?"

"Oh, I am fine Jean Luc, thank you, but the day has been long and busy, so it is good to quietly relax a while," Clothilde answered behind a cheery pretense.

"Indeed it has been an eventful day for everyone I suppose. Paul and I had planned to come here earlier and give you a hand, but soon after our return from lunch the irrigation system in the orchard broke and shot up water like a geyser; so we spent the afternoon working on it."

"Yes, I have heard. Your father is so pleased with your efforts."

"Thanks to Paul, I could not have fixed it without his help and I must add without his expertise."

"Your parents think he is quite a treat to have around," Clothilde said, aware that she could have gone on talking about Paul until time on this earth ended.

"Yes he truly is. With what regrets I shall see him leave. I would have enjoyed inviting him here often; he seems perfectly comfortable among us and ..."

Elise suddenly materialized behind them and blindfolded Jean Luc's eyes with both hands.

"Who could that be? Come and sit with us, impossible brat!" he exclaimed. He gently snatched her wrists with both hands and pulled her around.

"Here, take this chair Elise," Clothilde offered with an unsteady voice, "I'll go to the kitchen awhile; perhaps I can be of some use to our chefs," she managed to articulate through a smile as her heart sank into melancholy.

When Clothilde entered the house, she surrendered to the desire for a breath of privacy by withdrawing into the sitting room. She walked to the window, which opened wide on the dappled fields stretching far toward the distant hills. There, she stood and stared at the depth of the cloudless sky, as wild country scents wafted around her.

"Why have I grown into such despondency?" she mused. "Why does this sudden chasm so wretchedly afflict my soul? What do I want, what do I seek, what have I need of that leave me so dissatisfied?" Her pondering was soon interrupted when she heard Madeleine in the hall, mentioning to someone that dinner was ready. After a minute of hesitation instead of walking toward the kitchen, Clothilde hurried back outside and directly went to the dinner table. She wanted to make sure that no dust or whatever else had sullied the sparkling china and glasses, Elise made haste to help her. While giving a last minute review to their chef-d'oeuvre, Clothilde caught a glimpse of Jean Luc wearing a gleeful grin. He was approaching Paul who was just coming back from the pasture where he, Father Vernier and Charles had enjoyed a companionable moment with Canon d'Or.

"Paul!" She next overheard Jean Luc say, "I have the honor to inform you that my grandfather presently told me: *"If I had another granddaughter, I would absolutely insist that she and Paul fall madly in love with each other so I could proudly become his grandfather as well."* There you have it my friend. I knew you would immediately win his heart, and imagine you would then be my cousin! My! I would not mind this a bit!"

Paul kept his eyes on Jean Luc and with an immense effort, resisted to look at Clothilde.

"Well!" he replied laughing, "thank you, I could not be more flattered. I wish that too."

Clothilde lowered her eyes and awkwardly stared at the ground, grateful that thoughts could not be read on one's face.

Elise smiled.

Suzanne came out to graciously summon everyone at the table.

CHAPTER 19

As ALWAYS DINING at the Brisante was a rare delight. The food and wine were exquisite, the hosts and guests charming, the conversations lively. One topic weaved itself easily into the other without drawing out on ponderous deliberations or interfering with desultory talks. Everyone's interest was held alert in an exchange of pleasurable ideas. Since their knowledge was broad and varied, they were never short of subjects for discourses, which could range from Plato's Republic to the best recipe for red-current jam.

Paul was swayed by those wonderful people so devoid of pretense. They showed a noble refinement of character and knew how to respect and celebrate the gift of life. They stayed in harmonious rapport with themselves, with their fellow beings and with their universe, while cultivating a profound love for their families and honorable traditions. They were wholly healthy.

Madeleine was seated at one end of the table; Paul was placed directly on her right. Clothilde sat opposite him but more toward the middle of the table length. The inevitable meeting of their glances stirred within both of them the most mystifying emotions. Thank goodness, the dry yet mellow Chardonnay, which enhanced so well the delicate taste of the salmon trout, egged her on very favorably. Therefore she had the temporary illusion to have regained a certain control over her wayward mind. Finally, her heart was allowed repose from the riotous palpitations prompted by each gaze she laid on Paul.

All the same, after being in her company for sometime, Paul had come to observe that Clothilde's response to him suggested a nervousness he did not notice in the manner she reacted to others. Consequently, in the course of dinner he continued to be perceptive of her inmost discomfort that still prevailed over the pacifying effect of the wine, and in spite of however much she tried to mask it behind an air of studied ease. The thought of her being troubled awoke in him a strange desire to shield her against any distress.

The evening reached its zenith when upon the insistence of Jean Luc, Madeleine and Father Vernier united their tenor and soprano voices to sing in a duo of supreme counterpoint, the old ballads and folk songs of the Perigord. Suzanne accompanied them on the Piano. When Emile smiled at his "Amaranth," as he would endearingly call Madeleine, they drank from each other the love that inexhaustibly poured from their heart and soul, as countless memories were evoked by those charming songs.

Clothilde noticed that Paul had grown solemn as his eyes stayed focused on Madeleine and Father Vernier. She steered her gaze across the parlor window and watched the day slipping away. At the horizon, the vermillion and pink coral mist exhaled by the ebbing sun had completely dissolved in the lapis lazuli translucence of the night. Time did not relent from making the evening pass by. In a few hours, early the next morning Jean Luc and Paul would journey back to Dreux. How could she maintain her poise when what she had suppressed so bravely, now with full malice as it were gushed to the surface and rendered her helpless? Bemused, questioning her sanity, without being aware of it, her eyes followed the tallest foliage detaching itself from the background, like a festoon of wrought iron tracery.

Finally, the hour to part had come.

As they all went out on the front lawn to bid each other good-bye Clothilde wished she could have disappeared in the bowel of the terrace and fall into a mummified sleep to rid herself of all the throbs that crushed her heart.

Jean Luc sensed her dismay and took her in his arms thinking she was saddened by his departure.

"Cheer up darling! We will see each other again for your engagement only a few weeks away. Phillippe will be here in a couple of days, you don't want him to see you with a gloomy face, do you? Come now! Put on that radiant smile that fits you so well."

"They love each other like brother and sister. She misses him so very much. We all miss him. I shall be glad when this military business is done with," Suzanne said to Paul who was deeply moved by the sight of Clothilde's sadness. He strove desperately to withstand the pain that wrung his own heart.

Madeleine wiped her eyes with a pretty lace handkerchief.

"Now Paul, you must continue to keep in touch with us, there is no reason … no reason at all why you should not visit with us every so often. These days, traveling is made so fast and convenient." She tucked her kerchief in her dress pocket. "Distances are crossed quite easily, as if the world had shrunk," she added with an abrupt, nervous chuckle.

"It will be my pleasure," Paul responded warmly. "I shall readily plan on it, and I want to thank you for all your kindness, for …"

"Well, my friend, are we ready to tear ourselves away and give a big salute to the colonels?" broke in Jean Luc while pressing his grandmother against him.

Paul smiled and nodded in reply.

"Do go on. You need to be refreshed with a few hours of good rest for your long drive and don't forget to phone us as soon as you arrive. Now off you go," Madeleine encouraged. She gave an affectionate stroke to Jean Luc's cheek. "And Paul, I shall take very special care of those beautiful orchids."

Upon their farewell, Paul was not given just a formal handshake as he received at the occasion of his introduction. With sincere affection, he was hugged by the entire family including by Father Vernier. Repeatedly, he was invited to come again. When in turn he and Clothilde also embraced, he was overwhelmed by a profound desire to retain her in his arms for a while. She, almost in tears and unable to bear the intense emotions aroused by their closeness, hastened to withdraw.

"Perhaps we shall meet again," Paul said fearful that at any instant he should loose courage and his inner disquietude might belie his outer composure.

"Oh, yes we must! You will come back won't you?" Clothilde asked spontaneously. Driven by sorrow, she did not give a thought whether what she had said exposed her true feelings.

"Well, Paul! you have heard my cousin. How could you possibly refuse such a gracious invitation," stressed Jean Luc who had come back to join them.

"Yes, Jean Luc, I appreciate the kindness. Yes, I hope I shall return for a visit. Thank you Clothilde," Paul assented, all rather quickly as though wishing to eschew the painful moment. He had to exert the totality of his mental power to maintain command of his poise.

A gap of somber silence followed after Jean Luc and Paul drove away from *la Brisante* and their car disappeared in the darkness. Elise took Clothilde's hand to gently lead her toward the garden.

"We are taking a walk," she decisively informed.

"It's a lovely night." Suzanne acknowledged in reply to Elise. "How regrettable that Paul must leave for America so soon after we have met him," she then said following Emile and Madeleine as they walked back toward the house."

Clothilde and Elise having by then reached an ash grove, which bordered the orchard, sat on a bench and while Clothilde wept, Elise held her close. Neither of them spoke.

Meanwhile, Paul had found himself alone in his bedroom at *la Madrigale*. He welcomed the few hours of solitude the night offered him before he and Jean Luc would set forth on the road. Pensively, he opened the window. The moon hung high amid the shimmery darkness of space studded with pulsating stars that seemed to throb from a heartbeat radiating life throughout the universe. His gaze drifted slowly over the landscape plunged in a calm slumber. For the first time ever he viewed the days ahead overcast by a heavy gloom. Everything seemed void of purpose. He felt a change in him that reason was unable to explain. He prepared for the night, and then lay on the bed.

"A friend kindly invites me to spend a weekend in his family and heedless of all scruples, in a few hours only I have become obsessed with a woman who not only is his cousin, but moreover is just about to be betrothed. How could I, how dare I?" he questioned again in sheer exasperation. "And why such deep melancholy at the thought of having to part from her?"

He smiled as he then recalled their peculiar first encounter and with what surprise he met her again by the riverside. He remembered also the touch of her hand during the storm, or how charmingly she wore that chic little hat at church. Well, yes, he was a man and a free man at that and she was a very beautiful woman. But he was a man with principles and Clothilde inspired him only with the loftiest feelings and respect.

He stared at the sky, trying to order his thoughts. They seemed to travel back and forth and around and around among the stars, as if searching a way out of confusion through a maze. Exhausted, he fell asleep. When he rose at the first streak of dawn, there was by then a lot of bustling around the kitchen where Justine was already preparing breakfast. From the open window, he looked over the vineyards and the wheat fields still immersed in a violet penumbra. The roosters announced that the sun was climbing the slopes of the eastern horizon and would soon pour out his lavish rays over the earth. He heard the song of the cuckoo echoing from the depth of the wooded hills. Oh, but how desolate it all seemed to his dejected heart, how terribly lonely; like a cold winter morning on a barren land.

Twice he tossed his head around and loosened his shoulders as though aligning himself to defy the reality of the new day. After he had dressed himself and had made sure that the room was left tidy, he grasped his suitcase and wearing a feigned smile he went to meet his hosts. It was not yet daylight when he and Jean Luc took leave for their journey back to Dreux.

A few kilometers away, Clothilde had not found rest. Each time she closed her eyes the thought she would not see Paul again gave her the sensation to have slipped into nothingness. She yearned to speak with him, to apologize for the unbecoming attitudes he at time had displayed. She wished to let him know ... oh, to let him know whatever,anything ... anything, so long she could spend one more moment with him. At last, surrendering to weariness she dozed off in the chilling embrace of the void he had left behind

PART II

CHAPTER 1

IT WAS THE season of many activities for the landowners of the southwest of France. Their fertile soil thrived with the bountiful rewards of their spring toiling. From mid summer until well into the end of autumn there was very little respite allowed by the call of the earth. But extra hands were always available to face such an amount of labor. The buoyant energy that whirled in the air saturated with pastoral fragrances, and the land, which vibrated from myriads of colors and sounds, bestirred in everyone an enthusiastic spirit.

Already the hay and the wheat had fallen under the clangor of the giant mower. The hay had been scattered on the ground to wither; now and again it was tossed to prevent mildew. Its slender stems gradually turning to a metallic grey were spread thick like a silvery fleece over the shorn meadows. In the nearby parched-fields the cut wheat was girded into sheaves and heaped in glossy blond stacks. Forthwith, the thresher like a mighty earth-shaking Poseidon would separate the grain from the shaft in a cyclone of dust wafting on high. The plump crimson and gold grapes amid the luxuriant vine foliage portended a fine vintage year, so without delay the cellars and the vats were freshly scrubbed clean and given time to thoroughly dry. The barrels were set aside to receive the new wine.

In the kitchen, summer fruits and vegetables cluttered tables and counters tops. There women, amid the jangle of cooking utensils, busied themselves. For it was the time for canning. The steam rising from the vessels on the stove burners permeated the house with a fruity aroma, which unequivocally stated that jam was in the making.

Such worthwhile chores assured that the pantry shelves would be amply replenished for the winter days.

The tasks seemed endless, but they would be completed. Before the onset of the cold weather, barns, silos and hangars would be well restocked with hay, grains, tobacco, chestnuts and walnuts. Only the best in quality could be expected from the annual harvests so abundantly bestowed by this blessed land.

Husbandry at *la Brisante* excluded any kind of animals to be utilized for food, work or whichever financial purpose. It would have been an unthinkable practice in view to fatten the bank account. The revenue came strictly from the cultivation of the soil, which brought a more than substantial yearly income.

Jean Luc being deprived to partake in those seasonal occupations, gave a cheerless farewell to Grolejac as he left. He and Paul had already covered a considerable distance faring northward when at seven o'clock in the morning, Madeleine and Emile sat at the breakfast table in front of their first cup of coffee.

"At this time next year, Jean Luc shall be back home permanently," said Madeleine absently buttering a slice of toasted bread. "What am I thinking of, not next year but the year after." she calculated and rectified to her discontent. "Ah, still such a long, long time to wait for his return home!"

Emile deemed so too, but was prompted to comfort his wife. He sighed and affectionately reached for her hand across the table.

"You know my dear, we are quite fortunate really. Imagine if Jean Luc had been sent to some remote place far from his own country and was denied the privilege that permits him to return home as often as he does. We will see him again in three weeks or so for Clothilde's betrothal, then I am sure for Christmas if not sooner."

"Yes, of course, yes," conceded Madeleine lightening up to a more optimistic point of view. "You are right Emile, if we think of it that way, we are lucky indeed." She reflected upon a frown for a moment.

"Why, what on earth makes me so egotistically minded? My goodness! If one takes in consideration how difficult it must have been for Paul and his mother to be separated by such a distance and moreover for a requirement of four years at that, indeed I have no cause for complaints. If only the opportunity had been given us to meet him sooner, we could so readily have become a substitute family for him." she bemoaned, as if voicing her regrets would atone for her self-centered outlook and her lack of gratitude for her grandson's favorable situation.

Emile nodded to indicate he fully shared Madeleine's feelings, then helped himself to a small dish of fruits while she looked at him with aroused interest.

"Emile?"

"Yes dear."

"Did you say last night that Paul's mother owns a farm somewhere in the Beauce? Do you know if she and Paul ever go there to review their position as proprietors, for I would think that even as absentee landlords, their presence should be essential on occasions, shouldn't it?"

"I should imagine so. Being near Dreux it has been rather convenient for Paul to keep regularly in touch with the tenants. Now that he has left France, either he or his mother must have in mind to every so often check on the property."

"Well I am sure that Paul would not fail to stop by even for a short visit if he should come to oversee it himself."

Madeleine motioned to get up from the table.

"Where are the girls?" Emile asked. He tossed a searching look around as if they might have been somewhere in the dining room and he had not seen them.

"After feeding Canon d'Or, Suzanne went directly to Sarlat for some errand. I haven't heard a sound from Clothilde's bedroom. I suppose she is still asleep. The poor child must be exhausted. She came home late the night before last, she was up yesterday morning with the first twitter of the larks and did not rest a single minute until bedtime."

Emile rose and drew near Madeleine to kiss lightly her brow.

"Good! Let her sleep. I'll go and see if my boy is happy today; will you come along with me?"

When they crossed the front threshold of the house, they were confronted by the rumbling engine of an old rusted truck slowly coming to a stop in the driveway. Two brawny young men stepped out jovially. One of them was so enormous, no doubt he carried some cyclopean genes, although he had two beautiful blue eyes and was as magnificent as an oversized Adonis. They deferentially greeted Madeleine and Emile. They were sons of local families and old pals of Jean Luc. Employed by Emile during summer, they had come to receive specifications about their job assignments for the day.

CHAPTER 2

T HE RUCKUS CAUSED by the old truck as it parked in front of *la Brisante* abruptly awoke Clothilde after she had managed only an hour of light rest at the most. Being still under the influence of the turmoil she had suffered during the night, she was completely disoriented. Her room seemed as strange as if she had landed there from another planet or a different time. Mystified, she lay upon her bed and stared at the bleak whiteness of the ceiling while wading through her confused thoughts. Finally, she sat up and leaned her back against the headboard. All at once a recollection of the painful emotions she experienced before falling asleep vividly flashed back to her consciousness.

"Oh, no! No!" She whispered, distraught with rebellion and shame. "Why this yearning? Why this vacant space in my heart? Why this gap in my soul? What is the matter with me?" she again questioned. "Is not today the tomorrow I waited for yesterday, hoping it would bring me relief since now Paul is gone. Shouldn't I resume my life as it has always been? Oh," she lamented, "what shall I do with all those feelings that torment me like an agonizing thirst in the midst of a desert?"

She closed her eyes tightly, tensed herself and shook her shoulders as frustration and reproof rallied upon her. Discouraged she dropped her head forward as a gesture of discouragement.

"Phillippe! Phillippe!" She inwardly cried, "I am unworthy of you! I am a sham, a deceiver!"

As her gaze pensively followed the sunbeams dancing along the blue curtains gently swayed by a breeze, she was invaded by a sudden panic lest her love for Phillippe should prove to be only superficial and therefore insincere.

"No!" she protested again. It is pointless. I cannot continue to encourage this madness; let it stop now!" She clenched her fists to give more thrust to her resolution.

"Let it stop now!" she repeated. And gathering all the conscious fibers of her being, she took an emotional leap as it were, to view the events of the previous weekend as an insane chimera that must be obliterated from her memory.

She sighed, closed her eyes, sank back down into the softness of her pillows and emptied her mind of all thoughts even if only for a second at a time.

Gradually, her awareness yielded to the mirthful animation of the outside world. She listened to a dog barking in the far distance, to children laughing in courtyards, to the hearty voices of farmers at work in the fields amid their clanking machines. She heard a horse cheerfully neigh and the even-tempered cows placidly moo while they roamed in the green pastures. She smiled at the lambs' sweet bleating as she visualized them gamboling about the neighbor's farms. She listened to it all and it sounded like a lullaby that dispelled the dismal shroud she had spun around her soul.

After she had reached a certain inner quietude, she began to contemplate Phillippe's return. "Not long to wait now, only a few days," she then pondered over the festivities her engagement would occasion. It gave her a nervous twitch. She did not care much about everyone's attention streaming upon her. But the two families were bent to make a big fuss about it. She certainly had no intention to impose otherwise and disappoint them. She looked forward to the completion of the Museum; and most certainly to the work required by *la Brisante*. None of it seemed too burdensome. There should be enough to do to keep her days busy and her spirit free of the neuroses to which she had lately given in with marked propensity.

"Yes, everything will be all right." Encouraged to perhaps have reclaimed a more confident outlook, she got up, went to the window, drew open the curtains and let her gaze soar over the hills, the orchards and the meadows. All of them clad in their most sumptuous midsummer garbs unfurled in the dazzling sunlight as far as her eyes could see.

"Oh, how beautiful, how beautiful!" she sighed, as if she beheld it for the first time. She was about to walk away from the window when her grandparents returning from the pasture appeared at the curve of a footpath bordered by boxwood. They held hands while strolling nonchalantly. They were lovely together. So completely content in each other's company doing simple things. She felt teary at the sight of them. She envisioned Phillippe and her bonded by the same closeness. For the split of a second, it was Paul and not Phillippe who in her imagination appeared at her side. She calmly interpreted it as being an illusory effect, which often happens after one has too tenaciously focused upon an object or a person.

"No, I shall never stand as a deceiver. I shall be a good wife, a true and congenial companion to Phillippe. Together we will build a relationship upon the same foundations my grandparents have achieved the beauty of theirs.

After a quick shower, she dressed in a pair of navy blue shorts and a white sleeveless top. She brushed her hair letting it casually fall about her shoulders. Not hungry, she passed by the dining room door, entered the kitchen to prepare herself a cup of tea and taking it along with her, went to meet her grandparents who had sat on a bench under the linden-tree. They smiled when they saw their granddaughter step out on the threshold of *la Brisante*.

"Ah! There you are! Good morning to you!" Emile greeted cheerfully.

"Good morning sweetheart!" Madeleine joined in.

"Good morning Grandmaman, good morning gGrandpapa!" Careworn as she was, Clothilde managed to answer with an alert and gay tone of voice, watchful not to spill her tea.

"Come and sit with us, won't you?" invited Madeleine. She moved away from her husband to make room for Clothilde. "Did you get enough rest?" They exchanged a kiss.

"Yes, thank you, sorry I slept so late."

Emile teasingly gave her a light tap on the cheek.

"We are glad you did. You needed to catch up with a few restful dreams after those late soirees in such unruly society."

Clothilde laughed.

"Very unruly indeed, Grandpapa, but it was wonderful. How do you feel this morning? You must be a little sad of course as we all are after Jean Luc leaves," she inquired before she huddled between them and took a sip of tea.

"Yes, we miss him very much," acquiesced Madeleine. "But let me tell you, since we can't change the circumstances, your grandfather and I have therefore chosen that instead of wallowing in a useless pathos, we will do better to rejoice at the thought of his return in a few weeks. We must also be thankful he is stationed so near us in comparison to Paul for instance, who has had to bear with a long separation from his own home."

Clothilde's facial expression sobered.

"Very good Grandmaman, I'll try to do the same."

"You try darling, for I know it is not easy for you either."

Madeleine caught a repressed grin and a sigh of satisfaction from Emile amused by his wife having taken notice of his advice. She looked at him as he slowly scanned the horizon with a delighted expression passing across his face. She unfolded her arms and embraced the space that spread in front of them.

"Isn't it a glorious day?"

"It is. Indeed it is," approved Emile. He fixed his eyes on the highest branches of the acacia swarming with chirping cicadas.

Madeleine took Clothilde's hand in hers.

"Have you had breakfast, darling?"

"Not yet. I saw you from my bedroom window, so I thought it would be nice to first sit with you for awhile. But where is Maman? The house was completely quiet before I stepped outside," Clothilde asked gazing around *la Brisante*.

"She is gone to buy some pectin; I thought we had plenty, but we are short of it. This afternoon we have planned to make some cherry jam. She should be back soon," replied Madeleine giving a gentle but decisive tug to Clothilde's hand. "Now you go on and have your breakfast. We have left all the necessary for you in the dining room."

Promptly, Clothilde rose shifting her attention toward the pasture.

"I will Grandmaman, as soon as I have brushed Canon d'Or."

Emile put a straw hat on, drove to the fields in his jeep and with wholehearted stamina set himself at work with the daily laborers.

Madeleine followed Clothilde to help with grooming Canon d'Or.

Clothilde spent the next couple of days in the intimacy and bustles of family life and amid sighs heavy with regrets over the absence of Jean Luc or manifestations of effervescent joy elicited by Phillippe's homecoming.

Clothilde sought stability upon outside stimuli. Therefore, after she took part in domestic duties, which lasted most of the morning, in the afternoon she gave herself wholly over to the museum. There, for hours on, she documented slides of prehistoric artifacts and cave paintings together with various art objects from subsequent periods.

When alone at night, the quietness of her bedroom seemed like a vacuum too large for her thoughts to retreat in solace. So, she read until her eyes closed on the pages and the book slipped from her hands. At times of mental inaction, if any sentiments relating to Paul threatened to surface they were suppressed at once. She inflexibly substituted them by a willed contemplation of her future goals consistent with the life she and Phillippe had planned to share.

CHAPTER 3

THE FOLLOWING WEDNESDAY Phillippe with his two colleagues Eric and Jerome landed in Paris on an Air France jet. It was already late in the day. Being in no mood to rush, they decided to spend what was left of the afternoon at the Louvre; get a good night rest then early the next morning rent a car to complete their homeward journey.

They had a number of stops to make along the way, consequently, it was almost midnight on Friday when at last they approached the peripheries of their final destination. Phillippe not wanting to keep everybody up had phoned his parents as well as Clothilde to ask them not to wait for his arrival.

The responsibility of the car rental having been delegated to him, he duly took leave of Jerome at Limoges and of Eric at Beynac. Finding himself alone to cover the last kilometers, which separated him from Grolejac was a welcome relief. He had an urgent need to confront those unbearable trepidations he had so patiently suppressed in company of his friends. Yes, a few moments of solitude before he would reach home was truly a necessity. He could then freely follow the ebb and flow of his thoughts as they welled to his mind. "So many changes have taken place since I have left and it all has happened so suddenly," he contemplated.

The night was calm and transparent. At this particular time he was the sole traveler on this country freeway he knew well.

Passing a trail that led down to a narrow glen gently sloping down towards the Dordogne, he slowed his pace, came to a stop and backed up his car to park in an area away from the road. He then penetrated the woods where he tarried for a while.

Along his path, he met with a few deer as they grazed on patches of green grass or nibbled at shrubs. He stood motionless for a moment taking great precaution not to frighten them. In a graceful stance they turned their delicate head and beautiful eyes to alertly watch him; then undaunted they immediately resumed their nocturnal rummaging.

"How can man slay them?" he reflected moving on.

Phillippe loved and respected animals. One of his most venerated Saints was Saint Francis of Assisi. He was himself a vegetarian in the sense that he would abstain from any meat or products which involved the slaughter, abuse or injury of animals and was a relentless advocate of their protection.

As he walked further in the valley, from time to time the call of an owl soared then faded in the depth of the diaphanous darkness. The opaline moon together with the flickering stars had spun a silvery web over the branches where the birds nestled in the foliage, now and then awoke with a slumberous twitter. Phillippe smiled as he listened to their sweet murmur. Lukewarm whiffs emanated from the dried hay scattered over the fields across the river and mingled with the fragrance of wild lavender and dewy moss. The Dordogne rippled against its shores.

After such a long absence the scents and the sounds of his village were like a balm to his soul and he prayed. He earnestly prayed and entreated that above all, Clothilde, her family and his family be spared any grief at the news he was to announce them. He implored that their life be guided to a happiness commensurate with what he anticipated from his own. In absolute faith, he entrusted his dearest cares to the Divine protection. Soon, all anxieties seemed to have been dispelled. Reassured that neither he nor his loved ones would be abandoned to face alone the transition caused by this eventful mutation of circumstances, he finally reached the state of inner peace he had sought. He gazed at the sky as he dabbed the tears from his eyes.

"Yes!...Yes! None of us are ever alone," he whispered as he headed on home.

In the meantime, Clothilde had drifted into a peaceful sleep. The constant occupations to which she had dedicated herself in the course of the last days had sufficiently sapped her energy to make her long for some privacy and relaxation in the evening. Therefore, when she went to her room that night, she welcomed her solitude. In spite of the restlessness the next few hours should have aroused she remained undisturbed. Thank heaven once more her life was about to recover a sense of normalcy. Now and then her heart had fluttered a little when a few recollections of Paul had flashed amid her thoughts. He either smiled or held her in his arms when they bade each other farewell, or he offered the orchids to her grandmother in such a charming gesture, or ... well, it was nothing to really worry bout, she justified. (The fluttering part was overlooked.) Besides, it did not unleash that emotional feud she had had to contend with and only Heaven knew why, had possessed her so obstinately. Yes, now she was again fully in harmony with her world. The promises of happiness were almost palpable in the air she breathed. In a few hours, just a few hours, it would be a tangible reality. She would see, she would touch, and she would embrace Phillippe and never, ever again let him go away. Content, she reached for a book on her nightstand. It was not because, her mind needed evasion. No, her brain was functioning perfectly well now. It was simply by reason of a new compelling habit. Before she could finish reading the first page her eyes were shut until sunrise.

For Phillippe's parents it was certainly not likewise. They found it impossible to relax. What was their son thinking about when he suggested they carry on with their usual nightly routine? They had not set their eyes on him for three long months, how could they sleep at the thought he should arrive at any time soon? Surely, it did not seem right nor imaginable. As the hours advanced nearer to his arrival, they grew more and more impatient. Over and over again they listened to all the outside noises, watched for his car headlights to flare up in the driveway and checked the clock. They were in an ecstatic frenzy. It had well struck half-past one in the night when yes! ... yes! ... there he was!

"Here he is!" cried Veronique. She and her husband rushed to the front door. At last, their handsome, intelligent, wonderful son was home.

As they embraced each other and gathered in the living room to repair over tea, joy overflowed from their heart and glowed all around them.

CHAPTER 4

PHILLIPPE WEARY FROM his journey and his emotional dilemma, felt like God was granting him a taste of Heaven when after bidding good night to his mother and father, he lay in his own bed letting the nocturnal murmur of Grolejac lull him into a deep slumber.

Veronique and Frederick drifted asleep with a smile lingering in their eyes.

When Veronique awoke, Frederick next to her was as still as a mole hibernating in its burrow. The daylight seemed mighty brilliant and the birds much gossipy in the trees outside the window. "Was it already so late? Had everyone overslept?" she wondered. She looked at the alarm clock; it was not quite seven. "Well, good, it was still early," she thought, yet she felt completely restored. Indeed, she had no desire to idle time away by tossing and turning in her bed when she could think of a thousand things to do. Her gladness was more than enough to compensate for the lack of rest. With great care not to disturb her husband, she gently slid out of bed. She wrapped herself in a robe, which she had conveniently placed at reach on the back of an armchair, she took her slippers in her hands, she tiptoed out of the bedroom and went into the kitchen to switch on the coffee percolator. As she leaned forward to open the curtains draping a little window above the sink, inadvertently her sleeve brushed past a piece of paper set on the counter. She gave no attention to it at first until it followed the movement of her arm and fell on the floor. She casually picked it up and was about to discard it when she recognized Phillippe's handwriting. With a frown denoting intense curiosity, she read it.

"*Good morning Maman. I went to early Mass, and then I should like to pay my respects to Father Vernier, if he is available after the service.*

Love,

Phillippe."

"*P.S. Hope I was quiet enough when I left and did not disturb your rest. See you soon.*"

Veronique read the note once more, she put it in her dressing gown pocket and impulsively walked to the front of the house to verify if Phillippe's car was gone, as if the message was not explicit enough. Yet unsatisfied, she went to his bedroom. She noticed he had taken a shower, for in his bathroom droplets of water still trickled along the glass partition.

"Mmm!" she mumbled. "Well, I suppose he was driven by some kind of necessity after being too long estranged in a country where the culture and religious creed are so different from ours."

Upon further reflection, her heart billowed with tender maternal sentiments.

"Oh, how wonderful of him to have thought about going to mass so early in the morning even after having had so little rest! Ah, what a blessed gift is a son like mine! He has always been a joy. He has never caused us any problems, not even when growing up as some boys do!"

She then stopped in the guest bathroom to comb her short curly auburn hair and upon hearing footsteps in the hallway; she stole a look through the door left ajar.

"Is it you Frederick?"

"It is love!"

"I shall be with you in a second."

Once she judged herself reasonably presentable, she joined her husband at the kitchen table. While waiting for her he had poured each of them a cup of hot coffee.

"Thank you dear," she said as she sat opposite him and relished in the delicious aroma pervading the room.

Frederick smiled.

"You are welcome love. It is the least I can do in gratitude for the pleasure I have in sharing this new day with you."

Veronique extended her arm across the table to press affectionately her husband's hand.

Frederick had spoken in a low tone of voice, heedful that his son might still be asleep, although Phillippe's bedroom was quite far from the kitchen area.

"There is no need to whisper, Frederick; Phillippe is not here at this moment. He went to Mass." Veronique informed.

"To Mass?"

"Yes."

She took the note out of her pocket and handed it to her husband. He casually read it, nodded and gave it back to Veronique.

"Very good!" he acquiesced," I could not think of a better way for him to start his first day back home. Had he told me, I would have gone with him."

Frederick poured himself another cup of coffee.

"You seem surprised, why? Phillippe has always been a very pious young man."

Veronique shrugged and reconsidered the circumstances.

"After all this traveling and such, he should be exhausted and in need of a few extra hours sleep. I am sure God would have readily taken all this in consideration and would have excused him if attending mass had been postponed until tomorrow."

"Now Mother, don't worry yourself. One does not so easily tire when in the full vigor of Phillippe's age. Moreover, motivation owns the wonderful property to revitalize a weary body or spirit. Our son naturally at this moment is restless and is now driven by the impetus to move forth with the plans that have been postponed because of his departure. Give him time to settle down again."

As her husband spoke, Veronique had listened with a feigned quiescence. She took a sip of coffee and absently stared at a sunray that glistened through a cut crystal vase placed on a pine buffet on her left. She then looked at Frederick with a sudden shudder.

"Oh dear!" she sighed, "this journey to Egypt has given me no peace and I have no idea why really."

Compelled to move from nervousness, she got up to refill the half-empty sugar bowl from a bag stored in the cupboard.

Frederick's gaze followed the motions of her hand.

"Well, it is over and done with. Phillippe is home now and in his own right ready to fulfill all what his life is meant to encompass."

"Yes, yes, he is home now. What is the matter with me? How silly," Veronique echoed as she sat again. She then tilted her head sideward and softly looked at her husband.

"You know what Frederick?"

"What dear?"

"I hope Phillippe and Clothilde will share a love as special as ours, and then I will grow old with peace in my heart and ... Oh!" she interrupted as she sprang from her chair at the sound of a car door being slammed, "I am sure it is Phillippe home from church. I must attend to breakfast, for he shall want to leave promptly. Clothilde is waiting for him and he must deliver the car back at the rental agency early this morning."

She turned the oven on to warm up the buttered bread she had prepared in an earthenware dish on top of the stove. Frederick gathered milk, butter and jam to carry it in the dining room. Veronique followed him with a tray upon which she had gathered cups, saucers and a carafe of fresh iced water.

CHAPTER 5

"GOOD MORNING DEAR," Veronique greeted as she stepped from the dining room into the hallway and saw Phillippe appear at the front entrance. How good it is to have you home!" she said with a sigh of contentment while they embraced. "Breakfast is ready, come and take your place at the table again, it has seemed so immensely empty during your absence."

Veronique put a finger in front of her lips.

"All right, I shall refrain from further sentimentality so that I do not annoy all of you to distress."

Phillippe put his arms around his mother's shoulders.

"You could never tire me Maman, I missed you too. I missed both of you very much," he added smiling at his father. "Indeed, it is good to be home."

They sat at the table. Frederick poured coffee in everyone's cup.

"We are anxious to hear in the minutest details all about your odyssey. Understandably not now, you have little time to sit before you take off once more."

Veronique unfolded her napkin upon her lap."

"Yes of course, not today, surely you wish to spend time with Clothilde. For this reason, we have postponed until tomorrow evening a dinner in your honor. Father Vernier will ... Phillippe?" she then summoned gazing at him with puzzlement while she distractedly stirred her coffee to which she had just added cream.

Phillippe, spreading jam on a slice of bread, for a moment had drifted into his own concerns and seemed indifferent to his mother's comments.

"Excuse me Maman, I did not mean to be rude. Yes I have heard you," was all he was able to articulate as he cast a furtive glance at his mother and looked back down at his plate. What caused Frederick to briefly scrutinize his son's behavior.

"Oh, I thought I had lost your attention," resumed Veronique after a short pause. "I was about to say that Father Vernier will join us for the occasion, he is family too and so fond of you."

Phillippe reached for the milk jar.

"Yes father Vernier told me. I am glad you did. I would have suggested it had you not already invited him."

"I can imagine his expression when he saw you. No doubt he beamed with delighted surprise."

Phillippe nodded and smiled.

"Yes, we were happy to see each other."

Frederick aware that a certain uneasiness had settled among them, helped himself to a peach from the fresh fruit bowl and began to peal it as he examined what could possibly be the reason for his son's aloofness. Perplexed, he glanced at Veronique then assuming a casual demeanor he looked at Phillippe.

"We will appreciate his company. Except for a word or two after mass on Sunday, we have had no opportunity to visit with him. He has such a hectic schedule during summer. How good of him to have granted you some of his rare free time this morning."

Phillippe slightly moved his plate aside indicating he was done with breakfast.

"Yes, he invited me in the sacristy. We spoke a while, but I did not want to detain him at length."

Veronique wiped her fingers and toyed with her napkin.

"I don't mean to change the subject, but let me tell you quickly before you leave. I have had Grandmaman Manouche's diamond ring professionally cleaned. It looks divine. What a joy it would be for my dear grandmother if from wherever she is at, she could witness the moment you pass it on to Clothilde."

"Thank you Maman, that was thoughtful of you," Phillippe endeavored to express affably with what he considered his last reserve of self-control, while he held back the tears that crushed his chest. "Stop Maman! Stop! You are chastising me!" he wanted to scream. "I must tell them! I must tell them! Now, not later. Now, at this minute!"

However, he remained silent and if a part of him wept he wished he could infuse their heart with some of the rapture, which stirred the innermost core of his soul. Veronique and Frederick by then understood that their son had other things on his mind than his great grandmother's ring having been polished.

As soon as breakfast had ended, they all stood up and began to clear the table. Phillippe proceeded to help. Veronique rapidly took a plate from his hand, and caringly stroke his right cheek.

"Do not bother with such a thing darling. You go on, Clothilde must impatiently be waiting for you by now. Go on dear."

He thanked his mother and went to his room to change clothes. He then affectionately took leave of his parents and drove off.

As Veronique tidied up the dining room, her fumbling gestures caused more chaos than order. She finally interrupted what she was doing to plant herself akimbo in front of her husband. She forcibly tapped her forehead with the tip of her right hand fingers.

"Is it partly my intuition, partly my correct observations or is it none of it or all of it or is it simply my imagination which creates those suspicions of mine? But Frederick, did you also notice a change in Phillippe? like he is sort of preoccupied by something?"

"Yes," asserted Frederick, "yes I have noted this also."

Veronique raised her arms to the ceiling and them flop down on her side in surrender to helplessness.

"Then what is it? What do you think has happened to our son while he was away?"

Frederick shook his head negatively.

"I don't know love. I don't know. I should think nothing to be alarmed about. I trust he will intelligently handle whatsoever is on his mind, then so be it. I am sure he will tell us when he is ready."

Veronique kept still for a few seconds.

"You don't suppose ... no ... I should not think Phillippe ... yet one never knows. You would not suppose he has grown romantically attached to someone over there in Egypt, would you? Someone who has caused him a change of heart about Clothilde?"

Frederick amused by Veronique's suspicion, shook his head good-humouredly.

"Of course not Veronique! I do not assume this at all. Perhaps his thesis did not go as he wished or he is weary from his studies and from the tedious work of those last three months. He might just be in need of airing out his brain with some healthy distractions. We must allow him time to readjust."

Veronique did not quite accept her husband's speculations and carried on with her own.

"Oh dear! what about if he caught some serious illness, like … like malaria and it is not showing yet, or … "

"Now, now!" interjected Frederick reprovingly. In spite of his easy nature, he had begun to get annoyed by his wife's defeatist attitude. "You could go on and on with those kind of ideas. I could even suggest a few more if you would care to listen. What has come over you?"

"Oh, I can't explain. I can only compare it to the fear sometimes one experiences at the end of a long journey. The fear that suddenly at the last moment, the ship might capsize or the plane might crash and all the anticipations for a happy landing are shattered.

What are you afraid of? Phillippe is back here safely is he not? and he looks rather healthy to me."

"Yes, he is here physically so to speak. The rest of him seems lost in another sphere, in a world estranged from ours. Have you seen his lack of enthusiasm when I told him about his great grandmother's diamond ring? This is not like Phillippe at all. What about if something unexpected has ruined all our plans?"

"It is always possible. Our plans may not be what destiny has reserved for Phillippe and we can't change it, regardless of our wishes," Frederick replied calmly."

"What?" exclaimed Veronique, "What makes you say that? What's the matter with you? do you have some kind of foreboding or … ?"

"No love, I do not have any kind of foreboding. I don't believe Phillippe has contacted malaria, or any other diseases, or has fallen from God's Grace. What I know is that the unexpected has hovered around this planet since the creation of time. If changes come about they are not always for the worse. Do not conjure ill fate it might oblige," Frederick admonished again, wanting to finally spur Veronique into a more optimistic frame of mind.

"Frederick, please!" she cried out, appalled by what her husband said. Exasperated with herself, she drew close to him and lightly pressed his forearm.

"Oh, I am sorry. I am thoughtlessly shedding gloom all around us."

"Well it is time you do away with it. Everything will be fine, just fine," Frederick encouraged. "So now, I shall go and dress myself appropriately for the day. Off with you, I suggest you do the same and then let's celebrate our son's return." He laid his left arm around Veronique's shoulders as he led her out of the dining room.

CHAPTER 6

Yes, PHILLIPPE WAS preoccupied and yes, he had much to tell about his odyssey; but first he wanted to talk with Clothilde. Too restive to keep still after knowing he was on his way, she had begun to walk down the orchard to wait for him.

In Grolejac, it was one of those glorious summer mornings. Brilliant hues dazzled the eyes and lavish scents drenched the air throbbing from the sounds of rural activities. Clothilde embraced it all.

She wore-ivory white pant and a jade green short sleeve top. A pretty ensemble, which flattered her graceful femininity. Dainty gold earrings dangled and glistened amid her flowing hair. She never cared to apply make up to her face.

When she passed by the bench on which she broke in sobs beside Elise the night of Paul's departure, she was suddenly filled with regrets. But there was no time to ponder over such inopportune sentiments, for at the same instant she perceived Phillippe as his car entered the orchard road. Instantly, she quickened her pace toward him. When he saw her looking so lovely, so candidly gleeful, he was overcome by such poignant emotions, he nearly lost control of the steering wheel, swerved to the right and almost tumbled into a ditch. Upon their encounter, he hurriedly stepped out of the car to receive her in his arms.

"Clothilde! My dearest Clothilde!" he cried out. He held her close to him in a very tender but all the same far too dispassionate embrace for a fiance to be. Clothilde, completely absorbed by the moment, did not discern any difference.

"Oh, Phillippe!" she exclaimed. "Oh! how wonderful to see you!"

They remained silent for a brief moment clinging to each other. He was unable to utter another word; it was better to leave things unsaid than to create misinterpretation by expressing too ardently the profound love he still felt for her.

"Let me look at you!" she said gaily as she took a step back. "Yes! Yes! You are here, truly here! It has been so lonely without you! How I have yearned for this day!"

In a spontaneous resurgence of love, and so pained by the severance that now separated them, he drew her near him again.

"It has not been easy for me either," he gravely admitted.

A pickup truck loaded with bails of hay huffed and puffed uphill. As it advanced on their path, it disrupted her elan of enthusiasm and temporary rescued him from the oppressive impasse.

"We are blocking the way," he indicated slightly amused by the situation.

"Oh," she laughed when the truck came to her view. She really had not been aware of it. He took her hand to motion her toward the passenger's door of his car.

They both had agreed that from *la Brisante*, Clothilde would take her Fiat and follow Phillippe to Sarlat where he was due to return the rented Peugeot he drove from Paris. Then, at Clothilde"s suggestion, they had planned to spend the day together and drive along the scenic sites. They probably would stop for a light *aperitif* in some picturesque area on the way before taking their lunch at one of Phillippe's favorite restaurants in Castelnaud, a village agglomerated at the base and up along the slope of a steep hill. Then, they would climb to the highest peak where stood the colossal vestiges of a feudal castle. They enjoyed to leisurely stroll in the splendor of its ruins that still rose lofty and magnificent above enormous tumbled stones amassed around its foundations like petrified entrails expelled from its bowel. It still seemed to be watchful over the Dordogne valley, lest some ominous phantoms of old foes should suddenly loom at the horizon. There, from high above, Phillippe and Clothilde never tired to delight in the breathtaking panorama unfolding as far as their eyes could see.

After Phillippe and Clothilde had spent a few moments of gladsome reunion with Clothilde's family and naturally Canon d'Or, off they went.

Clothilde was in a blithe spirit as she journeyed along the freeway unwinding through wooded areas, open fields and grasslands scattered with dwellings from humble cottages to elegant domains. She was ready she thought, to receive all what the day had to offer. Now was the time she had been waiting for. Now was the time she could finally bask in her happiness. Phillippe drove ahead of her. A somber shroud of melancholy hovered over his thoughts; so decisive was this day. The notion that he was capable of hurting Clothilde devastated him. At times, he wavered, even doubted upon the trueness of his transformation. He reached Sarlat oblivious of the kilometers he had covered.

Finally, the Peugeot was delivered to safe haven.

"Would you rather prefer I drive, Phillippe? You have sat behind the steering wheel for hours since you have left Paris," inquired Clothilde, as they walked hand in hand to her car.

"No, I'll drive if you don't mind. Jerome and Eric drove part of the journey as well, so each of us could rest in turn; but thank you."

He gently smiled at her and thought how beautiful she was.

"All right then," she acquiesced in a cheerful tone, and gave him her keys.

"Now the rest of the day is ours," she said with a deep sigh of pleasant expectancy while she settled comfortably near him. He proceeded to maneuver the car out of the jammed parking lot.

"Oh, Phillippe darling!" she went on in a transport of joy "it is so wonderful to be and to do things together again!"

Phillippe did not know what to say; or rather, he had too much to say and was unable to voice it. Dismayed, he wished he could have stopped the car wherever he was at, take her in his arms, love her as he had in the past and tell her that "yes it seemed completely normal to share their life in the manner they had thought it possible." He had truly loved her. He had loved her in the full magnitude a man has the capacity to be in love with a woman, why couldn't it continue so? And now, why this drive to Castelnaud, which only prolongs the pain? Yet, could he have confronted her immediately after his arrival, thus abruptly get the entire ordeal over with?

Although he did not want to project indifference, he nevertheless remained silent and pretended to concentrate upon the street signs as if he was not familiar with the area.

Clothilde at this point began to sense a certain oddness in his demeanor.

From under a furrowed brow she briefly glanced at him, and then deep in reflection she fixed her eyes on the freeway they had now entered. On such occasions, during those leisurely country drives, he always held her hand or drew her near him. Why did he continue to act as if the road was crammed with traffic when at this time of the morning they were yet the sole travelers?"

"Ah," she thought seeking an excuse for what she didn't want to admit, "truly, my imagination lately, has been exceedingly fertile in much too many uncertainties and suppositions."

The tension was dispelled by Phillippe who asked her if she spent a nice weekend in company of Jean Luc. He then inquired about Paul.

Clothilde caught herself hopelessly blushing. Seized by the fear that his mind with the accuracy of an ex-ray instrument might perceive in the minutest details what she had experienced in the presence of Paul, she turned her head away from him. After a few seconds she managed to recover some poise, and ineffectively tried to answer him in a casual tone of voice.

"Yes, Paul is great. A good friend for Jean Luc. He has now left for the United States. We hope he will return for a visit. Grandpapa was at once taken by him. You probably would like him also. He is quite charming," she explained nervously in a staccato manner, so to speak, due to a surge of unwelcome emotions.

"I am sure I would," asserted Phillippe, a bit distracted by his own inner battle, but smiling at her.

For sometime, their conversation continued amicably, although at times overcast by intervals of sullen silence that forewarned of a romantic disconnection between them. Nonetheless Clothilde was still disposed to eschew any additional disquiet on her part, and since lately she had become so good at rationalizations, she looked for more excuses besides.

"Well, no doubt his mind is still cluttered with all that cryptic Egyptology which must indeed cause him to feel a bit hazy. Furthermore, he should be exhausted from so much traveling and probably from not enough sleep."

She glanced rapidly at his solemn profile.

"Yes, he looks somewhat weary and drawn," she observed. "Oh, how very unkind of me! I should have considered all of this before I proposed an outing to which he may have consented only to please me. It could well have been delayed until a later day."

She knew too that when tired, he had the fortunate ability to find retreat within himself. Then, even if only after a short while, he would spring back invigorated like someone would from a swim into a bubbling stream, or a meditative walk in the tranquility of a deep forest. Therefore, with the intention to allow him time for a peaceful respite she withdrew upon her own thoughts. Quietly she watched the scenery unfold, but to no avail. A grim strain constricted even the silence between them. Clothilde at last rebuked all former and further probabilities and sank in a dejected mood. Reality did not measure close to even her most reasonable expectancies. She had tolerantly waited, but the hours did not yield to the sweet moments one anticipates from being reunited with a beloved after a long parting. Something was bizarre. Something had gone wrong. "What is the matter with us?" she wondered. She then remembered the mutism, which incapacitated her by the river, after she had come across Paul in Sarlat. Could it be possible that by an irony of fate Phillippe was equally troubled by a similar experience? The fear that he might have fallen in love with someone else while he was away, crushed her.

She looked at him inquisitively. At last she was ready to ask questions. Phillippe noticed her edginess. He was well aware that by now they both had grown too uncomfortable in each other's company. Unquestionably the time had come to disclose the truth. It was absurd to hope for a more favorable opportunity.

"Clothilde," he said reaching for her hand. His face had turned pallid.

"Yes Phillippe … are you feeling well?" she inquired, deeply concerned by the change in his facial coloring.

"I am all right darling," he replied with a sad smile. "but I need to talk to you before we go further. It is senseless to keep on driving so. I shouldn't delay much longer what I must tell you."

"What is it Phillippe? What is it?" she asked insistently.

He kept his teary eyes fixed on the road.

"Please bear with me a bit longer. We will get off the freeway as soon as possible and stop in a quiet area for privacy."

She quietly abode by, and with great effort kept her poise.

CHAPTER 7

THEY SILENTLY DROVE through an agrarian stretch between farmhouses, until they turned into a side lane Phillippe had sought and he knew led to a grove bordering a pond. As they parked under an oak tree in the midst of opulent green pastures, a herd of cows followed by their frisky spring calves remained undisturbed and placidly advanced toward them. Phillippe proposed a stroll along the path forming a narrow festoon around the edge of the pond. A sense of suffocation caused by his burdensome feelings urged him to move in the open air.

As they began to walk, he surrounded Clothilde's shoulders with his right arm, whereupon keeping her gaze lowered to the ground; she nervously waited for him to speak.

"Clothilde," he said at last, while his blood churned in his veins, "many changes have happened during those past three months."

She listened while her heart fluttered from apprehension.

Defying his dread, Phillippe took a deep breath, mustered all his courage like someone about to plunge in a pool of iced water, and all at once uttered the words:

"I have decided to be a priest."

She lifted her head and inclined it sideways to look curiously up at him.

Being influenced by her own guilt due to her feelings for Paul, and dreading that Phillippe might have another woman in his life caused her to misconstrue what he said.

She waited for a more explicit disclosure of what she thought he was leading to, but he didn't give any more details. After an unbearable lapse of silence, she shrugged her shoulders. She didn't know what to say. To break the increasing strain, which was creeping between them she awkwardly stated:

"That's good, Phillippe."

He stared at her, wordless, transfixed by the amazement to have elicited such an unconcerned response.

"Well," she added, too troubled to think of something more intelligent to say. "It is always wise to see a priest when one seeks counsel."

"Clothilde!" he called to her attention, when he finally became aware of her misinterpretation. "You did not hear me well. I did not say: "I have decided to SEE a priest." I said: "I have decided to BE a priest."

"What?"

"Yes, BE a priest. I have decided to BE a priest, he asserted emphatically.

"Be a priest? she repeated at a complete loss. "A priest?"

Paul remained silent.

She removed his arm from around her shoulders and swiftly stood in front of him.

"What did you say?"

"I want to be a priest." Phillippe restated.

All colors drained away from Clothilde's face.

"You … Did you say … ? What are you talking about?"

Phillippe was unable to pronounce another word.

But now she had understood what he meant. She melted in utter stupor, as in a flash she visualized him emulating a priest when being a little boy. Struck dumb, as though transfigured into a statue of ashen stone, she fastened a bewildered look upon him.

"You…you are telling me you want to be a priest! When have you decided to be a priest? When … ? Do you mean a Catholic Priest?"

Phillippe nodded affirmatively.

"But, Phillippe you can't. How could you? … A Catholic priest must vow celibacy!" she cried out baffled.

"I know," Phillippe said gravely.

"Why, in that case we can't get married?"

"No," he heard himself reply decisively with a firmness of voice which sounded like it was not his own. He was well aware it was meant to offset the insufferable desire to hold her close and reconsider his decision. Oh, how easy it seemed possible at this very moment!

He had been mesmerized and dazzled by his lofty calling. His spirit soaring in visionary contemplations, had dimmed all other aspects of his life. But, when he approached nearer to home, his human vulnerability began to waver under the pull of his earthly bondage. Did he not still love her? Could he truly be sustained by enough fortitude not to relent?

The renouncements he was required to shed on his path to priesthood sorely distressed him.

He stood there facing her, wordless, besieged by a maddening impetus of emotions.

Clothilde perceived it to suggest only cold indifference on his part. As she looked at him, she had the impression that her life had stopped in front of a sealed, cold marble door.

"Why?" she questioned through a sudden shiver. "But why would you want to be a priest now? And why haven't you told me earlier … before we went so far on a drive?"

"I dreaded this moment," he responded at last, with a stern inflection of voice. He made a slight movement forward.

"Do not come near me!" she signaled with the palm of her raised hand as if blocking the distance between them.

"No, no, do not come near me!" she repeated. Her tears glistened under the stroke of a sunray filtering through the foliage.

"Oh, Phillippe! You have gone mad!" she lamented.

Incensed, she turned around sharply and scurried away on a lane in the thick of the grove.

"Clothilde!" he cried out rashly pursuing her; but it was like a dream in which despite all efforts one feels helpless to reach a love one in distress. He neither could see nor hear her. Disheartened he slowly went back on his steps.

Running amok, she wanted to shake the trees off their roots and pound her fists against the hills. She wanted to evaporate in the clouds, do away with all she was, and all she had been. Through her attraction to Paul, she had deeply sinned in thoughts. Surely, she carried the seeds of an adulteress and was being punished. Yes, now unworthy of Phillippe, God had deservingly anathematized her. Dejected, she broke into grievous sobs while she sank heavily upon a tumbled rock under a chestnut tree.

Phillippe mortified paced back and forth along the edge of the pond, glancing at the whereabouts like a lost sheep. He stopped by a stone bench, stood there dazed for a moment and then sat with his head cast down and both arms folded upon his chest. The weight of affliction had drawn a dismal veil across his handsome face and had faded to a hazy grey the spirited blue of his eyes. He vacantly stared at the reflection of the flaxen weeds in the glassy water, unable to pray, unable to elucidate his confused and divided thoughts, oblivious of time.

A lone beetle came to whirl in the midst of the reeds, and then flew away. Phillippe watched it meander over the meadows as it vanished into the distance like a floating speck of dust.

"Regardless of his apparent freedom, it too is locked up in an inescapable carapace, as we all are," Phillippe pondered.

Half an hour or so had slipped by, when the sound of dried fallen leaves crackling under approaching steps, suddenly brought him back to reality. He looked over his right shoulder and rose at once.

Could it be Clothilde returning from her flight? He was disappointed when instead a farmer from the vicinity loomed out of the under brush. As he passed through he lifted his hat and saluted Phillippe.

"Good day! Good day Monsieur!"

"Good day, Monsieur," Phillippe greeted in response.

The stranger put his hat back on and with a brisk stride went his way.

Phillippe sighed despairingly; likewise, he too had to be moving on. Surely, he could not continue to remain hopelessly there. He turned toward the hillock where Clothilde had fled and with a heavy heart he went to search for her.

CHAPTER 8

DURING HER FEW moments of solitude, Clothilde was tossed around and around in a whirlwind of shock, rage and utter confusion.

"How could this be happening? How could she imagine going on existing on this planet without Phillippe on her side? She had built her entire future happiness upon the vision of their life together. Must her long time dream dissolve into the nothingness of a mirage?"

As her initial anger was beginning to lessen in turn an escalation of guilt gushed upon her conscience and unleashed the most absurd reasoning constructed by a sane human being under enormous stress. No doubt, she argued, she had fallen from God's Grace. She was chastised for her covetous temptations of the previous weekend. Perhaps even she could fully take the blame for the radical shift of circumstances as well, and take complete responsibility for what had determined Phillippe's fate. Surely, God wished to protect him from her evil influence. If she had remained pure in thought none of this would have ever happened. However, she considered further, through the cleansing of her heart and soul from all wrongs, couldn't she then own the power to alter the course of events?

"Oh, dear, dear God, forgive me. Please do not take him away from me!" she then implored, sincerely repentant, ready to bargain with her Maker. In a solemn promise, she pledged to expiate for her sins, to convert into an earnestly reformed woman as did Marie Magdalene after being redeemed from her decline into depravity. Then indeed, she should be most deserving of Phillippe's love. In addition, she vowed to be a very, very devout Catholic. She would go to mass and take communion every single day for the rest of her life. In other words, she was ready to embrace sainthood. Having grown so praiseworthy virtuous, God would have absolutely no reason to worry about Phillippe. He could be reassured that she would be capable of bringing him as much blessedness as though he were among His anointed ones.

She was contending in this manner, when again she remembered her mother's anecdote about phillippe impersonating a priest. Instantly she plummeted from the denial fashioned by her faulty reasoning into the harsh revelation of reality.

"Oh, my God!" She pressed the palm of her hands against her lips to prevent herself from a cry of astonishment. "Since he was a child it has always been a part of him, an intrinsic, dormant part of him, like a smothered fire that now has been reignited into an almighty, decisive yearning he is unable to oppose!" she contemplated with awe as though spellbound by a wondrous mystery in the course of being unveiled.

"Oh, how wrong of me to have been so unduly angry at him!" she then conceded, filled with contrition as though she had committed a sacrilege.

Mercifully exhausted, her brain refused to deliberate further. She was unable to think anymore. Her unfocused attention soon drifted over the tiny wild flowers, which like brilliant multihued droplets sprinkled the purple verbena spreading thick at her feet. She distractedly followed the contours of the trees and the lacy patterns their branches formed against the sky. She nonchalantly glanced over the valley scattered with farms hooded by burnished red tile roofs. She almost smiled as she glimpsed at the satisfied bovine shapes sprawled on the meadows for a late morning siesta. Finally, her gaze led by a flight of birds, wandered in the infinity of the transparent horizon. It was then that a feeling of immense peace fell upon her and without having given a thought to it; she softly uttered a few verses on *"The excellence of love,"* from Saint Paul's first epistle to the Corinthians:

"Love is patient, love is kind and is not jealous. Love does not brag and is not arrogant. It does not act unbecomingly, does not seek its own, is not provoked, does not take into account a wrong suffered. It does not rejoice in

unrighteousness but rejoices with the truth. Love bears all things, believes all things, hopes all things. Love never fails."

"Why, of course," Clothilde concluded. "Of course, love does not seek its own but bears all things, believes all things, hopes all things, rejoices with the truth and never fails or else it would not be love. It must not be a self seeking gratification at the expense of another who then becomes an object of repudiation if the egotistic expectancies are not met. Love must be absolute and unconditional. It is upon those principles that I must love Phillippe and release him to fulfill his own destiny unbound from my own selfish desires. This doesn't make me a martyr, but on the contrary it releases me from the burden of trying to shape him to my liking and from all the negative emotions this kind of expediency breeds. It sets me free.

Therefore, incredibly in less than an hour, Clothilde felt gently swayed from despair to a magnanimous spirit of acceptance.

Without knowing why she had a vague, uncanny impression that from all this recent chaos in her life some kind of order was striving to resolve itself. But she didn't care to seek further into it. In the midst of so much confusion nothing seemed intelligible by logical reasoning. Moreover, she was tired of analyzing all those strange feelings and happenings. She had experienced too many of them lately.

She stood up, swept off the leaves from her clothes, tidied her disheveled hair and looked around trying to retrieve her sense of direction. As she stepped cautiously through the thorny bushes and brambles creeping over the rocky underwood, she began to find her way back. She had no recollection of having penetrated the wilderness so deeply.

CHAPTER 9

PHILLIPPE FOUND CLOTHILDE slowly walking down the grove in direction of the pond, evidently with the intention to rejoin him. She thoughtfully looked at what she passed by. Her face was a little haggard and flushed from weeping, but she seemed calm.

When she saw him, she vaguely smiled and came to a stop. He looked so downtrodden. She wanted to take away his suffering and if only for a moment she wished to see his beautiful blue eyes sparkle once more with the happiness he thought to have found in their love for each other.

Phillippe also longed to obliterate the distress he had brought her and rekindle on her face the radiant smile of a beloved. He did not speak. He outstretched his hand to her and withdrew it while she continued to stand still. He deemed that her absence to respond indicated a sustained hostility toward him.

Hesitantly at first, she met his gaze and then dashed in his embrace.

"Oh, Phillippe!" she said in a rueful tone of voice. "I am so … so sorry. I have behaved like a child. I did not mean to be so angry with you. Oh, I am so very sorry. I should not have …"

"Hush, hush!" interrupted Phillippe as he pressed her closely to him. "My dear, very dear Clothilde, you did not behave like a child. Please do not apologize when it is I who is causing you so much grief."

It took her a supreme effort to repress a flow of tears, for she did not want to give the impression she was still unyielding.

"It is so difficult but really, nothing is definite at this stage. Oh, Clothilde, I don't know any more!" he finally uttered in a moment of desperation.

She placed a finger on his lips to silence him, then stepped back a little. While she enveloped his face with tenderness, her beautiful dark eyes glistened with the residue of aborted tears. She understood that from a profound empathy for her affliction he had succumbed to a moment of weakness. She shook her head negatively a few times.

"No, no, Phillippe," she objected with affected firmness, although her heart throbbed. "No, no, I could never find peace knowing I have selfishly influenced you to bend to my wants or that you felt the urge to protect me from sorrow. Inevitably, this would surface anew and cause a lot of unhappiness along the years to both of us. You must listen to the voice of your soul, for it is the voice, which speaks the truth. You ought to do away sensibly with the nature of our past attachment so you can freely move on towards the lofty pursuits demanded of you. For my own part, I wish to give you my full support and assure you I shall not persevere in futile, self-centered whimpers, even though I so dread to loose you."

Her sudden change of demeanor, her display of absolute selflessness and her equanimity astonished him. He looked at her, profoundly moved, and wandering for an instant if she had been mysteriously counseled by a compassionate angelic intervention. A grave expression shrouded his face. He took both her hands in his.

"My sweet Clothilde, you will never loose me and if the Holy order is my true calling, you will find me all the more, for otherwise I would live a lie. I would be a false man, and if not deliberately, no less real for that. How could I pretend to be what I cannot be? How can one build mutual trust, genuine friendship and love upon deceit? However, come what may, you will forever be an important part of my life, and if it is in my power I shall always be there for you. It would be insufferable if as a result of a change in our relationship we should become alienated from each other, for I too would dread to loose you."

He released Clothilde's hands from his and quietly turned a reflective gaze toward the open space spreading over the valley.

"Love has many configurations. My love for you is everlasting and transcends the boundaries of our present existence on this earth," he stated pensively.

"What does he mean by "our present existence on this earth?" Were there any others? Is he converting to Elise's beliefs?" she questioned silently. Does he think he was on this earth before?"

"In moments of profound meditation," Phillippe continued, "oddly, I seem to sense that my Calling has been prompted so to speak, by a need to atone for certain long forgotten yet still haunting wrongdoings. Something like an alter consciousness takes hold of me and leaves behind blurred memories of personal iniquities that pursue me with regrets. It is so difficult to explain!" He abruptly shook his head with impatience, exasperated by the impossibility to put into words what he wished to convey.

"What in the world is he talking about?" again wondered Clothilde. Have we all lost our mind? She stared intently at him to only mirror his puzzlement through a baffled silence.

"Yes, I know," Phillippe sighed, meaning to agree with her mystified expression.

Wanting to give him comfort, she put her hand on his forearm and pressed it gently.

"Don't let this disquiet you. You know that often when under stress our mind may transiently experience some uncommon perceptions, but it will all subside when you have settled in more stable circumstances."

"Yes I suppose so," he simply approved, while a sudden nervous smile fluttered across his weary face.

"Or!" he exclaimed, "or perhaps I have gone mad after all!"

"Oh, Phillippe please do not say this!" Clothilde objected. "I am so angry at myself for having pronounced those awful and unfair words I did not mean!"

"I know, I know," he reassured her.

"And," she added with sincerity, "you will be a wonderful, kind hearted priest! the very best ever!"

He lowered his brow then looked up and away.

"Well," he said turning his head back toward her, unconcerned to hide the tears he could no longer suppress. "Shall we return to the pond?" He took her hand and they descended the hill.

As they reached the meadow, they stopped for a moment and could not resist a smile as the cows and little calves tranquilly came to meet them. Phillippe released Clothilde's hand and raised his arm to surround her shoulders. Both being emotionally exhausted, they had reached a state of numb resignation. Everything seemed at a standstill. They knew there was no turning back, but were not sure where exactly they were going from then on.

The bell of a solitary church rising from the depth of the valley, began to toll, apparently for no reason at all, since it was well past noon and at this time, there was no religious observance to abide by. They walked to their car. Before Clothilde took her place in the driver's seat, Phillippe on an impulse yearned to hold her close to him. His heart ached at the thought he couldn't mend their shattered plans. He withdrew his arms from her shoulders and opened the car door for her.

"It is almost one o'clock," he informed Clothilde as he settled behind the steering wheel. "Would you still care to have lunch?" he then inquired after a moment of indecision.

"Would you?" she asked in reply. "Well, actually, yes, I am absolutely famished," she assented with a bit of exaggerated good humor. She was not hungry. But she felt remorseful for having unleashed so much anger towards Phillippe earlier on. She wanted to repair some of the hurt she had caused. She thought that a peaceful respite for both of them while still together, was necessary before they returned home where no doubt, more uneasy confrontations were awaiting him.

They spent a few more hours in each other's company. At first, it was with a certain simulated ease but soon in spite of a heavy heart, their deportment became more relaxed and spontaneous. They did not pursue the drive to Castelnaud. Instead, on the way back to Grolejac, they stopped in a little inn for an *aperitif* and a light lunch much needed for their writhed nerves.

They were able to enjoy a few pleasant moments.

In answer to Clothilde's many questions, Phillippe found himself quite involved describing the many fascinating wonders of Egypt. In turn, Clothilde talked about what had happened in Grolejac while he was away. She gave a brief summary of her work at the museum to which phillippe listened with intense interest. He expressed his hope that in time he would be able to contribute to it, as he had intended long before this change of circumstances when the project was still in the planning.

Finally Phillippe found the quiescence of spirit to disclose how *"In the calm of the morning, just at the break of dawn, upon awakening he felt uplifted by a sense of infinite bliss. It seemed that while asleep his own will had surrendered to a glorious imperious force, whereas his innermost self had been unlocked and released."* He told, how *"a vision of himself celebrating the Eucharist appeared to his mind's eyes. How, an inner voice beckoned him to the sacerdotal duties of a priest and ever since had taken command of his soul, of his entire being, as if he were reborn into a new consciousness."*

It was drawing toward late afternoon when they reached the driveway at Phillippe's house.

"I should come to *la Brisante* later on and speak with your family. Please phone me to let me know if they can receive me," Paul said gravely as he gently pressed Clothilde's hands tensely clasped together on her lap. She only nodded. A dim smile froze on her lips.

While she stepped out of the car to take the driver's seat, she sadly watched him walk away. Before he opened the front door they waved at each other. His gaze rested on her for an instant.

"My dearest Clothilde, my beloved sister now," he thought with tender melancholy.

CHAPTER 10

CLOTHILDE CONSUMED BY fatigue and shivering from dejection, was unable to think anymore. She wished she could sleep and sleep then wake up on another planet in the bosom of space where life was kinder and things made more sense.

Although she had dozed off only for a couple of hours in that gloomy frame of mind, she had awakened upon a fleeting impression of joyful expectancy at the recollection that Phillippe was back home. Remembering further, she assumed for a brief instant that what had happened the previous day, of course, must have been the most ludicrous nightmare. As the dreary reality like a sharp sword pierced through her memory, she sank into despair. She had the impression of having just crossed a bridge that had collapsed behind her. Now, the unknown stretched in front of her like an infinite void. It seemed so threatening without Phillippe. She resisted falling asleep again lest she would have to go once more through this painful process when awakening, so she sat on a chair by her bedside. To appease her anguish, she had the sudden impulse to talk to him at once. Well, she realized it was too early and would have to wait, for she was not about to selfishly wake him up at the break of dawn. But she had to speak with him soon. Perhaps there could be some kind of compromise after all. Certainly she did not wish for him to revoke his Holy pursuit if she should be the cause of it. "What about if remaining a Catholic at heart he would outwardly convert to some other Christian denomination that would allow him to marry?" she proposed. "This imposed celibacy that rests chiefly on conventions, has it not been laid down by man? Wasn't the Beloved Apostle Peter chosen by Christ to build His Church on earth, a married man? Thank goodness all men are not anointed to Catholic priesthood, or if so what would become of the human species?"

Soon however, she became aware of her derisive thoughts.

"Oh, dear!" she uttered aloud appalled by her covetousness to wheedle Phillippe into deceiving the Catholic precepts, which are as inherently a part of him as are his own genes."

"Oh, dear!" she whimpered again. Standing up she leaned against her nightstand and buried her face in the palm of her hands.

"How could I? Oh, how an innocent intent can easily stray from one's scruples when coerced by desperation!" Feeling deeply repentant, she made the sign of the cross all around her head and shoulders. Promptly, she recited the Mea Culpa, asked Jesus, the Virgin Mary and all the saints for pardon. She had to think of a better solution than having recourse to this wicked means for a compromise.

She walked to the window, drew the curtains open and let a fresh breeze infused with moist night scents, stream in the bedroom. She took several long deep breaths, like performing a rite of purification.

In the penumbra of early dawn the last stars had waned to a timid twinkle. From the oak trees and the hawthorn on the hillock behind the terrace, the caroling of the larks in concert with the rooster's call from the neighboring farms, heralded a new day. The rising of the sun already tinted the eastern horizon with a delicate pink and amethyst wash.

Clothilde sat again on an armchair near a small round table placed in front of the window and stared at the deserted orchard road. Her face bore the saddened expression of a lonely soul who hoped for a friendly visitor to come into view. Soon all the birds began to sing in merry repartees amid the cooing of the pigeons and the doves. The sound of human voices mingled with the plaintive bleating of lambs, the languorous lowing of cows and the spirited neighing of colts. Indifferent to Clothilde's pain the cycle of life had sprang again into its daily bustle after a nightly repose.

As she heard a stump against the wooden wall of the stable Clothilde glanced over in direction of the pasture. She listened attentively when a forceful "Brrrrrrr" gushed from Canon d'Or's nostrils. Her face instantly lit with a warm smile. No feeling of loneliness could possibly linger now in her heart. She leaned forward over the windowsill and examined the daylight breaking across the full magnitude of the sky. In no time she was dressed. She had a strong suspicion that Canon d'Or was anxious to go for an early outing in the countryside, as he always did during summer. Noiselessly she went to the kitchen, took three sugar cubes and left a note on the table to inform her parents that she had gone for a ride with Canon d'Or. She then stepped out of the house and hurried toward the stable.

When Canon d'Or saw her he frantically began to pace from side to side in front of his stable door. The upper section of it being separate from the bottom part was left open during the summer nights.

"Hello my big darling! It is yet so early, why are you not asleep?" she asked approaching him. "Have those inconsiderate roosters awakened you from your dreams of enchanted meadows? Hush! Hush!" she whispered as she gave him sugar. Once he had calmed down, she cupped his head between her hands to lay a kiss on his warm velvety muzzle while he gazed at her adoringly. Content he then went around his corral, neighed, kicked his hind legs with a rocking motion and came back to her. Clothilde laughed.

"You are a silly horse. You think you are still a little colt, don't you?" she sighed. "Oh, you look so beautiful in the light of dawn!"

He tossed his head, went to the gate and insistently pounded the ground with his right hoof. Clearly, he wished to communicate that he had sufficiently slept and was in perfect condition for a promenade.

"All right! all right! I understand," she said while she rubbed his flanks. "You want to go and gambol about, never mind about your breakfast yet? Well, along our way we may find some sweet clover for you to nibble on. Come then."

In perfect agreement they walked abreast to the tack shed.

Although Canon d'Or was in great physical fitness, because of his age he was only ridden by Clothilde whose lightweight was merely like a feather resting upon his back. She refused to torment him with a mouth bit, or with a tight saddle strap fastened around his stomach. A halter with reins and a riding blanket were sufficient.

"Now where would you like to go?" Clothilde asked as she mounted Canon d'Or after opening the gate of the pasture. "It is you who will decide," she then conceded, giving him free reins. He gave off a saucy neighing, pranced a little and shook his head a few times before calmly turning left to enter a lane which led to a brook. There, he very cautiously walked over a narrow bridge to reach the other side and in a smooth gallop sprang forth across the full span of a meadow. As he anticipated the sharp tortuosity of a trail he knew well, without being told he changed his pace to a slow canter then to an unhurried amble. Clothilde bent forward to pet his neck and thanked him for being so sensible.

They soon penetrated a woodland through a footpath and went on leisurely. Along those delightful rides Clothilde now and then hummed childhood songs and old lullabies to Canon d'Or while he listened alertly pricking his ears back and forth.

Above their heads, the leafy branches of the trees interweaved in soaring curves like arches of Gothic cathedrals. In the crisp sunrise the foliage glittered with the radiance of emerald green stained glass.

As the hawthorn and the wild roses lightly brushed upon Canon d'Or, tiny shudders passed across his flanks in waves of golden ripples while the marjoram and the sweet heather rustled against his legs. On both side of them the wild flowers displayed the entire range of colors nature could possibly dream up. The fragrance of it all permeated a breeze as delicate as the breath of a newborn fawn. Surrounded by this idyllic setting Clothilde and Canon d'Or conveyed a rare beauty to behold. Together they embodied a living poem that only heaven could translate into words.

At the limit of a glade very familiar to Canon d'Or, he came to a halt and tapped the rocky terrain with his right front foot. Most definitely he questioned whether they should go forward or perhaps dally nearby a while. For within this area he was always allowed to gambol at his pleasure. It was so irresistibly tempting to frolic unrestrained amid a countryside so pretty.

Clothilde understood him at once. She fondled his neck under his blond mane.

"But of course, of course we will spend some time here and you can play to your heart's delight," she agreed, laughing at his adorable way to express his desire. She dismounted, unhooked the reins from the halter, removed the blanket and let him go loose. He followed her to a source that bubbled gaily out of the earth. In the small eddies of water that had formed near by, a few quails were bathing, flapping their wings and pecking briskly at the wet ground. Frightened by the intrusion, they suddenly flew away. But soon they returned to alight a little further on withered branches scattered around the underbrush and curiously they watched their unexpected company. Clothilde sat on a tree trunk, which had been cut down long ago. In the fissures of its parched bark moss and tiny flowers had grown here and there spreading over like poultices on open wounds. Canon d'Or took a drink of fresh water and swiftly fled in the distance at full gallop. His cheerful neighing echoed in the full amplitude of the forest. He never ventured very far though. He continuously returned to Clothilde, sensing as it were that if he disappeared too long, she would worry. During those precious moments when she looked at her horse frolicking about in sheer delight, she transcended beyond the consciousness of her own being and lost herself completely in the joy Canon d'Or experienced. Nothing else existed, time stood still. But, on this particular morning the effect was of short duration; the fangs of reality persisted in tormenting her. However with the passing of the hours the need to speak with phillippe had lost its initial exigency. The reflection over which she had given herself in the solitude of the night, appeared ridiculously impulsive and irrational. She again took comfort in Saint Paul's Epistle to the Corinthians on *"The excellence of love,"* and directed her endeavor toward becoming accustomed to the bleak change.

The sky had lost its subtle tints of early dawn to gradually deepen into a brilliant blue. When Canon d'Or calmly came to graze on a patch of grass growing by the rivulet, already the sunrays poured a warm golden light over the countryside. Immediately Clothilde rose to reach for the riding blanket and halter she had hung on the stump of a torn branch.

"I think you are ready for your breakfast," she stated with a smile as she approached him gently. He nudged at her side while she fastened the halter on his head.

Unhurriedly they walked back home. Canon d'Or contented from frisking around was full of yummy thoughts about the sweet oats waiting for him in his manger. Clothilde now face to face with her separateness from Phillippe, was coming to the realization that up to then she had identified herself mainly through the nature of their relationship and wondered "who am I really?"

CHAPTER 11

AT THEIR RETURN home, Canon d'Or was groomed from mane to hoofs and then released in the pasture. After a certain interval of relaxation he was fed his alfalfa and his much-anticipated sweet oats, not to forget a bowl of fresh carrots.

Clothilde was surprise to find everyone bustling about at *la Brisante,* as if it were any typical day. It seemed that life went on for the whole world but for herself. Madeleine, with a brisk step came from the garden. She carried a basket filled with newly picked, luscious tomatoes.

"It is strange," she was thinking, "how sometimes the same circumstances, yet completely unrelated, repeat themselves through different generations of the same family. Although Baptiste and I never reached a deep involvement, it bears an amazing resemblance to the new developments between Phillippe and Clothilde."

To Clothilde though, her grandmother seemed rather carefree with nothing other on her mind than looking forward to the next thing to do.

Suzanne was in the kitchen hurrying to wash the dishes, for she wanted to prepare a dessert from a recipe passed on by a neighbor. It consisted of fruits, Bavarian cream, hazel nuts, plus other diverse ingredients. It required a few hours of refrigeration before being served. She hoped to have it ready for lunch.

Emile wearing a smart suit and tie, gave the impression to be in a pleasant mood. He was on his way out to attend a meeting at the town hall.

It certainly was not indifference on their part. Their heart ached for Clothilde. They grieved the son and grandson they had hoped for through this marriage. As disappointed as they were and however much they instinctively wished to shield her from pain, the implacable truth that all plans don't come to pass, that all dreams are not fulfilled, that all desires are not actualized stood supreme against them. They were well aware also that regardless of the beneficial influence generated by the empathy of well meaning people, ultimately it is from the aloneness of our inner self that we must endure and process our lot.

It had been discussed at the breakfast table that within the family, all feelings concerning the situation should be freely expressed and respected. However, in their objective to support Clothilde any display of persistent melancholy, dejection and other negative inputs among them should be deterred at once, whereas an atmosphere of discerning kindness favorable to a sound recovery ought to be initiated. With impartiality they bore in mind not to disregard Phillippe. Surely, an etched pathos in every one's face would only aggravate the hardship of his position. He too was in need of their encouragement.

All the same, when they saw Clothilde, they couldn't restrain themselves from showing their concern. They hugged her, kissed her, inquired how she felt, told her that breakfast had been put aside for her in the dining room and urged her to repair with some sleep. A few hours of rest was now an absolute necessity after having been up since so early.

She responded warmly and reassured everyone she felt just fine while she ran a glance from one to the other as if assessing their state of mind. She was relieved to notice that no visible signs of deep affliction showed in their demeanor. As they had intended, their self-possession and thoughtfulness acted immediately like a tonic on her weary spirit. She had worried about them. Moreover, she was harassed by the blame from having failed to bring to actualization the happiness they had contemplated.

She walked to Emile, surrounded his waist with her left arm and rested her head on his chest, heedful not to wrinkle his clothing. As tears began to seep through her eyelashes, she turned her face away from him, careful also not to stain his shirt. Emile pressed her softly close to him; Suzanne and Madeleine gathered around them.

"My sweetheart!" cried Suzanne stroking her daughter's hair while Madeleine looked at them speechless.

"I am afraid I have let you down!" Clothilde sobbed. "I am causing you so much disillusionment!"

"What?" asked Madeleine as she drew closer and took Clothilde's left hand in hers. "Why, of what nonsense are you talking about? Oh, my dear, dear child, you should not feel accountable for what is happening. No, no, you must not let these thoughts torment you! It is well beyond your control, well beyond any one's control. It would even be much unmerited to lay the least reproach upon Phillippe. All this is larger than him, larger than you, larger than us. It is God's Will. He has other plans in mind for you also."

Clothilde sighed.

"I'll miss Phillippe so terribly. Oh, how I wish! … How I wish, it was only a dream!"

Emile smiled kindly.

"Well, we wish that too, but even so it is not a dream, Phillippe will always remain a part of your life and of our life as well. Differently than what we had imagined but all the same he will. With regard to you my dear, naturally at this moment everything will appear insipid as you look ahead but you must trust life, it may take away, however it too gives generously. As all of us have, you will experience sadness but I am sure you will receive also your share of happiness. We cannot escape this irrevocable law by which our existence on this earth must abide by."

There was a silence.

"I have never forgotten," went on Emile, "what my dear father floridly told me once when he was in one of his philosophical inspirations. He wished to arouse me from a deep brooding over a high school infatuation for a girl who discarded me in view of someone else."

"My son," "he said," *"life unfolds much alike the seasons, it brings forth dreary days, but it bestows sunny days also and the cycle goes on. Ah, what do you know, you are so young! Sometimes, an apparent adversity may carry hidden promises of a new beginning just like a spring storm conceals the transport of new seeds, which in time shall bloom into beautiful flowers."*

"That sounds exactly like the sort of thing great Grandpapa would say," commented Clothilde as she drew away from Emile. She looked at him with an amused expression.

"Yes it does and he was so, so very right," stated Emile as he tenderly looked at Madeleine. "Then one day quite soon after, my heart was stolen by your grandmother, needless for me to tell you anymore. Of course darling, I don't mean to compare your love for Phillippe to a merry infatuation."

Oh, I know Grandpapa," reassured Clothilde with a new sparkle in her gaze.

Emile noticed it and smiled. However, Madeleine discerned he had not been able to stop the tears that glittered in his own eyes. He pulled a pocket watch from a slash on the upper left side of his waistcoat.

"Now ladies if you permit me, I regretfully must take leave of your charming company or else I'll be late for my appointment. That would be a very serious offense. It could disqualify me from the mayoralty and bring the worse disgrace upon my family," he then said good-humoredly.

Clothilde went to take her breakfast in the kitchen in company of her mother who busied herself with the preparation of the dessert as she had intended. Madeleine sat with them to enjoy an extra cup of morning coffee.

CHAPTER 12

CLOTHILDE WALKED INTO her bedroom feeling fortunate to have been born in such a precious family. She thanked God for it.

As she tidied the disorder left behind earlier and dressed for the day, she missed Jean Luc. Moreover, Elise had unexpectedly left Grolejac on the eve of Phillippe's return. She and her mother were now in Biarritz, spending a week near her maternal grandmother who was in need of help as a result of having taken a fall from a ladder while gardening. Elise had gone with a cheery smile, wholly partaking in her friend's joy at the thought that Phillippe would be home the next day. "Why did she have to leave now when I needed her most?" Clothilde bemoaned. "Well if she was here, surely at first I would have to patiently listen while she would analyze the situation by inferring again that Phillippe was remembering a past life when as a boy he stated: *I want to be a priest like I used to be.* and consequently for some uncanny purpose, he might be compelled now to experience priesthood again." Clothilde considered briefly with disapproval. "Thank God her esoteric escapades don't last too long and she soon abandons her absurd. arguments for a more practical reasoning," she then fondly conceded. For she knew that Elise would join her and Jean Luc to realistically confront the issue. They always had faced their difficulties together in the past. Even simply talking about it collectively was therapeutic.

Clothilde looked at the telephone on her nightstand.

"Would Jean Luc still be in his B.O.Q?" (Bachelor officer's quarter) she wondered. "His work hours are irregular. Sometimes he his assigned to an afternoon shift which leaves him the morning free. But again, he might be on an errand or playing tennis." Impulsively without more deliberation she dialed his phone number.

"Oh!" she exclaimed taken aback when Jean Luc picked up the receiver after the very first ring, as though she had not expected him to answer.

"I didn't think you would be …"

"Clothilde!" interjected Jean Luc immediately recognizing her voice. "What a pleasant surprise! All is well at home?" he hastened to ask.

"Yes, yes, everyone is well," she informed him at once to put his concern at rest. "Sorry I didn't mean to alarm you."

"Good! It is so rare to hear from you at this time of the day. Is Phillippe back as planned?"

She hesitated for a second.

"Yes, Phillippe is back."

"And so now at last you are ecstatically happy!"

"Not quite, Jean Luc."

"Not quite? What do you mean not quite? Any complications? Nothing too severe I hope."

"He wants to be a priest," Clothilde announced without any euphemistic disguise. A nervous quiver in her throat brought her voice down a bleak octave from its normal pitch.

"What? …What did you say?" Jean Luc asked amused by what he thought to have heard.

"I said, Phillippe wants to be a priest."

"A priest?"

"Yes, that is exactly what I said."

Jean Luc not believing for a moment that Clothilde could be serious, assumed that she was in a playful mood. Although he deemed her joke to be a bit odd, he decided to go along with the game.

"My, how funny! What has inspired you to such a wit so early, my dear cousin? But, why have you singled out a priest among other far out choices such as a clown for instance? that would have been infinitely more hilarious. Well, I must acknowledge it is always good to know someone in a position affiliated with the all-powerful. Who knows, we might get a free passage to Heaven! So now ... what's new?"

"Jean Luc, listen, I am telling you what is new. Phillippe wants to be a priest," Clothilde stated again slowly and clearly. "A Catholic priest. There will be no engagement and much less a wedding for all that. He is a profoundly transformed man. He wants to be a priest."

There was a silence.

"All right, stop all nonsense and tell me the truth, "asked Jean Luc.

Clothilde's persistently assertive tone of voice was beginning to give him a suspicion that perhaps it was not a jest after all.

"I am telling you the truth," insisted Clothilde.

There was another silence.

"Honestly, it is the truth," she reinforced, in an effort to convince him beyond doubt.

"Ah," ... was no more than Jean Luc could utter,

"It was revealed to him during his stay in El Cairo," went on explaining Clothilde.

"Oh, I see," Jean Luc sighed pensively as the story often heard about Phillippe impersonating a priest when being young, flashed through his memory. It grounded some insight into Clothilde's account.

"You are not joking?" he questioned once more, although at this point he had come to believe that indeed, Clothilde was serious.

"No, Jean Luc, I am not joking," Clothilde replied with a forceful tone of voice.

Jean Luc finally out of hesitation, almost exploded from repressed bafflement.

"What on earth are you talking ... when did you find out?

"He told me about it yesterday when we went for a drive."

Clothilde took a moment to recollect her thoughts.

"I should have apprehended some warning signs when he turned even more devout after Marie Joelle's accident," Clothilde then said dolefully.

"Well, none of us could have foreseen such a drastic change, and one can seek solace in religion without necessarily being ordained," Jean Luc stated. "Clothilde dear, I am so sorry!" he then apologized with heartfelt regrets. "Oh, my God! I have delivered pure absurdities when you are in want of comfort. I feel like a complete fool."

"Please Jean Luc, there is no need to apologize. I would have been very surprised if you had believed me at once. All this is so unexpected to all of us, but really I am fine."

"Don't you pretend with me. How is everyone else coping?"

"Our sole option is to accept gracefully," replied Clothilde in a tone that seemed to carry a certain mordancy so to speak, probably caused by a covert feeling of resentment at the thought to find herself so suddenly rejected from Phillippe's world. A world she had trusted as being constant.

Jean Luc reflected for a moment.

"I shall come down next Saturday," he stated decisively.

"No, Jean Luc, do not impose so much upon yourself. You have been on the road quite enough just a few days ago. We can talk on the phone, it has already helped me a great deal," Clothilde contested.

"I'll be there," he confirmed willfully.

"All right then, your company is always welcome," she conceded, knowing that her most vehement protestations would be pointless. "Drive carefully," she recommended.

"Besides," added Jean Luc, "I feel kind of lonely here without Paul."

The moment Clothilde was reminded of Paul's definite departure, her heart writhed in acute anguish as if she had received news of a great loss. Now life seemed to stare at her like an interminable yawn of aloneness. The phone receiver slipped from her trembling hand, bemused she looked at it for an instant then brought it back to her ear.

"Clothilde, are you there?" Jean Luc called.

"Yes, yes! I am here," she answered, quite unsteady.

"Oh, all right. I heard a clicking sound so I thought we had been disconnected."

"The phone fell," she said with simulated nonchalance as if she alluded to a trivial incident. She did not intend to be deceptive, never with Jean Luc, but why was she thrown in such a state of agitation; how could she rationally explain what had happened?

"I was saying, …" resumed Jean Luc.

"I am sorry Jean Luc, I know you will miss him terribly," rejoined Clothilde in haste, while pretending to be in full control of herself by reconnecting appropriately the sequence of their conversation.

"Yes, he is a very special person. Listen my dear, we will speak about all this at length when I see you in a couple of days. Although I deplore to end our talk, I must set myself off to work. Be brave! Until Saturday, my fondest embrace."

"The same to you from me," Clothilde replied on the verge of pathetic sobs. She hung the phone and beset by indignation, slumped in the armchair next to her bed. She leaned her head against its high back, oblivious of the tears that flowed along her face and dribbled upon her clean white blouse. Overcome by the poignant sensation to be completely forsaken by God and His living creatures she clenched her fists and angrily pounded against the armrests.

"How did I come to this?" she questioned angrily. "My nerves are as feeble as the thread of a spider's web tearing to bits under the slightest touch. Why am I thrown into those frenzies at the least aggravation?" She grimly looked outside and for a while, reflectively fixed her gaze upon a cherry tree at the entrance of the orchard. Then, like if taking a long sip of fresh water out of a glass, which by chance would happen to be within her reach, she inhaled deeply the lush fragrance exuded by the outdoors. She began a thorough review of her reactions to the recent events. Her excessive inner agitation aroused by Paul's company went beyond all comprehension. It was an affront to her principles, to her integrity. Then yesterday, she had shamefully flared up with wrath at Phillippe and now she was shattered like an empty eggshell hurled against the wall, when she was told that Paul had left Dreux. Didn't she know it? Didn't she said goodbye to him last Sunday night? She was so tired of waging battles against so many emotional conflicts. It all felt as if at least a hundred years of tribulations weighed like a clawing albatross upon her young shoulders. She longed for peace, even for solitude. And no, thank you! no romantic attachment ever again! To stay single, grow to be an old spinster would be immensely more sensible than all those unpredictable, tiresome, consuming entanglements, no doubt.

CHAPTER 13

"CLOTHILDE!" CALLED SUZANNE, as she gently knocked on her daughter's bedroom door. "Come, dear! Grandpapa is home. We are serving lunch."

"Yes!" Clothilde answered startled by her mother's voice. She promptly stood up.

"Yes, Maman, I'll be there at once."

"Already noon!" she realized. There again, she had been riveted to immobility by her dilemmas. Her blouse looked like it had been worn for days. She changed into a different one, a coral pink one that challenged her mood. She peered at her appearance in the long wall mirror, patted her eyes with cold water, brushed her face with her fingertips to erase any trace of shed tears or gloomy expression and went to the dining room.

Suzanne was pouring Evian water over ice cubes, which crackled in everyone's glass.

"You look lovely, darling," she complimented Clothilde who approached the table with a sober countenance while directing a gentle gaze from Suzanne to her grand parents.

Emile nodded with an air conveying he agreed entirely.

"Thank you, Maman," she graciously acknowledged and then took a seat by her grand mother.

"Yes, that color suits you well," Madeleine emphasized. She softly ran her fingers over the material of Clothilde's sleeve. "Wait until you taste your mother's dessert, it is purely divine! Although it has subjected me to many disrespectful reprimands for sampling it a bit too often. I declare! what have we come to!" she feigned to complain with mimicked displeasure mixed with a playful expression.

Clothilde amused, smiled fondly at her mother and at her grandmother then excused herself for not having helped in the kitchen on account of her phone conversation with Jean Luc. No one was surprised, when told that Jean Luc would come home the next weekend. Doubtless, they guessed Clothilde had informed him about the drastic changes within the family.

Suzanne made haste to interrupt a short silence, which if enabled to last could have easily yielded to a dismal atmosphere.

"Well now Papa tell us all about your meeting?"

Emile put on a satisfied look.

"It went well dear, very well in fact. We unanimously reached the agreement to lay out a plan for a camping ground on the upper stretch of land opposite the castle; across the Dordogne. It belongs to the Rozieres who being too old to work the soil have let it go fallow. They gladly will sell it to the commune. The location is ideal. The whole area stands upon enough elevation to be protected against inundations. An abundance of trees will always provide plenty of shade. It will include a large swimming pool, a tennis court, and a playground with a merry go round, swings and all to occupy the younglings."

Madeleine delicately stroked her lips with a white damask napkin.

"Oh, my, it sounds so grand!"

"And …" continued Emile, "next to it, a comfortable kennel as well as stables will be installed for those who should desire to bring their pets along, including horses. An assistant will be attending at all times to assure the well-being of the animals.

A sudden glow of delight and pride in her grandfather, lit up Clothilde's face.

"What a wonderful, thoughtful idea, Grandpapa!"

"Excellent, excellent arrangement!" interjected Suzanne. "Too many pets are left behind at vacation time, either neglected or discarded to aimlessly roam the streets like dejected vagrants."

Madeleine was horrified when reminded of animal cruelty.

"Ah, how dreadful. How can anyone treat those dear helpless

creatures so heartlessly whereas we are all accountable for their welfare?" Instead of protecting them as we should, we use them, abuse them, persecute them, discard them. What a disgrace to our human integrity. In the future, at the rise of civilizations more advanced than ours, we will be considered like primitive barbarians due to our based conduct toward animals. I really think that mankind is fated to be doomed so long human beings give themselves the right to perpetrate those abominable acts against them."

"I know," Emile sadly acknowledged; then he continued in a more encouraging tone of voice, "well if we can make a difference, all the better. Everything should be ready by the end of next May, so you, my dear girl," he urged, addressing Clothilde, "you and Elise have much ado in that museum of yours! Next summer should be a busy season. This addition of conveniences surely will bring an increase of tourists who regardless of where they come from, as you are well aware, never fail to express their earnest interest in the history of our heritage."

After an undivided rapture over Suzanne's dessert, Clothilde with insistence considerately sent her mother and her grandparents to the drawing room, for coffee, while she offered to clear the table and wash the dishes to compensate for her lack of participation in the morning household tasks. Even though all of them equally doted on her, she remained unspoiled, always eager to show her gratitude. It gladdened her to give back some of what she received. She had inherited their beautiful nature.

Once the dining room and the kitchen were restored to order, Clothilde went to sit by Suzanne on a sage green settee facing one of the windows giving view upon the front garden. Almost immediately, she took notice of a light blue car, which had turned into the orchard road.

"It was Veronique driving up to the house."

They all rose and hurried outside to welcome her.

Since the news about Phillippe's change of plans, Veronique had been incapacitated to visit anyone. She only had a few brief conversations on the phone with Clothilde's family. This was the first time she ventured out of her house. She stopped abruptly in the driveway and seemed to be out of the car while it was still moving. Her careworn features and pale complexion in contrast with the sun gilded surroundings, gave the impression that a hazy penumbra had spun a mournful veil over her face. Dumb by the throe of her emotions, she hastily approached Clothilde then drew her close in a long embrace. Striving in vain to muster her self-control, she at once gave way to uncontainable sobs.

"Oh, my sweet girl!" she was at last able to bemoan. "How are you enduring? I am so sorry; I am so pained for you!"

To reach for a handkerchief out of her handbag she released Clothilde who now being so moved by Veronique's dismay silently wept.

Veronique gazed at her with a compassionate smile.

"My dear child, your lovely face is bathed in tears, whereas it should glow with radiant happiness! Ah, how the objects of our love can so suddenly become the causes of our great sorrow!" she sighed as she lastly hugged each in turn.

She was then invited in the house for tea. A strong after lunch liquor was recommended and readily accepted.

"I'll prepare a tray," offered Clothilde with a little bounce in her voice. It was meant to lift the pervading melancholy. She then swiftly motioned toward the house.

As they walked in direction of the front porch, Emile affectionately put his right arm around Veronique's shoulders, and coming to a stop he shifted to face her.

"Veronique, dear," he promptly counseled with fatherly solicitude, while Suzanne and Madeleine listened, "true we are all saddened by having to renounce what we had contemplated for our children's future; yet we must not go on and desperately cling to what is not meant to be. It would be pure absurdity. How terribly unfair if we should keep them bound by guilt for not complying with our selfish wishes. Both of them need our encouragement and our blessings to move forward."

"I understand that," uttered Veronique. Her sobs had by then abated to a mere whimper. Oh, but it is so hard! I have lost my Marie Joelle, now I am loosing Phillippe."

Emile gently tapped her shoulder.

"I know, I know, but in a sense, you have lost neither of them. Marie Joelle in her own way has let you know that she is not everlastingly separated from you. Phillippe, indeed a pure source of joy is here now and even if it is not quite in accord with what you had in view for him, he deserves the right and the dignity to meet unreservedly with his destiny. So does Clothilde who will always be like a daughter to you.

With faith in our heart, we must set them free to follow the path life has intended for them.

Veronique heaved another deep sigh. She stared at the distant hills beyond Emile, where reminiscences of bygone days seemed to loom in so clear visions. She clasped her two hands in front of her chest and raised her eyes to the sky.

"Ah," she lamented again, "how life can bless us so generously and then snatch it all away from us so chillingly!"

In response to her dramatic statement, Emile looked at her tenderly, while together in one embrace Suzanne and Madeleine held her in their arms.

Clothilde appeared on the front steps to invite everyone in for tea.

When nearly two hours later, Veronique took leave of her kind friends, she parted less heavy-hearted. She was relieved to have found everyone, and even Clothilde, so indulgently understanding. Their wisdom in accepting disappointment so compliantly was a true inspiration.

With Suzanne's help, she bravely went to prepare dinner for Phillippe's homecoming.

CHAPTER 14

"HEAVENLY FATHER, WE humbly thank You for the gift You have bestowed upon our beloved Phillippe by bidding him to be anointed as one of Your shepherds. Under Your Divine Guidance, may he serve You with devotion and sanctity in his desires. May the voice of the Holy Spirit extol this blessed calling by rejoicing in the heart of his loved ones. Glory be to the Father to the Son and to the Holy Ghost, Amen.

Thus prayed Father Vernier when he had come to sit at the dining room table for the Saturday night dinner given by Veronique to celebrate Phillippe's return. Under lowered brows, all eyes were bathed in tears. Then, the Abbe upon whom was always conferred the honor of saying Grace when invited to dine in his parishioners' home, relinquished this customary deference to Phillippe, in recognition of his imminent ordainment.

As if God had answered the good Father's prayer, the austere ambiance which hovered about the room was steadily dispelled giving way to a faint gaiety that soon lit up Clothilde's and even Veronique's eyes. Gradually the atmosphere grew more relaxed and cheerful. Every so often if silence seeped through the chatters, either it was instantly prevented to linger by Charles' incurable charisma or by the delightful wit of Jean Luc or the spirited verve of the Abbe which at all times drew everyone in a stimulating conversation.

Phillippe was more a listener than a talker. Therefore, it was difficult to differentiate whether he drifted away lost in his own thoughts, or if he simply pondered upon what was being said while his eyes wandered pensively. But overall, he remained socially alert and readily replied to the many questions about his journey to Egypt, which fascinated Jean Luc's mother. She was passionately interested in Egyptian ancient history and claimed that her attraction doubtless was due to a past life spent as Nefertiti, the beautiful wife of Pharao Akhenaten. Charles would then concede that indeed, if so, such beauty had been well preserved throughout the centuries. But certainly, his humor conveyed as well a sincere praise of Justine's stunning good looks.

Nothing was mentioned on the subject of Phillippe's mystical experience. An adventure to be shared during more intimate moments.

The following day after church, Jean Luc passed some time with Clothilde and Phillippe. He could stay only a few hours in Grolejac, for he had to drive back to Dreux. However it was beneficial. To be in close contact with the situation rendered him more insightful of Phillippe's mental state, and to find Clothilde in a relatively mellow spirit appeased his anxiety. Nonetheless, he was profoundly saddened to leave his family behind in such critical impasse.

While Elise was attending to her grandmother in Biarritz, Clothilde had chosen not to burden her with all that madness. The next Monday when she returned home and it was with a considerable shock that she learned about the developments, which had taken place in her absence. Clothilde was right to deem that her friend would connect Phillippe's behest to priesthood with a past life, as was projected by Phillippe himself when he was young. However, Elise had enough subtlety of judgment to discern that then was not the time to debate on the issue.

Then at the end of the week, a letter from Paul came in the mail. He wished to express his gratitude for the kind reception he received upon his visit to Grolejac and his sincere regrets for his departure from France. Clothilde found herself compelled to read it over and over again. She searched for a certain nearness with him through his handwriting. She perused between the lines as though some kind of hidden message addressed to her personally might be disclosed, and she ran her fingers over the paper like one would stroke the relic of a dearly loved soul. She knew it was outright absurd, but she could not stop. And so the days slipped into weeks, and the weeks finally added up to a month.

During this interval, Clothilde and Phillippe openly sought to elucidate their emotions still in a stage of utter puzzlement. But it all remained unresolved. Neither of them could understand why they felt so helpless to change their situation or to accept it completely.

Ultimately, at the end of August the time had come for the last preparations of Phillippe's departure.

Then he was gone.

During the week prior to his leaving, Clothilde believed that she had prepared herself to reasonably bear with their separation. But when confronted by the final rupture, her illusory courage plummeted into a bottomless chasm of gloom. She had forgotten every single words on *the excellence of love* from Saint Paul's first Epistle to the Corinthians. An empty space within her felt like a deserted immensity where all flowers, all verdure, all life had suddenly withered. Although she was surrounded by the love and solicitude of her family and Elise, she sorely felt like a forlorn wanderer without a sense of direction. At night when she sat by her bedroom window, she took notice of neither the silvery glow streaming from the moon, nor of the throbbing twinkle of the vibrant summer stars, nor of the soft chatter of the somnolent birds, nor of the fragrant breaths exuded by nature at rest. She stared at a dense silence and nostalgically reminisced all the happy moments she and Phillippe had shared since their childhood. He had been like a brother, a best friend, a guide. Then one day they grew aware that between them a nascent attraction had begun to stir certain feelings, which deliciously swayed their heart far beyond a platonic friendship.

Yes, they had fallen in love with each other.

Oh, how she missed him. There will never be the same anticipation for his homecoming after his absence. Never again!

Lately, when he was in Egypt, too often, the wait for his return had seemed unendurable, yet how sweet was this yearning in comparison to the void left on the wake of their last goodbye.

Everything reminded her of him. There was not a room in *la Brisante* where he had not entered, not a chair in which he had not sit, not a door he had not passed through, not a blade of grass he had not trodden on the front lawn, not a hair on Canon d'Or's head he had not caressed.

She remembered when at one point, he gave some indication to waver; apparently tempted to surrender under the sway of the love he felt for her. Torn by a spell of piercing regrets, she crossed examined all the "whys." which perhaps had conclusively influenced Phillippe's final decisions. Why hadn't she been more forceful, less tolerant? Why did she relent so easily, much too easily? Ah, why hadn't she voiced more assertively the real intensity of her feelings for him? it might have prevailed over his indecision. She went on blaming herself for not having done this and that, or such and such. Had she given way to a senseless pride? She recalled how she had encouraged him in moments of hesitancy and how she had promised her support. Was she a glutton for self-sacrifice?

She also, sorrowfully wondered how he managed to bear the situation. What was it like for him now that he was permanently separated from his family, from Grolejac, from her, from everything to which he had been accustomed? Oh, and she was not by his side to comfort him!

CHAPTER 15

ARRANGEMENTS HAD BEEN made for
Phillippe to pass an indefinite period of seclusion with his uncle Aristide
Dumonteil and his aunt Celine Aulnier at their quiet home near Arles
in southeastern France, before he would enter the seminary.

Aristide Dumonteil was the younger brother of Frederick's mother,
therefore Phillippe's granduncle. Now at the age of eighty-one, he was
a retired priest sharing with his sister Celine, a small ancient house
surrendered by beautiful lands and woods inherited long ago from his
godfather. It offered an ideal sanctuary for Phillippe's retreat.

Father Dumonteil persistently declined to climb the ecclesiastical
hierarchy, preferring to stay in the intimate ambiance of a small parish.
He wished to grow old among those he had baptized, married, or had
preached to from the days he was a young man himself. Celine, five
years younger than Aristide, due to a fatal train derailment, had become
a childless widow during the fist years of her marriage. Having had no
desire to enter into matrimony again she chose instead to live with her
brother, and each was contented to watch over the other.

As a boy, in the course of his summer vacation, Phillippe had
enjoyed many happy moments under their vigilant care at the time
when they still lived in the presbytery. During this recent sojourn with
them, Phillippe regularly phoned his mother and father then Clothilde
and her family. At the very beginning, Clothilde entertained the hope
that he would announce a change of mind; that upon reconsidering

he would come to the realization that priesthood was not his vocation. He would then admit he had made a mistake and finally would return home to take up again their former relationship. She would be on the verge to tell him how she wished it would be so, but there again, the words remained mute on her lips, for she really wanted him to make the decision without being influenced by her desires. Alas! As the days went by, Phillippe showed no change in his intention. Clothilde forced out of denial, resigned herself to relinquish all hope.

Had she known how sad Phillippe was! Had she known how desolate he was from being so decisively separated from his loved ones! His early morning hours were particularly filled with anguish, for at night, what he had repressed all through the day rose to the surface in his dreams and cast a heavy gloom upon awaking. Probably at that time, God had His Hands tied up elsewhere, because Phillippe believed himself completely forsaken from the touch of Grace. How often was he then tempted to pack his suitcase and rush home to reclaim the love he had renounced. However, invariably an innermost, persistent bidding insurmountable it seemed, pressed him to resist those impulses. "How could I?" he would reflect when later those urges were reconsidered. "How could I expect Clothilde to once more commit herself to someone like me? Someone she then could only perceive as unethical, inclined to alter his mind at the whim of any fancy regardless of other's feelings or consequences. How could I?" Even his mother would live in the racking torments of uncertainty. His mother, his very dear mother! Feeling so helpless to console her constantly tortured him.

At one time, like Clothilde, he had come to question how justifiable was the necessity of celibacy imposed by the Catholic church upon its clergy. "Why couldn't a man have a family and serve God well at the same time?" Consequently, he would then be appalled by his impudence to cross-examine the tenets of the Church. Was he befitted to be a good priest or rather did an uncanny need to sublimate his self-image tempt his imagination into some kind of fantasy? So many inner discords caused him such an insufferable emotional schism. He was torn between the hopelessness to atone for the pain he had caused and the guilt provoked by the thought of rejecting God's bequest, as a son would refuse the generous gifts offered by a loving father. Finally driven by the exigency to unburden his heart and to confess as it were a contrite soul, which he feared did not measure up to the sanctity of his calling,

Phillippe decided to confide in his uncle. Therefore, one evening after dinner, as they both took a stroll side by side in the spacious garden, the good Abbe with a placid compassionate expression, readily listened to his grandnephew. Passing by a cast iron bench huddled in a rosemary hedgerow shaped like a half circle, he invited Phillippe to sit, so they could quietly talk uninterrupted for a while.

"My dear son," he said, (he always called Phillippe, his son.) while leaning his cane against a tuft of boxwood next to where he sat. Father Dumonteil turned toward Phillippe whose prolonged silence seemed to suggest he was waiting for his uncle much anticipated advices. "I am glad you did not hesitate to open your heart to me. I have wanted to ask if you were troubled by some thoughts, for I did notice an apprehensive look unusual about you. Indeed I am not surprised by what you have told me. A very sudden and dramatic change has come upon you when your plans were set upon a different course with someone you love deeply. It is quite natural that this would create a worrisome disparity between your sentiments, your conscience and that imperious new desire to unreservedly consecrate your life to the Almighty. However, your circumstances are no rare exceptions. How many have been in a similar situation at the onset of their spiritual journey! It may surprise you, but I too once had to contend with my share of struggles. Our trials when in doubt are necessary means to an end so to speak, particularly on the occurrence of an instantaneous spiritual awakening as has happened to you."

Brought back to the basic awareness that he was not alone to face such tribulations, Phillippe drew a deep sigh of relief, as if all at once he had been delivered from a sense of isolation.

"Yes," continued Father Dumonteil after a short pause, "yes, notwithstanding the disquietude aroused, this critical phase should be appreciated as an essential process. It is quickened by the intervention of a God-sent prudence to help you cast off any reservation about the direction conclusively pursued."

Father Dumonteil watched an acorn drop to the ground then smiled at Phillippe.

"But I am not speaking of any matter that you don't already know," he said thoughtfully.

"Recently it seems that my judgment as been blurred by my emotions." Phillippe voiced with an unassuming smile. "But, listening to you Uncle Aristide never fails to enlighten me. I have always found a source of inspiration in your wisdom. May it be God's desire that I follow in your footsteps."

"Oh, my dear son! If you are destined to be one of His servants, you will be the best by virtue of your own merits. Do not be further distressed. Do not resist yourself. Flow with your feelings, which are very sound and appropriate. Pray, calm your soul. It is from the deepest stillness within that the voice of the Holy Spirit shall speak to you with perfect clarity and gently shepherd you to a more transparent vision of what concerns you. Concerns, my son, which can only arise from the heart of a principled, sensitive and caring man such as you."

The Abbe gazed at the milky depth of the sky shedding a pearly glimmer over the September twilight. Reverently raising his hands, he pointed at the infinite.

"Every single one among us is an active part of God's all encompassing design. If He has elected you to a Holy mission on this earth, it is therefore in view of a broader and better purpose than what would have been fulfilled by your marriage to Clothilde. Then you must trust that as the future shall unfold, your dear ones will be justly guided as well, and will find in your enterprises worthy causes for many new and abiding joys. However, be as it may, in like manner for all else, one must wait for God's auspicious timing."

Tears had spread a mist over Phillippe's eyes.

A chilly wind swept up the fallen leaves in crimson and gold eddies all across the garden.

Phillippe stood up and promptly indicated it was best to return inside lest his uncle would catch cold. He reached for the cane, which had fallen on the ground and gave it to the Abbe, then gently assisted him to get on his feet.

"I thank you Uncle Aristide for your sage advices. Again, you know how much I value your sensible judgment," Phillippe sincerely expressed as they began to walk.

"It is my pleasure, dear son, my greatest pleasure!"

Father Dumonteil looked far away at the horizon. A glow of pure delight illumined his beautiful furrowed face.

"Surely, it was a sin to be so proud of one's nephew," he thought.

They had barely taken a few steps, when they caught sight of Celine's silhouette briskly advancing toward them. She was endowed with an excellent health and tireless energy. She carried a garment that hung on her wrist.

"The evening has turned awfully nippy to still wander outdoors, I have brought you a shawl, let me lay it on your shoulders."

Father Dumonteil stopped for a moment.

"I thank you. You are very kind."

As they resumed their walk, Celine went by her nephew's side and wrapped her arm around his.

"It is so good to see you here Phillippe, your uncle is in heaven when you visit us. So often we speak about you; time and time again we reminisce the joyful days when as a young lad you stayed with us in summer."

"I too fondly look back upon those memories, Aunt Celine. I always felt so sad upon parting from both of you and wished you lived nearer to us all.

They gathered for tea and pastry close to a fire in the large and rustic drawing room. The stern expanse of the white washed walls was brightened by brilliant reproductions of Leonardo de Vinci's Last Supper and the Madonna of the Rocks as well as Raphael's Holy Family with lamb. A massive brown sofa faced two armchairs of the same color around a low walnut table in front of the hearth. Some wood chairs were placed here and there. A few scattered porcelain objects passed down by the family from way back in time, glistened upon small tables.

On the mantle piece, a miniature replica after Michelangelo's Pieta stood next to a statue of Saint Francis of Assisi preaching to the birds. Both statuettes were in pearly white alabaster.

Above, nailed to the wall, a bronze Crucifix attested the ultimate sacrifice of the Christ to expiate and redeem the sins of humanity.

An old grand piano, which had belonged to their mother, took over the entire opposite west end corner of the room. Celine enjoyed playing. While the music flowed from her fingers, her brother read but quite often dozed off irresistibly lulled by the beautiful melodies. He loved Chopin's preludes and Bach's fugues, so she never failed to thoughtfully include them in her repertoire.

Celine kept everything dusted and polished. Lovely lace dollies of all shapes, bouquets of the many flowers she and her brother passionately grew in their garden, added a delightful feminine touch.

When they bade each other good night after having joined for prayer, Phillippe's handsome face, which recently had been too heavily stilled in somber expressions, at last was animated by a bright smile.

While he passed in the first stage of sleep, the words of the Abbe repeatedly echoed in his semi consciousness and jumbled all other unwelcome thoughts. For the first night in eternity it seemed, he finally fell into a serene slumber.

In the course of the next few days, Phillippe was thankful for the opportunity to pass many more hours in inspirational discourses with his dear granduncle.

It was within a couple of weeks after pious hours of meditation, as he beseeched peace and gladness of heart for his loved ones that Phillippe found his own. Seized by the unquestionable trust that yes … yes indeed, God had broader and wiser purposes for the good of all, than what could have been fulfilled by his marriage to Clothilde, he felt delivered from any traces of ambivalence. He was reconciled with himself, with his Maker, with his fate. At last this certainty manifested itself as clearly as a brilliant sunray suddenly piercing through a heavy dark cloud.

He had found his path now, he was sure of that. He might have encountered misgivings and temptations, but yes, Uncle Aristide was right, it had been a necessary test to clearly be assured of the Divine Will. Oh, yes, when his spirit was exalted to a rapture up to then unsurpassed, he was sure that he was restored by a heavenly wellspring, and was made whole.

CHAPTER 16

"PLEASE SAY YES," Elise insisted repeatedly as she searched for a sign of affirmative reaction in Clothilde's profile fixed on the road. They were on their way to Sarlat, having in mind to spend some time browsing through the bookshelves at the library.

Elise wished Clothilde would attend an afternoon outdoor party given by her neighbors the Girondos. Henri Girondo, a native of Grolejac had been one of the village doctors since his graduation from medical school. Now retired, he and his wife Simone always found a good excuse to organize some cheerful social events at their house. Their grandchildren living in Gourdon, were of Clothilde's age. If free from their own obligations, they never failed to participate in those pleasurable occasions, and their young friends were always welcome.

The weather being unusually warm for the season, their bon vivant nature found it perfectly justifiable to host an open-air gathering for no other reason than to enjoy the outdoors in good company. If so desired, one could always compete in a brisk game of tennis or take a plunge in their spacious swimming pool, which like a mini lake in the midst of a meadow, reflected brilliantly the ever-changing moods of the automn sky.

Naturally, Clothilde and Elise had been invited.

"You know they will be terribly vexed if you refuse," went on Elise. "They are very fond of you."

Clothilde frowned and flashed a glance at her friend.

"Now, don't play on my sentiments or on my conscience!"

"I wouldn't dare," retorted Elise with an elfin smile, which conceded she might very well have used such devious means after all to motivate a positive answer.

There was a silence.

"All right! Yes, I'll go, just to please you," at last Clothilde consented with an affectionate tone of voice.

In a joyful impulse, Elise threw her arms around Clothilde's shoulders.

"Thank you! Thank you! I am so glad!"

"Be careful!" warned Clothilde, "or I'll drive us both off the road."

"Oh my! Sorry!" interjected Elise, as she happily settled back in her seat.

"Oh, thank you! I am so very glad!" she repeated, as if she had received the most exciting news. She then switched into a more serious attitude.

"Really Clothilde, you have behaved too long like a disillusioned old maid pathetically secluded. Isn't it time to end this austere modus vivendi, and begin to take a peek at the world where the rest of us still live?"

"Yes, it probably is," Clothilde acquiesced amused by Elise's analogy while she thought "but why? what for? what is there anyhow?" Everything seemed so distant, so impersonal.

Ever since Phillippe's departure now more than two months ago, Clothilde had gradually slackened into a daily treadmill much at odds with her rather spontaneous and versatile personality. Perhaps it gave back to her life the sense of predictability that so many disappointments had recently taken away from her.

Those around her understood she had arrived at a very difficult junction, causing her to be temporarily immobilized. With that in mind, without questions they continued to give her their loving support. However, they quietly wished she would pull herself out of the monotonous pattern from which lately, she had not even once deviated.

Elise, who had shown much patient sensitivity about her friend's lot, had decided it was imperative to initiate a change. She judged it unsound for Clothilde to abstain from all social activities and narrow her world to the non-stimulating repetition of a much too rigid routine.

Day after day, Clothilde invariably rose at six o'clock every morning. First, she attended to Canon d'Or. She bathed and groomed herself before joining her mother and grandparents for breakfast, then as she normally would, she contributed to household or any other domestic responsibilities. After lunch, she went to work assiduously at the museum with Elise or alone. Occasionally father Vernier would team up with them as he had promised to do in the fall. He also discretely maintained a close surveillance over Clothilde's recovery, which was a great concern of his. He stood always ready to offer her, spiritual as well as secular guidance.

Veronique, her grandparents, her mother or others would stop by frequently, either to help or have a chat, never leaving without expressing a well-deserved praise for her and Elise's accomplishments. At five o'clock in the evening she returned home, sometimes accompanied by Elise who now and then would stay for dinner and a short visit. At nine o'clock, Clothilde was ready to retire in the privacy of her bedroom where she read until her eyes refused to stay open.

Sunday after mass, alongside Madeleine and Suzanne, quite reluctantly she intermingled with people within the precinct of the church. At first, she did suffer from a certain shame, like a forsaken woman exposed to public ridicule. However, she soon realized her mistrust was unfounded. She never heard one derogatory comment addressed to her situation; on the contrary, because Grolejac was like a large extended, caring family. They all understood that life is full of uncertainties and wished the very best for Phillippe and Clothilde like they would for any of their own. It was even noticed that many eligible young men aware that Clothilde was unattached, lately had rallied around Emile hoping to ingratiate themselves in his good favor. Compelled by their eager intent to date his beautiful granddaughter, they thought his influence could be propitious in attaining the realization of their desires.

Every Sunday afternoon, Clothilde had tea with Phillippe's mother. During these moments they spent together, Veronique warmed her heart in cherished reminiscences of happy days long gone. Although everyone else had exhausted all discussions about Phillippe, she could still extract some more regret she longed to share.

After taking leave of Veronique, if it were not too late or raining, Clothilde would hurry home, change clothes and take Canon d'Or out on his favorite trail. That year, even though it was already the end of October, all the trees still clang to most of their gold, crimson and vermilion foliage. It seemed that the countryside had borrowed time on the wintry days to orchestrate a grandiose pageant of flamboyant colors. As a result, toward evening when the fiery amber of sunset unfurled at the low horizon, one had the illusion it was the earth's rays, which illumined the sky. In those enchanting hours, Clothilde enjoyed peaceful outings with Canon d'Or. She then found a welcome reprieve from the dreariness of her present quasi-sequestered existence and from some of her concerns yet unresolved. The splendor and tranquility of nature slipping into twilight exhaled a magnificent melancholia, which predisposed her to serene pondering. As they ambled leisurely, Clothilde now and then verbalized her thoughts to Canon d'Or. He would let her know that he listened by nodding or flipping one or the other ear back and forth at the sound of her voice.

He was the only soul to whom she had disclosed the secret hermetically locked in the innermost recess of her being for she didn't dare tell anyone else. Yes, only Canon d'Or knew that an unappeasable longing for Paul still lingered in her heart. Who else would understand her madness?

For heaven sake! She had been around the man for merely a few hours then he had vanished farther and farther away. Surely, by now he had even forgotten her name. What was going on in her head? How could she intelligibly avow to any one that against the mightiest resistance of her will, thinking about him threw her in a turmoil as intense as a volcanic thrust on the threshold of flaring up from its ashes.

Could she present herself at the breakfast table, and nonchalantly announce, "oh, by the bye, lately, over and over again I have been dreaming about Paul. What could that mean?" and expect an indulgent response from her perplexed family?

Could she admit to Jean Luc, "oh, each time you phone, I desperately hope you will announce that Paul miraculously has returned to France?"

What could she say to Veronique? To Father Vernier? To any one? No doubt, everybody would conclude rightly that she had lost her reason. For, logically it seemed that it was for Phillippe and Phillippe only she ought to languish.

Elise, of course might have been more receptive since she was already in her confidences. But Clothilde harassed by a certain sense of culpability didn't wish to mention the issue, lest it would give it greater purport. Moreover, Elise, bless her heart, with all her kind intentions would at once reason everything out by her absurd theory on reincarnation. Somewhat Clothilde, in spite of her religious intolerance on that subject, occasionally, would give in to be amused by her friend's "metaphysical eccentricities" in the same manner she would humor the paradoxical swearing of a profoundly pious nun being no less devout for that. She really held Elise to be fundamentally a good Catholic. However, she viewed her own situation as sufficiently peculiar the way it was, and therefore didn't care to render it more so by exposure to some esoteric interpretation. It seemed too appallingly cryptic when applied to her personally.

Conversely, inasmuch as Paul had not been mentioned lately, all in all Elise thought it a propos not to kindle more disturbance in the midst of already enough upheaval and let the matter rest.

Therefore, Paul was not discussed between them.

Nonetheless, if Clothilde gave others the disconcerting notion that she had withdrawn into a dejected state, for the most part her outward attitude was only illusive. Her mind was far from stagnant. She aggressively sought to examine the thoughts and emotions, which in those recent months had dominated her as if they had belonged to an alien personality forcefully trespassing upon her own. She wished to explore beyond it. She felt that an alter consciousness seemed eager to emerge and aspire further than the former sense of self she had until then experienced. It was still indefinite though, like striving to come out from a cocoon while still deprived of sight. However, it was worth not to be ignored.

Again she was left on her own in quest for answers. As a result, when alone in her bedroom at night, reading moments were not a gluttonous absorption of soppy novels she had picked up at the supermarket. She had no desire to relive through an imaginary character that which reality had usurped from her.

Deep from within, a driving force sparked her spirit to yearn for a regenerative energy she was unable to obtain from her immediate circle of interaction, mainly due to her secretive conduct. Therefore, until all hours in the night she immersed her mind in any philosophical or psychological treatises available.

She had always enjoyed to explore objectively and critically the writing of the finest minds in the world or simply read their work for the sheer pleasure of it. She now approached their thoughts for therapeutic purpose, so to speak. Her brain thirsted for rational thinking, which of late had not been simple to apply effectively. Their reasoning process absorbed her intensely. She would lose herself in the development of their ideas until quite weary for want of sleep. Of course, her Holy Bible stayed permanently at her reach, for she never bypassed the notion that in it laid the true Fountainhead of all enlightenment and wisdom.

She did not expect to see Paul ever again; neither had she any hope that at this point Phillippe would change his mind. To strive for structuring anew her unstable world into a tangible reality favorable to her emotional autonomy, certainly seemed to be the most sensible alternative.

CHAPTER 17

As CLOTHILDE WAS getting ready to attend the Girondos' afternoon reception, she felt a pang of intense loneliness. It was her first social function since the breach of her relationship with Phillippe. She nearly changed her mind, but decided she would go. She wanted to keep her word, for she had promised to accompany Elise. Anyway, wasn't it time to face the world again with what was left of herself? Was it why on an impulse, immediately after she and Elise came out of the library in Sarlat, she went to buy something new for the occasion, as if symbolically wishing to break away from the past? Her family was elated. It was indeed a positive sign, a good progress no doubt showing an imminent recovery. Regretfully, neither her mother nor her grandparents were able to join her in this diversion. On that particular day they were committed to partake in the celebration of some long time friend's wedding anniversary. But they beamed with gladness as they waved at her when she left.

She looked so pretty in her new lilac blue summer dress and her hair pulled back in a french braid.

Elise looked no less exquisite in a mint green skirt and white sleeveless top.

The weather held its pledge to stay bright and warm. Accordingly, the party was given in the front gardens. Upon their arrival, chatter, carefree laughter and lively music filled the air and resounded joyously over the gold and ruby sun-splattered vale.

Clothilde and Elise's appearance elicited a sweeping wave of cheers and smiles. The hosts immediately met them with affectionate embraces. They were introduced to a few guests they had never met before, while many eyes lit in admiration of their striking beauty.

At the start, Clothilde felt awkward. Even though she knew most of the people, she had an impression of estrangement from everyone. The world they lived in seemed so far remote from hers.

Almost oblivious to the kind consideration received, she nevertheless responded graciously. She felt like an automaton following her own shadow. Her glance hovered absently about and was captured by a couple who held hands while being lost in each other's gaze. A shudder of lonesomeness chilled her heart. She wished Phillippe were by her side. Everything was so uninviting without him. Then at a little distance further, the silhouette of a tall young man engaged in a conversation with a group of other men, arrested her attention. The style, the color of his hair, the manner in which he carried himself, altogether bore such a remarkable resemblance to Paul, that she could have sworn it was he standing there. She was spontaneously invaded by a brief sensation of extraordinary joy and an irresistible urge to rush toward him, when at that very moment he changed his stance. From the new angle of vision she could well see his face. What was she thinking of! Of course, it was not Paul. She knew all along that it could not be Paul. Yet only with great effort, she repressed the tears already burning her eyes. Was there anyone around plagued by such a concoction of paradoxes? They all looked so happy, so cozy in their fate she mused. Thank God there was no time to sink into long dismal reflections, for Francis, the doctor's grandson, had come to greet them. He instantly offered refreshment. Elise was in the mood for champagne. Clothilde without hesitation accepted a gin and tonic. In no time, a flock of gallant young bachelors was already gathered in their company. They were delighted to see them both and ecstatically surprised by Clothilde's unexpected presence.

The fist few sips of her drink sprayed her nostrils with a pleasant iced mist and promptly dispelled her qualms. Before long, caught in the contagious high spirit of her entourage, she felt quite light hearted and astonished at herself that she would find a certain appeal in the attention showered upon her. All this seemed so new. She dared to confess silently that it flattered her vanity, and even if essentially shallow, she liked it. However, as superficial as it appeared, this sensibility to compliments was not just a frivolous reaction of her ego. It was rather a welcome indication that she was awakening to a need she had undesirably denied herself. A need to be Clothilde; to be human, loving and vulnerable. A need to open herself to life again and to merge in the will of her destiny, without further pointless questions or resistance.

The rest of the afternoon was spent with ease. She and Elise mingled agreeably with the other guests.

All the while, the tennis court, the swimming pool and even the billiard room remained silent. People had tossed their worry aside for a few hours by passively entertaining themselves in pleasurable chatters and enjoying a choice of lavish food and refreshments. Clothilde pensive watched families' members who ate, laughed, and every so often embraced. She wished her grandparents and her mother were there also.

"Oh!" she inwardly cried out, as though suddenly aroused from a long torpor. "Oh! how selfishly I have been heedless of others. How I have allowed my own wants to consume me while I went on whimpering over regrets for what I thought I possessed but never had the right to own. Meanwhile I have thoughtlessly taken for granted the dearest beings who matter most in my life."

Overwhelmed by repentance, she wanted to run home to apologize for her egotistical attitude, to tell her grandparents, her mother, Canon d'Or, Veronique, Father Vernier, how much she loved and cherished them. She would have liked to put her arms around Elise's shoulders right then, and tell her likewise.

The evening sun had sunk in the western horizon, spilling out on its trail, streams of flaming colors along the far edge of the forest. The company had begun to disperse. Time had come to part from the charming hosts.

Although Simone had help from a village woman, Clothilde and Elise stayed a bit later among those who kindly lent an extra hand to put things back in order. When they were left alone after being escorted to their car by Francis, Clothilde took Elise in her arms with the same ardor as though she had found a beloved sister after a long absence.

"I love you Elise, please, forgive me!" she stated apologetically.

Elise was taken aback.

"What is this all about?" she exclaimed bursting into a puzzled laughter, "forgive you for what?"

Clothilde stood still and silent, and then released Elise.

"You know what I mean. I am sorry for not having been my true self lately. I have behaved most inconsiderately toward the ones I love.

Elise gazed at her friend with profound affection.

You have been drawn into an extraordinary situation and have born it superbly. Please do not chastise yourself so unfairly. I hope my support measures up to your courage and dignity. We all hold you in our heart with great respect and so much love."

Elise gently laid both hands on Clothilde's shoulders then asked directly.

"You still think about him, don't you?"

Clothilde stunned by Elise's unexpected question, tensed rigidly as if posturing in a defensive reflex, then she slackened like a reed drained of its sap.

"I … Yes," she admitted, perfectly aware of who was the "him," Elise was referring to.

In turn, Elise gathered Clothilde in her arms.

"I have wondered."

Clothilde for a moment put aside the difference on their spiritual interpretation of life, She was so glad to have Elise back in her confidence.

"Thank you," she said kindly "Thank you for your discretion, thank you for your friendship and your patience, thank you for being you." She freed herself from Elise's embrace, and then added in a lighter tone of voice, amused by her effusion of "*thank yous.*"

"And I thank you for having tugged me along today. I really enjoyed it."

"You are welcome," said Elise, with a smile that glowed from deep within, for she too felt she had reunited with a dear sister.

With a refreshed spirit, Elise took her place behind the steering wheel, and Clothilde settled herself in the passenger seat.

When Clothilde arrived at *la Brisante*, she found her mother and grandparents having tea in the drawing room. At once she ran to them and in the midst of heartfelt embraces poured all the sentiments, which earlier in the afternoon had given her so much remorse.

They wept and laughed together in a whirlwind of released emotions that had been temporarily silenced until ready to be expressed. Because in that family there were no locked cells available for long secretive brooding. If the right of privacy was respected, concerns could be shared at any time and caring advices were always accessible.

This spontaneous reunion was intensely uplifting to everyone.

That night, there seemed to be a different aura permeating the atmosphere at *la Brisante*; as if it were charged with a latent energy that yearned to assert itself, like the elan vital of a new spring still hushed up in the last days of winter.

The next day, upon arising, Clothilde went to her bedroom window she had left open. She stretched and breathed deeply in the coarse autumnal scents emanating from the fallen leaves and the moist soil. At the east, the ascending sun sprayed a gold and rosy mist across the pale horizon and over the nacreous fleece of fog enveloping the land beneath. Still a little hazy from a deep slumber, she sought to summon up her thoughts and reflect upon the events of the preceding day. Then she remembered.

She remembered she had the most vivid dream about Paul. While sitting in a chair by the window, bewildered but intrigued she gave her full attention to the recollection of its content.

"He was running toward her from far, far away. She was unable to move but could extend her arms to him. While approaching her, he appeared and disappeared time and time again. When almost close enough to touch each other's hands, they were suddenly separated by the same distance he had initially come into view. She cried out his name, but the sound of her voice remained trapped in her chest yet she could hear him call her also. The boundless span to be covered between them seemed to symbolize a never-ending, unattainable wish."

She found herself sinking into the most profound discouragement, as if her confessions of the previous evening had provoked a defiant genie to challenge the sincerity of her contrition.

"What is it in me?" she questioned. "What is it that attracts my mind to those kinds of absurdities?

She stayed still for sometime, trying to void her mind from further disturbing thoughts.

"No," an inner voice soon asserted. "No," you will not be lured again into the obsessions you have suffered lately. You will gain complete control over the deplorable power you alone have given them. "Heaven!" she implored while raising her gaze toward the sky, "may I dwell in the joy of what I have been granted, and not be tormented by covetous desires."

She corrected her slumped posture, got up from the armchair, dressed herself and went to feed Canon d'Or.

CHAPTER 18

THE PULSE OF the land was at rest and Grolejac heaved a deep sigh of relief from the satisfaction that all essential tasks had been well completed. The village was ready to take repose until next spring, when the seasonal sway once more would burst astir.

Yes, at *la Brisante*, everything had been put in good order for the advent of winter. The grapes had been processed and their juice had filled many barrels. The new wine stored in the cellar, was already ripening its exquisite bouquet.

The tobacco leaves scattered to dry upon long folding tables set around the loft of the barn, soon would be gathered in small bunches, then hanged at the ceiling until thoroughly parched. In the silo, next to the wheat and corn, the walnuts had been put aside; within a month or so they would be cracked and the nut separated from the shell. There, the chestnuts as well had been packed away in sacks. The bulk of it all would be delivered at a wholesale price to the local merchants who in turn would retail it according to the consumers' needs.

Preserved fruits and vegetables filled the pantry shelves with more than enough to provide for the family and plenty left to be given away.

The woodshed stacked with fire logs, was drenched in scents of cedar, pine and oak sap, which along the wintry evenings would sizzle among the crimson and gold flames swirling up the hearth of the large chimney in the rustic kitchen. It was here, in this large but cozy room that the family, during the cold season gathered to read, chat over tea or hot chocolate or dreamily watch the chestnuts roasting upon the glowing embers, and sometime even, just laze awhile in a recliner like Emile did.

Since the onset of September, Suzanne had resumed teaching at the elementary school. Once a week, Clothilde assisted her with a drawing and watercolor class followed by an art history mini-course accordingly simplified to befit the student's level of comprehension. Both Clothilde and the children loved it.

To the great pleasure of everyone, Clothilde's attitude had well improved. Her cheerful voice and laughter again echoed around them.

However, despite her new self-willed behavior, concerns, which in all appearance had been effectively overcome remained ever-present and unresolved. This was simply because regardless of her endeavor, the answers were meant to remain sealed in the limbo of time yet to come. At times though, nature can be merciful and beguile us to think we can deflect from the tests coming on our appointed path, so everything gave the impression to have resumed a normal life at *la Brisante*.

Clothilde's night reading did not bring her the result she had hoped to obtain. All the same, she never tired of such past time, which nonetheless continued to be a source of stimulation to her keen intelligence.

The reception at the Girondos' home had proved to be an encouraging prelude for Clothilde's renewal of social contact. From then on, she participated in most of the diverse entertainments organized for the sound recreation of all ages.

Every first Saturday of the month, from September to Lent, an orchestra was hired for a public ball given at the city hall. Emile being the Mayor, by tradition it was expected that he and Madeleine honor it with their attendance. He was yet the swifter dancer on the floor. What a rare marvel to see him whirling his wife, his daughter or his granddaughter in a waltz, like if each were a whiff of spring breeze in his arms. All generations able to stand up vertically on nimble feet, or whosoever else wished to sit there for the pleasure of it, were welcome. So children no older then ten or twelve were seen having the grandest time as they danced with their parents or between themselves. Even father Vernier would now and then make an appearance. To everyone's delight he would sweep off one of his childhood friends into a few dance steps, then would walk to the stage and accompanied by the musicians, would enrapture his audience with a song or two.

Some betrothals and weddings were also celebrated in a similar manner.

Every year, a masked ball on the weekend preceding Ash Wednesday, was the last but not the least of the season. A carnival of the most spectacular disguises gave rise to much merry making. Persons from different and distant eras were miraculously resuscitated to meet for the occasion. Accordingly there would be Marie Antoinette temporarily reunited with her head, conversing with Anne Boleyn, both apparently having a lot to talk about. On the other hand the empress Josephine in attendance also, would be casting soft glances at the duke of Wellington, while he and her husband, Napoleon Bonaparte were engaged in the most fascinating conversation on military strategy.

No one had reason to suffer from ennui during the cold season. The joyous disposition of those fine people, would not allow their sprightly spirit to idle away from the lack of initiative in creating sound diversions.

Frequently a piano recital or other musical evenings would be organized in which Clothilde and Elise took part as piano soloists.

Often, either at *la Brisante* or at other dwellings one would be invited for dinner. On other occasions, in the evening a few friends would simply gather for tea and a game of cards or chess; usually, an enjoyable polemic about politics, religion, philosophy or whatsoever would follow. Then time fled away well into the night but seemed to have passed only in an instant.

Those moments weaved memories of incomparable charm upon which one tenderly leaned throughout the passing years.

It was a joy to see Clothilde participating in all those diversions.

Then Christmas was not far away. Jean Luc and Phillippe would come home for the holidays.

With renewed enthusiasm, Clothilde and Elise drowned themselves in many hours of work dedicated to the museum. They wanted to take advantage of the winter months to advance their project for, at the start of next June, the museum should be ready to receive the public after the exciting ceremony of a private viewing. Their ardor was consistently supported by well-intentioned family members and Father Vernier.

From such reservoir of sound influences, Clothilde's life every day seemed to become more and more stable. She missed phillippe, but she had grown accustomed to the unalterable circumstances. When she thought about Paul, however much her emotions stirred, to overcome their compulsion she applied a firm self-discipline to repress them instantly as unacceptable. She wanted to believe that at last a sense of stability had begun to crystallize upon the ruins of her past.

CHAPTER 19

LATE IN THE afternoon, at the end of October, on the eve of "All Saints' Day," Clothilde was alone at the museum as she sat at a desk in the old parlor, which had been transformed into an office. She was typing an invoice to purchase an extra large glass case needed for the display of some stone artifacts, when Madeleine arrived and directly went to take a seat in an armchair by the window.

Clothilde at once interrupted her work and turned slightly sideways to face her grandmother.

"Hello Grandmaman!" she greeted with a bright welcoming smile."

"Hello darling!" Madeleine responded cheerfully, but a certain amount of agitation was discernible through the intonation of her voice. "Ah," she sighed, "the more I age the quicker time goes by me. It seems only like the twinkling of an eye, since we celebrated the last New Year, already Christmas is upon us again and soon it will be time to seed new flowers in the front garden."

"Yes, to me also, it looks like the days do not stretch as far as they used to when I was younger," agreed Clothilde.

"Come now, they should not have shortened that much for you yet!" Madeleine exclaimed amused by Clothilde's comment. For, that granddaughter of hers naturally would forever remain a little girl. "I am returning from the nursery where I extravagantly bought a bag full of bulbs I was helpless to resist. Already, it is time to plant them. We should have pretty blue and mauve jacinth as well as lovely pink and yellow tulips in profusion this coming spring," went on Madeleine.

Clothilde clearly detected anxiety behind her grandmother's effort to maintain a casual demeanor.

"Grandmaman, what is the matter? You seem bothered by something."

"Do I make an impossible nuisance out of myself to burst so, amid your busy schedule dear?" Madeleine questioned in reply, admitting in some way that yes she felt a little troubled, while indirectly inquiring if Clothilde had a moment to spare.

"Of course not Grandmaman, you know you are always welcome in here."

"Thank you darling. Well yes, I am a bit puzzled about Veronique. Yes, it is about Veronique. I wanted to ask you, how did you find her on Sunday when you had tea with her? Did you notice anything odd in her behavior?"

Clothilde thought it over for a moment, then shook her head negatively.

"No, not really, she was her regular self."

Clothilde paused again to reflect further.

"Now that I think of it, perhaps she was a bit more absent minded than usual. But she has acted like this before, so there was no reason to suspect anything that could cause any alarm, why Grandmaman?"

"Well, this afternoon, on my way back from Gourdon, I saw her from the road. She was in her front garden, so I decided to pay her a visit. As I drove up to her house, she followed my car with a fixed gaze. It appeared she had not recognized me until I parked in the driveway and stepped out. At last, she reacted, first surprised then extremely pleased by my unexpected arrival. She invited me in for tea. We put cups and saucers on the kitchen table and sat there instead of in the living room. I observed a mask of immense sadness over her face. At times, she became impervious to my presence or was visibly distracted by some other matter than what we were saying. Her hands never ceased to be fidgety. I inquired if all was well with Phillippe since we last heard from him."

"*Yes, yes,*" "she answered rather impatiently. She turned pensive, stood up, walked to the window, briefly looked outside, returned to her chair, gravely lowered her brow and stared at the floor."

"*It is my Marie Joelle*," "she said in a low tone of voice."

"Marie Joelle? I asked, not certain to have heard her clearly."

"*Yes, Marie-Joelle, she, … Oh, I don't know Madeleine, sometimes I feel like I am loosing my mind.*"

"She grew silent. I waited but she did not speak. Why, please do tell me Veronique, what is it about Marie Joelle, that concerns you dear? I finally entreated. She looked at me unsurely as though cautious about my probable disbelief."

"*She has been visiting me. It sounds crazy, I know.*"

"It doesn't sound crazy at all, I promptly reassured her. She nervously reached for her cup, but placed it back on the saucer without taking a drink. I hastily drew a chair to sit near her. Tell me, I inquired, taking her hand in mine, how and when did Marie Joelle visit you, is she … ?"

"*It seems like in a dream*," "she promptly replied ignoring what I intended to ask her next."

"Well, I said, rather perplexed. We all dream about our loved ones don't we? Marie-Joelle has been in your dreams before, why should it now disturb you so?"

"*But it is different than a dream, Madeleine, very different. Though it is dreamlike, it is not a dream. It mostly happens when I am not completely asleep yet, but shortly after I close my eyes and I barely begin to doze off. Much in the same manner she spoke to me the day … the day she drowned, when I heard her say "don't cry mother, I shall return." I do not receive visions of her. It is her sweet voice only that reaches me, like an invisible presence that speaks from outside of me, but strangely also from within my soul,*" "Veronique tried to specify." "*Oh, I cannot explain exactly,*" "s he then yielded, with a sigh of exasperation."

"That's all right dear, you don't need to. I think I understand, I encouraged, wishing to ease her frustration. What does she say? I then asked. Veronique smiled dimly. Her eyes dulled by melancholy, took a tender expression."

"*She says, "maman, I shall soon return. We will see and recognize each other again."*

"*I am almost certain that I heard Clothilde's name on one occasion. But her message came through completely jumbled and faded away before I could grasp any meaning out of it. Oh, the sweetheart, the precious sweetheart!*" "bewailed Veronique."

"At that moment Frederick drove up. She hurriedly smoothed away her face to erase the strain. I rose to embrace her."

"We will talk again, I uttered reassuringly as I regained my seat at the opposite side of the table. She thanked me for listening and we changed the subject of our conversation. Soon after Frederick had arrived, I took leave. Poor Veronique!"

"Oh, Grandmaman!" lamented Clothilde, "how very peculiar, how dreadful! What can this mean? One could easily believe she is undergoing some kind of psychosis, perhaps because of Phillippe. Do you think she is trying to fill the void caused by his last departure?"

Madeleine raised her right hand, held it up for a second and then dropped it on her lap.

"You know what darling, I haven't the slightest notion of what has provoked this."

"How long has this been going on Grandmaman?"

Madeleine took time to think for a brief moment.

"For a couple of days, I believe."

Again, Madeleine reflected.

"Who knows, though unaware of it up to now, perhaps she is a medium. I have heard that this gift after having been latent until later on in years, may all at once be awakened subsequently to some trauma."

Clothilde looked at Madeleine quizzically and frowned, whereas her eyes smiled.

"Grandmaman! you don't believe in that, do you?"

" Sure I do. You know I do. Have you forgotten Amelia? She conveyed messages from the beyond with absolute accuracy, giving an exact description of whomever she communicated with even though she had never known them. She was reluctant to make predictions, but she did divine a few happy incidents, which came to pass with extraordinary exactitude. Besides, Amelie, is not the only medium known to us. Many convincing stories of people having such gift, have been recorded in the chronicles of our region."

Madeleine inclined her head sideways over her right shoulder. She softly looked at Clothilde as if a lovely song had been evoked to her memory.

"Ah, my dear child, I am a true daughter of our Perigord! its awe-inspiring mysticism is as much an intrinsic part of my being as is the blood of our ancestors in my veins. Darling, do not repudiate this part of your heritage, to severe yourself from it would only impoverish your life."

Madeleine rose decidedly and went to kiss Clothilde on the forehead.

"But now, I must go or your grandfather will wonder with whom I have eloped this time. Thank you for listening to me, my dear. I feel a bit less burdened from having talked this over with you. See you at dinner, sweetheart."

Clothilde escorted Madeleine outside and pensively watched her drive away. She had no desire to return behind her typewriter. Anyway, the afternoon was drawing to its end. She sat on a stone bench by the front entrance, her gaze followed a rivulet meandering gaily beneath the vaulted foliage and then disappearing in the distant shadow of a ravine. A sudden shiver overtook her by surprise. She was not cold. And, why this impossible wave of spontaneous euphoria, which enwrapped her, like the folds of a luminous cloud, when she was on the verge of weeping for Veronique?

Thank heaven, immediately after Veronique confided in Madeleine, and soon after in Clothilde and Frederick as well, her extraordinary experience ceased all at once without a trace of subsequent occurrence. Incredibly, her spirit was not affected by sadness. She rebounded all the better from it. Frederick viewed it with the kind of indulgence one would grant a child taking flight in a world of make believe. Clothilde interpreted it to mean that Veronique was turning to Marie-Joelle in a desperate attempt to compensate for what she considered her losses caused by the change of direction in Phillippe's life. This time Veronique knew otherwise. No, she wasn't insane. She wasn't dreaming either. Now, no one could alter with doubts her belief that Marie Joelle had not disappeared like a smile in the inaccessibility of the beyond, to leave behind only an eternal goodbye. This is why lately one would notice an aura of serenity about her. With a delicate handwriting she entered in a diary the bittersweet words spoken by the beloved voice, to seal them forever in her heart.

PART III

CHAPTER 1

W̲HEN AT HIS final home coming, Paul alighted
from his flight from Europe to set foot on the American soil, he was not
the same man who had left for France two years since, after spending a
week leave with his mother. His somber gaze followed a blue and white
jet as it soared in the celestial abyss, which drearily spanned the Atlantic
Ocean between him and France. Then, heavy hearted, threading his
way through the human shoal, he walked in direction of the exit gate.
It was past four o'clock in the afternoon. A delay of one and a half hour
would hold him in New York before his plane would depart for Los
Angeles, where Isabelle, his mother and a friend would await his arrival.
Then they would drive by car to Santa Barbara.

He went to the rest room, splashed his face with cold water, and
dallied in the restaurant over a cup of brisk coffee to do away with the
torpid sensation brought on by his long confinement in the passenger
seat.

Indifferent to the crowd, he was oblivious of whether anyone lived
behind those faces shoving around him. He felt alone, isolated. Absently,
he reached for the remnant of a .news paper left on a vacated table next
to his. He looked at a few headlines but he found it impossible to
concentrate. As he automatically glanced over the front page, he tried
to recapture the happiness he had so long anticipated at the thought
of seeing his mother again. Now, how could he enjoy their reunion to
the fullest with this pain throbbing in his heart? Knowledgeable of

183

the human psyche though he was, no acumen of his could objectively unravel back to their rational cause, the sentiments he so obsessively entertained for Clothilde. Try as he would, he could not push her out of his mind, which inevitably gave rise to a burdensome duality between his sensible judgment and his feelings.

He had wished nothing more pleasant than the dawning of this blessed day, when finally he would be on his way home as a civilian. Then, he had thousands thousand of exciting projects in mind. How it all looked so different now through the deep sadness that had increasingly stolen over his spirit. As he was confronted by aloneness during his flight over the Atlantic, he was constrained to realize that some profound changes were happening within him. He became aware that until then, a space within his heart had not been fully alive and that since he had met Clothilde new emotions were stirring deep in the innermost core of his soul. The dictate of reason could not subjugate their powerful influence, which moved and surpassed him beyond what he had ever known. Now and again, the mere fact to know that she and he existed on this planet at the same time unaccountably was sufficient to fill him with an extraordinary joy. To love her was forbidden, yet it could have seemed like the most natural impulse. It was enough to cause doubts about one's sanity.

He couldn't restrain a smile when he suddenly remembered a professor from an early psychology class, who when unable to answer unexplainable questions, would simply state:

"There are certain mysteries in this universe which remain inaccessible to the most astute system of man's logic or scientific expertise, the human psyche is one of them."

He was impelled to concede that if those delicate, beautiful, unique sentiments, which had blossomed in his heart, could no longer be denied, then at least they must be disciplined. He surely was no teenager hopelessly mesmerized by a fair maiden who had fluttered her eyelashes when gazing in his eyes at a prom dance. He was a grown, mature man, an intelligent man with a steadfast disposition and a sound mind. If he did not understand the cause of his dilemma, he at least was altogether quite lucid about its implications. Certainly, he knew that to sustain his mental soundness, necessity would coerce him to creatively redirect his emotional energy. It would be vital for him to remain undeterred in moving on with some plans and reconstruct his life.

Before landing he tried to allow himself time to recover his self-possession and prepare for a cheerful reunion with his mother. How disappointed she would be if he disembarked with a gloomy face. Although he often caught himself into melancholically reminiscing the moments of rapture he experienced in the pastoral ambiance of Grolejac, he endeavored to guide his thoughts toward the most potent antidote: work. Work only could rescue him from this unproductive impasse. Accordingly, he attempted to revise one by one all the goals he had projected for himself, now waiting to be achieved.

His few years as a psychiatrist in the Air Force, gave him a foretaste of being a member of the staff in a hospital, and it didn't bring him the vocational satisfaction he had expected. To open an outpatient clinic was perhaps more compatible with his temperament. Teaching was out of the question. Through the past years, he had taken time to reexamine, reassess and consider new ideas applying to his medical field. He had meticulously registered them in succinct notes with the intention to compile them in a scientific treatise on mental disorders, which should include several volumes. It would be a very advanced and informative dissertation valuable to anyone from undergraduates to licensed professionals dedicated to that science. The previous year he had already published a textbook on psychology for university students. Because of its great success, he was asked for an adaptation that would meet the needs of more advanced classes. Consequently, he had begun to prepare it during his last few months spent in France, and was committed to complete it upon his return home. Then, finally but most importantly he would buy a farm near Santa Barbara, live there with his mother, and eventually a family of his own. A cherished dream he had wished to realize ever since his childhood.

His mother had imparted her desire to sell a farm she fell heir to in France near Chartres, in the Beauce region and invest the money along with her son's venture. However, all this was a speculation to be considered much later in the distant future. Now concerns that were more exigent needed his immediate attention. However, if due to his dejected state of mind, certain things had lost some of their former appeal; his dream to till the soil could never leave him indifferent.

"Yes, one day, I'll have a farm," he reflected as his flight was approaching Santa Barbara, and he evoked once more the rustic charm of *la Madrigale*. "The slow winter days should allow me sufficient freedom to write, although I foresee no reasons that could prevent me from devoting my attention to it at any other time. What a desirable way of life this would provide to raise a family …a family?" he sighed, surprised at this contemplation. He did not dare to reflect further about such a possibility lest it would plunge him again in a deep sadness when he was just about to land.

CHAPTER 2

Upon his arrival at home, Paul allowed himself time for a restorative adaptation to civilian life. He wanted also to give Isabelle an opportunity to indulge in those maternal solicitudes she considered as her everlasting right. She tasted slices of heaven when she cooked those delicious special dishes for him. However, he knew how to reciprocate her kindness with affectionate filial regards. He often took her for a drive along the coast, and then to dinner in some cozy restaurants, while they enjoyed a spectacular sunset over the Pacific Ocean. During those early days immediately following his return, Isabelle asked quite a few questions relating to Paul's sojourn in France, and expressed her gratitude for the generous welcome he received in Jean Luc's family. Paul at times found it difficult to speak on that subject and at this point he thought it suitable to avoid any allusion concerning his sentiments toward Clothilde. He didn't wish to sadden his mother with his extraordinary adventure. But one day though, when the pain in his heart would be less acute, he would tell her all about it. Otherwise, they deliberately chattered about nothing very serious. No grand plans were discussed. It was an intended mini vacation pleasantly therapeutic for Paul who found great comfort in the presence of his mother. He deeply loved and respected her. She adored him.

However, at the start of his third week back home, some of the more pragmatic aspects of daily existence could not continue to be ignored. Paul felt ready to focus his attention on the academic textbooks he had in mind to complete. The revenue from the publication of the original version, plus the money he had wisely economized in the military provided him adequately with financial ease for a while.

Although in the early evening he still reserved himself a certain amount of freedom to visit with his mother, he mainly stayed in his apartment a few blocks away from her. There, he wholly occupied himself with his writing which virtually consumed most of his days and often a good part of his nights. Beyond this particular project, no other major decisions concerning his future had yet been formulated. Well, there he was where he had longed to be, doing what he had wanted to do only to find sadness and disquietude. Had he turned into his own enemy?

At the beginning, it was only with great difficulty that he could steadily follow a logical sequence of ideas. His mind, with renewed insistence repeatedly traveled back to Grolejac where he yet so vividly visualized Clothilde. However, if the passage of time could not erase his affliction, it mercifully allowed him to recover a certain inner strength.

As he obstinately disciplined his interest to pursue his objective, it became steadily less difficult and in a sense more natural for him to keep his concentration fixed upon his task.

After three months of diligent labor, he was surprised to observe that his undertaking had satisfactorily advanced. For the most part his thoughts about Clothilde were easier to repress. They had retreated into dreams or had become less intense and seemed to emerge only outside of his daily preoccupations. The familiar environment he had been accustomed to, the effect of "here and now" appeared to take precedence upon the adverse influence of what he considered his fantasies.

"He was encouraged by having steadily resigned himself into accepting what appeared to be the direction of his life. At this point, he did not wonder much about what fate had in store for him. Peace of mind was really what he sought most. "Would it be possible to ever attain?" he would sigh.

Meanwhile, unexpected turns of events stealthily unfolded.

In mid December, Paul feeling a little more relaxed was persuaded to set his work aside for a short pause and have a quiet dinner at his mother's.

Isabelle had insisted upon this for two valid reasons. The first, because her dear son had worked much too hard, she deemed he needed to repair on a good substantial meal, the second, because she wished to discuss with him a concern of great significance for both of them. Lately, they had seen each other in such great hurry. Some peaceful, uninterrupted time was necessary to talk over the matter.

Isabelle lived in a comparatively modest home up in Montecito, but she had come to find it too large for her alone. She had toyed with the idea to put it for sale or rent it and move into a small condominium. Recently however, new designs that seemed more attractive had taken form in her contemplations.

CHAPTER 3

IT WAS ONE of those radiant evenings at the onset of winter. The weather, even if cooler, was still pleasantly mild. The air transparent like polished crystal, unveiled the infinite as far as the eyes could see. Isabelle sat on the west terrace of her home, which overlooked Santa Barbara gently rolling downhill toward the ocean. She waited for her son to join her for an aperitif. The retreating sun, which had immersed heaven and earth in a flood of pink and saffron light, stroked her silvery hair with a delicate golden shimmer. Her inbred graceful bearing had not been altered by the years. Upon sitting down, she offered her face to a sudden drift of crisp breeze. For a brief moment she pensively gazed at the horizon, while in an elegant gesture she took a slow sip of her Martini.

Paul had been detained in the drawing room by a last minute phone call received soon after his arrival. It was his publisher who having been unable to reach him at his apartment had rightly guessed that in all likelihood he would be at his mother's home.

"Ah, here you are!" She said smiling as Paul stepped out on the deck. "Come and relax a bit here, before dinner."

Paul looked at his mother thinking how beautiful she was. Through his filial affection she was the paragon of excellence.

"Sorry, Mother," he apologized, lightly kissing her forehead. He then sat opposite her, across the round glass table. At once she reached for a cube of ice from the bucket, put it in a glass and passed it to Paul who poured himself some scotch over it.

"Thank you. That was my publisher. He could not wait until tomorrow to clarify some minor errors in the first edition of my book He didn't want to repeat them in the new publication. Hopefully we will not be disturbed again," he explained. After having allowed a few moments of relaxed chatting, his gaze took an expression of intent curiosity.

"Well, Mother, I am ready and very anxious to hear about what you wished to tell me."

Isabelle examined her watch.

Almost seven o'clock! she exclaimed. It will take me a while to explain, so let's wait until we are more at our leisure in the dining room after I have served dinner. I believe it is grand time or else the salmon will be burned whereas it was meant to be simply baked."

She energetically rose from her chair and dashed to the kitchen. Paul gathered the empty glasses from the patio table and followed her. After she checked that all was well with her cooking, she went to the dining room and put a pretty bouquet of flowers at the center of the table. Back in the kitchen, she displayed the food on serving dishes, while Paul uncorked a bottle of chilled Champagne. On an oval platter upon a bed of lettuce, Isabelle surrounded a steaming salmon by baked oysters. In an other dish she neatly arranged a heap of asparagus beside a sauceboat filled with a rich golden hollandaise sauce. She heaped tiny roasted potatoes in a terrine and put a few slices of crusty french bread inside a dainty wicker basket lined with an embroidered linen napkin.

"Dear Mother, you outdid yourself again, it looks absolutely exquisite!" Paul complimented enthusiastically as he helped carry the lot to the dining room.

"Darling, trust me I have enjoyed every minute of it," Isabelle stressed while, last of all she mixed a variety of colorful raw vegetables over a vinaigrette already prepared at the bottom of a cut glass dish. An assortment of cheese had been put on the sideboard, to let it absorb the room temperature. The dinner being rather copious called for the traditional hors d'oeuvres to be omitted.

Isabelle heaved a sigh of contentment as she and Paul gathered at the dining room table. From where they sat, their eyes could delight in the incandescent sky spreading a glow of fulgent colors over the ocean.

Isabelle served herself a portion of salmon, Paul in turn did the same.

"Now let me tell you about what I have been thinking," Isabelle directly stated while taking a sip of champagne. "I am aware that every so often my brain can weave fanciful, even emboldened ideas, however this seems to deserve some consideration from you as well."

Slightly patting her lips with a napkin, she paused briefly to reflect.

"I have been wondering about your plans. Since your return, we have never seriously discussed them. What I wish to know is, do you still intend to buy that farm here in the vicinity of Santa Barbara?"

This subject was virtually never mentioned. It was a project to materialize only far off in the future. Paul was caught unprepared for this unexpected question. Puzzled, he looked at his mother and shrugged his shoulders.

"Yes," he replied after a moment. "Yes of course, I am still enormously interested in owning a farm. However I cannot afford it yet, but yes, when my financial situation will permit."

Isabelle took another sip of Champagne and slowly put her glass back on the table as she took time to think about what she wanted to say next.

"Must it be in the Santa Barbara region?" she then asked quite straightforwardly.

"Well, Mother, we live here," replied Paul, still at a loss.

"All right, I'll get to the point," said Isabelle decisively. "The tenants from our property in France have reminded me again of their desire to retire. Their children not wanting to soil their hands, have gone to work in some office or other. Therefore they are not interested in the renewal of the lease, which is near termination as you have been informed upon your last visit with them. Why should we go through all the trouble to rent it again? We could sell it to help you acquire some acreage here. However the price of landed property in Santa Barbara being much higher than its equivalent in the Beauce, through the exchange the sale of our farm would therefore cause us a monetary loss. It would take years of hard work to compensate for the assets it represents in France and produce the kind of lucrative husbandry you have in mind."

"Oh, I wholly agree," consented Paul. However he was still unable to grasp what his mother meant to convey.

Through the dining room window Isabelle gazed longingly over the ocean.

"And frankly, parting with it sounds all so final. It would give me the impression of being irrevocably severed from France."

There was a silence.

"But it can be yours," she offered, briskly looking back at Paul with a sparkle in her eyes.

As his mother spoke, Paul's facial expressions indicated he was getting increasingly more confused.

"Do you mean Mother, that you want me to take complete charge of it?"

Isabelle reached for her water glass and pensively ran her fingers around its rim.

"Wouldn't you like to live in France?"

"Mother!" interjected Paul, with a hint of protest mixed with shock. "are you suggesting, that I pack up for France to take care of your farm?"

"Yes," Isabelle said as nonchalantly as if she had answered the most trivial question.

"And leave you here?" asked Paul seriously concerned about his mother's state of mind.

"No," she reassured with a gentle smile. "no, I mean exactly the contrary. It is I who would like to live in France again, but would not wish to leave you here. For some time now I have been yearning for a change and have considered moving into a smaller place. The guest house on our estate seems so ideal for me." Her arms swept the space around her. "This house gives me the impression to increase in size everyday. It is so much to maintain."

Paul stared at his mother with unconcealed reproof.

"Mother, time and time again I have suggested you hire someone to help you. I would pay for it."

"It is not simply the care of it. I find it lonely also. All these rooms sighing at me!"

"What if I would move back with you?" offered Paul.

"Ah, that was once our wonderful French way of life. Generations who cohabited in a family home, which adequately accommodated everyone's comfort. However, this beautiful tradition is not widely accepted in the American culture, and much less as time goes on. Besides, would you want to live with me, this house is not suited to offer you the privacy you require at your age and for your work. However, you could have it for yourself if you should wish."

"Mother, you know very well I …"

"No, no!" Isabelle interrupted, raising her unoccupied left hand to support a categorical rejection of her son's probable argument in favor of his offer. "Should you prefer to stay here, then a small condominium would be my best option. Actually, I liked the idea very much until this other quite tempting alternative dawned on me. Of course darling you don't need to worry yourself should you decline my proposal. My imagination could have been so active that I might have lost all good judgment of practicability."

There was a silence. Paul had grown quiet.

"Don't ask me why, but my motherly intuition," went on Isabelle, "on several occasions, has led me to discern how much you seem to miss France and the friends you have met there, I suppose this has encouraged me to put forth this idea."

Nostalgic recollections of France educed a remote expression in Paul's eyes. Aware of his emotional shift, he made an effort to recapture rapidly a brighter mood and smiled.

"Yes, I must admit, as always your discernment is accurate. It is true. I do like your beautiful country, Mother, and I keep lovely memories from my sojourn over there."

"My dear son, I sense your genes have awakened to the voice of your ancestors. They beckon you back to your roots."

Isabelle's face gleamed with a pensive smile as she drew a deep sigh.

"I should not forgive myself if for fear of a refusal, I had refrained from imparting my thoughts to you. However I can assure you, that it is your happiness which in the depth of my heart takes precedence over all other concerns, and not my selfish desires."

Paul enveloped his mother with a gentle gaze.

"I thank you for this incredible, absolutely incredible offer, Mother. I don't know what else to say at this moment, except that I shall give it the most serious and objective consideration."

"Oh, darling!" Isabelle continued with heightened enthusiasm, "would it not offer you the most favorable ambiance for writing? Furthermore, you are well versed in french semantic," she laughed at her choice of word, "I see no reasons why you could not practice your profession there as well as here, after all, psychiatry speaks a universal language. Of course, we would hire help to work the land. The property is sufficiently spacious to house a large family. Naturally I hope one day you will meet someone you fall in love with and wish to marry. I for my part, dream to live in the charming little cottage, the guesthouse that is. It is of the perfect size for me. The main building would be at your disposal. So reflect upon it dear."

Paul took a relaxed posture by leaning his shoulders against the back of his chair. He folded his napkin and put it beside his plate.

"Well, Mother, I am truly surprised. I thought you were deeply attached to this town."

"Bah, nothing holds me here, other than you."

Paul smiled affectionately at Isabelle.

As the twilight wore on, a few stars appeared in the sky and quivered like droplets of spilled quicksilver. The moonrays had polished the surface of the ocean water with a transparent sheen.

Paul and his mother went back on the terrace but only briefly, for the air had turned rather chilly. They spent the rest of the evening in Isabelle's living room, speaking about everything except of what they had previously discussed.

Meanwhile, in spite of Paul being unaware of it, the outline of his destiny was stealthily defining itself like the contour of an evolving form still captive in the sculptor's mind.

CHAPTER 4

AFTER MANY LONG and conscientious deliberations with himself and with Isabelle, at the end of January, Paul had virtually decided in favor of the move to France. Overall, he concluded it would be nothing other than a transfer to an area that held no fundamental bearing upon the sum total of his existence. He had no profound personal attachment to any one in Santa Barbara. Where he would go presented as many choices to his professional aspirations as was available to him in the United States. He had always been very adaptable. The world was his country and wherever he lived was a part of it. That was a very rudimentary, but nonetheless factual view of the assessed situation pertinent to his relocation, which appeared more and more seductive as time went by, and most importantly it caused his mother much joy.

They resolved to lease Isabelle's house and shop as well as Paul's apartment. The income from the rentals together with the revenue from the farm, which in relation to the cost of living in France was comfortably remunerative, and the royalties already received from some of Paul's writings certainly would assure an ample pecuniary security for both.

Would Paul have been completely honest had he not admitted to be influenced by his mother? Of course not. Would he have been truthful if he had acknowledged that most definitely he had not been biased by self-seeking purposes at the detriment of his mother's best interests?

Absolutely, yes. For if Isabelle's concern for the happiness of her son took precedence over all other matters, to watch over her contentment and well-being, was equally one of Paul's top priorities. A commitment that was very dear to his heart.

Of course, he was well aware that his life in France would restore a close relationship with Jean-Luc, which would inevitably expose him to Clothilde, who by then in all likelihood should be a new bride. However, by the force of circumstances the burden to adjust to it would again be his, and he would adjust.

Although a telephone call had been exchanged between Paul and Jean-Luc at Christmas, upon their conversation Jean Luc had withheld from giving Paul news of the circumstances, which had developed between Clothilde and Phillippe. At that particular time, he thought it would not be appropriate to discuss such a complex and sensitive family issue. Likewise, Paul on his side being still in the process of deliberation with his mother concerning their move, at this point had preferred to still wait a while before talking about the situation with Jean Luc.

In the course of all the arrangements for their relocation, Isabelle thought it sensible if Paul would travel to France and act as an emissary, so to speak, for the settlement of legal matters between tenants and proprietors. He would also assess the situation to ensure satisfactory accommodations for their imminent arrival, now fixed for the coming September. It was not until the end of February that such journey was finally decided to take place in the first days of April. Thereupon, as soon as the date was definitive Paul phoned Jean Luc to impart his intention. Jean Luc then, in the course of their conversation, thought it suitable to inform him of the changes with regard to Phillippe and Clothilde's relationship. However, the manner in which Jean Luc conveyed the news gave Paul reasons to think that the situation between them was not conclusively settled.

Paul transcending his personal feelings, sincerely deplored this set back in Clothilde's life, for to imagine her in distress was more than he could endure. He would have given his last breath to protect Clothilde's happiness.

As might be expected, Paul's announcement gave Jean Luc occasion to invite his good friend for a visit they would spend preferably in Grolejac.

CHAPTER 5

IT WAS STILL early in the morning. The air was brisk but slightly warm. When Clothilde came to brush Canon d'Or, he acted rather frisky from having taken a good rest after breakfast. He definitely indicated that he would rather go out for a walk than stand there behaving like a well-mannered, patient horse while being groomed. Clothilde glad to oblige went back in the house to dress adequately, and off they went in the countryside surrounding *la Brisante*.

As they ambled along the bubbly brook or over the nearby meadows, Clothilde nonchalantly went through the repertoire of old children songs she always like to hum when they wandered about. Canon d'Or listened to the pretty tunes and seemed to keep in rhythm with the gentle tempo by placidly swinging his head from side to side.

The earth seethed from the leavening seeds eager to sprout. Every new bud feverishly quivered at the expectancy that soon they would bloom into radiant flowers.

A multitude of finches, wrens and sparrows having gone wild from the vibrancy, which galvanized the air, jubilantly fluttered in tremulous prattles amid the verdant shrubs. Already some dragonflies whirled about like sparkling gems under the sunrays while a few white butterflies frolicked above the stream admiring their reflection in the water. They could not believe their eyes to see themselves so magnificently metamorphosed since they were released from their chrysalides.

Now and then, a crisp breeze carried gusts of coarse scents emanating from the humus and the newly ploughed fields.

It was the dawn of spring.

Clothilde looked longingly at the cloudless sky so transparent that in the depth of its immensity, one could almost have expected to perceive other galaxies neighboring ours. As they followed the stream, she turned her gaze toward the water. It splashed gently against the banks strewed with mossy rocks and conveyed a cold sensation by its metallic glitter.

She alighted from Canon d'Or, picked the stickers from his shins, removed the reins from his halter, ran her fingers through his luxuriant blond mane and let him go where he wished. He followed her like a faithful dog and stopped only to nibble at a few young shoots.

They slowly went on walking along the creek. Soon Clothilde drifted into recollections of the days Phillippe spent in Grolejac between the previous Christmas and New Year. She smiled at the wonderful welcome he received. His visit was the cause of many joyful celebrations, not only for his parents, Clothilde and her family; but also for the entire village. Unanimously, everybody requested that he be ordained in Grolejac and be assigned as the parish priest when Father Vernier would go into retirement. There was no prouder mother walking the face of the earth than Veronique. Frederick and Father Vernier were no less elated.

However, Clothilde was sadly moved when she fully realized the change, which had taken place in her heart. She no longer looked at him as a man with whom a romantic involvement could be possible. In her view, he was now a man of God. He was among the selected few, whose life was dedicated to the spiritual and not the secular. He did not seem to belong to this earth. Yet this separateness from him, she thought, would leave a void to pervade enduringly in her soul, as an unmendable rift caused by hopes never actualized. On the other hand, she was so immensely proud of him and was rather pleased with the manner in which she withstood the circumstances overall.

She was not dissatisfied either, from the control she had finally attained over her emotional response to Paul. He had sent his season greetings for Christmas. She did admit that her excitement stirred by the recognition of his handwriting had rapidly plummeted when she painfully realized it was a warm and polite gesture from his part, but nothing else. A similar reaction occurred when told that he and Jean Luc had exchanged a telephone call over the holidays, for a moment, she hoped he might have given Jean Luc a special message for her. But thank goodness she was able to subdue promptly her absurd thinking and her disillusionment.

"I made it through," she thought. "Yes, I made it through. One way or the other, I have ridden the storm."

She mounted Canon d'Or again and idly rode toward home. She was struck dumb when she suddenly realized she was casually chanting an ancient *Pastourelle* * in the poetical dialect of the region as it was always traditionally sung, and which told of: *a lover calling across the river to invite his girl, a shepherdess tending her sheep, to join him so they can talk about their love. She answers it is not possible, for she has no boat. He replies she can easily obtain one, or anything she wishes since she is so beautiful.* It was a song dear to Marie Joelle. Her beloved great grandmother Manouche, who was Veronique's paternal grand mother, used to sing it to her and it had remained a cherished memory in her heart. After her passing, it had been silenced from the lips of all those who knew her and loved her. To hear the very first notes of the melody would have rent one's soul.

"What has possessed me to? ...What is up with me?" Clothilde asked herself startled that the *Pastourelle* had come out of her lips as though by its own volition, and she had not been conscious of it. What was she thinking? Or clearly, she was not thinking at all.

Her thoughts were abruptly disrupted when she saw Elise waving at her while hurrying down the path, which led to the stream. Clothilde and Canon d'Or pressed forward to meet her.

"Jean Luc is on the phone, hurry!" Elise called out.

"My goodness! What's so important?" Is he all right?" interjected Clothilde.

"Yes, yes, he is fine," reassured Elise.

"Couldn't he have given you a message? Can he wait? ... Did you tell him I was ..."

"No, I mean yes," interrupted Elise, almost out of breath. He is talking with your grandmaman."

"Oh, all right, come along Canon d'Or," Clothilde motioned.

Arriving at the house she leaped inside and went directly to the parlor. Whereupon Madeleine took leave of Jean Luc, gave her the phone and went her way.

Elise led Canon d'Or to his corral. She had barely time to clean his hooves, before Clothilde reappeared entirely transfigured. Her face was livid. Too astonished by the news announced by Jean Luc, she could not speak. Her heart was whirling from palpitations. She retreated into the tack shed to collect herself, and sat upon a cedar chest in which Canon d'Or's winter coat was kept. She lowered her head and raised her right hand urging Elise to wait a moment.

Elise compliant to her friend's request anxiously stood in front of her.

Clothilde finally less frantic looked up at Elise. Her face had regained the earlier pink flush quickened by the fresh air.

Paul might come back to France," she uttered with a controlled calm, "He might come back in about three weeks."

Elise drew a deep sigh and smiled quietly such as someone who had received a tiding long expected. Moved to tears, she was speechless.

"Elise darling! Canon d'Or my love! Clothilde exclaimed, rising to her feet, "did you hear? ...Oh, my God! ... Paul will be here in three weeks!"

She hugged Elise, twirled her around a few times, ran to Canon d'Or, took his head in her hands and covered it with kisses.

"Oh! Elise, is this a dream?"

Elise, in a spontaneous, ecstatic embrace wrapped her arms around Clothilde's shoulders and drew her close.

"Oh, how wonderful! How wonderful! I am not a bit surprised though. Somehow, I have always had a little hunch whispering that he would come back ... and quite soon." She released Clothilde, then added as if amazed by her keen astuteness, "isn't it something?"

"I would have never thought ... ," uttered Clothilde. Before she could finish her sentence, a thousand fears arose before her and all at once shrouded her gladness with a somber cloud.

"Oh, dear! She bemoaned as she withdrew from Elise to lean against one of the fence poles. "Why should Paul's return bring me so much joy? How can I be so impulsive, so childish? In an instant, Clothilde's exultation had crashed into dismay. She felt ridiculous and laughed at herself contemptuously.

I should be ashamed," she declared, seized by a sense of indecency as though she had violated someone's privacy. "At my age, to be so naïve. I thought I had recovered enough reason to fit with the rest of mankind. For goodness sake Elise, the man might be married by now or engaged or whatsoever else in between, and come here accompanied. "Oh!" she sighed, "Am I now doomed to regress into the turmoil I have so battled?"

Elise had listened quietly.

"Calm yourself darling and don't be so cast down. May be the beginning of those sunny days your great grandfather spoke of, has finally come for you," she then felt compelled to say in a cheerful tone voice, to lighten Clothilde's spirit.

CHAPTER 6

CALM YOURSELF! HOW could Clothilde follow Elise's advice and calmly wait for Paul? What an insane, inhumane, unrealistic proposition! How could she even think rationally when her spinning mind refused to give her a single moment of peace? Why did her grandmother leave so rapidly after Jean Luc's phone call? She might have some more information. She might know if Paul is coming alone or accompanied by someone. Oh, if she could only hurry back!

Jean Luc had just communicated to Madeleine the reasons for Paul's passage through France. He assumed she would impart the glad tidings to everyone, for when he finally spoke with Clothilde he was too pressed by time to repeat himself at length. However, Clothilde was able to learn, that yes Paul would soon be on his way to France for a review of his mother's property in the Beauce, that yes he had accepted an invitation to spend a weekend at Grolejac, and that Jean Luc had been granted leave at this intention. Since he was in so great haste, she was unable to ask further questions.

Elise was spending most of the afternoon meeting with a group of local artists who wished to present some of their work to her, in the hope of exhibiting them at the museum.

Madeleine by then was in Sarlat for a dental appointment. Upon her return, she would assist Clothilde with the display of a few paintings in the section reserved for the art gallery.

Clothilde went to dress appropriately for the rest of the day while giving in to all sorts of persecutions from a host of forebodings. Nothing could be resolved into good sense.

"What if Paul now engaged and accompanied by his fiancee would come here to announce his approaching wedding and personally invite Jean Luc to be his best man? What if already married, he and his bride were traveling to France for their honey moon?" What if? What if? She positively knew her brain was coming apart but she couldn't put it back together.

Then for a moment, she gave herself up to some pleasant fantasies, which subsequently mortified her for their supreme audacity. She dared to conceive she could be the reason why Paul extended his journey to Grolejac. She even envisioned if somehow they entered into a relationship. Up to then her feelings had always struggled against Paul's inaccessibility, which subconsciously shielded her from any probable risks. However, what about if now, what had appeared impossible became possible? wouldn't it still remain a hopeless situation as a result of being separated by the full span of an immense ocean? What would she do? Oh, God! She could never ... Oh, Heavens no! She could never part from her mother, from her grandparents, from Elise and certainly not from Canon d'Or. The thought to move across the world so far from them whirled her into a vertigo, which at once blocked all such speculations.

She had put so much effort into bridling all those insane emotions that had consumed her since their meeting of last summer. Now in the space of an instant she was helplessly thrust back into the same dilemma. She wished Paul would change his mind or that at the last minute Jean Luc's leave would be declined. She prayed she could tumble into nothingness and reappear again on the earth only after those few weeks ahead had well passed.

Then again, she visualized the time she had spent in Paul's company nearly a year ago, nine months ago to be precise; merely long enough to say hello one day and give a farewell embrace the next. Yet he had stayed in her memory ever since as if bonded by a profound affection. She had not forgotten how it felt so right when he took her hand or put his arms around her. The sheer thought of it drowned her eyes in tears. She finally conceded that whatever the outcome, the joy to see him once more would be worth the risk involved. Will she ever survive those three weeks of waiting for his arrival? Surely, it will seem longer than eternity itself.

Thank goodness her hands and her head had sufficiently to do at the museum. The date of the grand opening was set up for the first Saturday of June. She shouldn't find time to idle in sterile reveries .

Due to the busy schedule she and Elise had sustained lately in preparation for this much-anticipated occasion, her family, Father Vernier and even Elise's parents were always available to land a helping hand. Consequently, on that particular day, Madeleine had offered her assistance for a few hours in the afternoon.

CHAPTER 7

AFTER HAVING RECOVERED from the emotional chaos caused by Jean Luc's phone call, Clothilde went to the museum and waited eagerly for the arrival of her grandmother.

When they met, Madeleine soon noticed that a transformation had taken place in her granddaughter's attitude since she had seen her earlier in the morning. She dropped objects, she acted preoccupied and altogether she seemed quite nervous. After a short while, as if prompted by a canny little sensor setting off an intuition, it came to Madeleine's mind that last summer she had observed that Paul and Clothilde now and then had exchanged a few sweet glances. She had even sensed the possibility of a certain attraction between them. Well, at that time, she had simply attributed it to a very normal response elicited by their respective good look; for she had an absolute trust in Clothilde's loyalty to Phillippe. However, now Clothilde was uncommitted. Madeleine wondered if the anticipation to see Paul again could therefore be unsettling. She discerned rightly that her granddaughter might be in need of encouragement to release some latent feelings, which had been repressed by the force of circumstances. She took the opportunity offered by those few moments they were spending together to address the issue.

"Your grandfather is overjoyed at the thought that Paul will visit us again. You would think he waits for the arrival of a long lost prodigal grandson. He has grown so fond of him like the rest of us have."

With an air of vague expectancy Madeleine cast a sideway glance at Clothilde, who now did not have the courage to voice even the most trivial question concerning Jean Luc's phone call. She feared it might disclose something she did not want to hear, so she pretended to be busy by picking up a hammer nearby on the floor. When she rose, she faced the wall and drove a nail into the area designated to exhibit the oil landscape Madeleine held at hand. Clothilde took the painting and hung it up.

"Don't ask me why I deemed so," pursued Madeleine, "but I always have had the presentiment that we would see Paul again soon in spite of the apparent finality of his departure."

Clothilde gave her grandmother an inquisitive look that she sustained for a brief moment, as though on the verge to question:

"What other presentiments did you have Grandmaman?"

Again, she did not dare to ask.

Both took a few steps back to overview the display.

"Well, how does it look so far?" Clothilde questioned, pretending to be thoroughly involved, and satisfied with the result.

"Perfect dear, absolutely beautiful. You always do everything so well."

"Thank you Grandmaman, I had a great teacher," said Clothilde referring to her grandmother with an affectionate smile.

"The student has far surpassed the master," Madeleine rejoined, not without pride.

They went on with their assessment, carefully situating the rest of the pictures in a pleasing arrangement.

Madeleine gazed thoughtfully at a still life.

"I do hope Jean-Luc can be allowed time off to attend the opening ceremony. We will miss Phillippe terribly. Wouldn't it be lovely if he would surprise us with his presence? What a pity Paul's visit does not coincide with the occasion." She heaved a deep sigh. "Ah, well, no doubt from now on we will have many opportunities to see him quite often and share pleasant moments together, given that he and Jean Luc are so good friends and we like him as we do."

Clothilde was suddenly taken aback by Madeleine's last comment. What was her grandmother talking about?

"And I think," went on Madeleine gaily, "I think he might enjoy your company too. The way he sometimes looked at you last summer gave to think that he might have been sensitive to your charms."

'Grandmaman!" exclaimed Clothilde thrown into a spontaneous laughter, so amused and surprised by Madeleine's remark, "he knew I was virtually engaged!"

"He could still look, couldn't he? and I don't blame him, you are a beautiful young lady."

Clothilde laughed again.

"How shocking, Grandmaman!"

"Please forgive my mundane badinage dear, but I also speak of the inner beauty a wise man sees far beyond appearances. Paul has impressed me as a very sensible man. No wonder he was attracted to you."

"Grandmaman! What has come over you? do you wish to throw me in his arms?" asked Clothilde in a feigned careless manner.

"Of course not darling. I would not dream to do such thing," Madeleine protested playfully.

"That Grandmaman of mine, her mere presence can immediately lighten up a burdened heart," Clothilde thought.

Impulsively she laid her tools aside and embraced Madeleine.

"Oh, Grandmaman, you are forever so kind to me, and it is indeed such inner beauty I too behold when I look at you."

Perplexed, unable to wait any longer to clarify what she wished to ask, she drew back for a brief moment stared at Madeleine and shrugged her shoulders awkwardly.

"I am not sure if I have heard you correctly, Grandmaman, but did you mention we might see Paul often from now on? Why? What was that about? she at last inquired.

Now it was Madeleine who became puzzled by Clothilde's question.

"Yes, I suppose we will. I hope we will."

Clothilde shook her head in confusion.

"Why should that be? Why so?"

"Well, darling from my long experience with the logic of things, since Paul has decided to move to France, because of his close friendship with your cousin, I have concluded we might see him quite frequently. Don't you think so?"

Clothilde stared at her grandmother, stupefied.

"Paul ... to France? ... Who told you? ...

Madeleine peered at Clothilde trying to make sense out of the strange development of their interaction.

"Why, Jean-Luc naturally."

"Jean Luc?"

"Yes Jean Luc." Madeleine reasserted surprised by Clothilde's apparent confusion.

Clothilde stared at her grandmother with questioning eyes.

"You mean Jean Luc did not tell you?" inquired Madeleine at a complete loss.

"Tell me what, Grandmaman?" Clothilde uttered. She was barely able to speak.

"Well dear child, that Paul is moving to France!" Madeleine finally clarified.

Clothilde stood there sottishly, as if dispossessed of self will.

"Ah!" Madeleine exclaimed, "didn't you know? Oh, and all along I thought Jean Luc had informed you also of the news."

"Jean Luc told me that Paul would journey to France to check on his mother's property and had accepted an invitation to spend a weekend here. He was in great hurry and had no time to give me more details."

Madeleine sighed as she began to grasp the cause of their misunderstanding.

"Oh, my dear, I am sorry, I thought you knew."

"Grandmaman please, let me know all about it," Clothilde requested impatiently.

"Well, from what I have gathered, Paul and his mother, intend to permanently settle in their estate near Chartres. They have decided to take charge of the property themselves as soon as their tenants' lease will be terminated."

"Are you sure Grandmaman? Just Paul and his mother?"

"That is what Jean Luc said, darling, just Paul and his mother," Madeleine specified, understanding Clothilde's fear.

Clothilde was unable to contain her excitement. Whatever guise or pretense she had resorted to, more by modesty than by hypocrisy, was lifted instantly from her demeanor. An outburst of sheer joy poured out from her heart.

"Oh! Grandmaman!" she cried out as she hugged Madeleine. "Oh, how wonderful! Imagine! Paul permanently living in France! Oh, thank you!"

Madeleine laughed.

"Don't thank me darling, I don't have much to do with it. Although if it had been in my power, I would have arranged it exactly as such. You like him don't you?"

"Yes very much," replied Clothilde quite candidly.

Madeleine smiled at her beloved granddaughter.

"I reckoned so and I have a notion he likes you also. Now let us finish hanging these few paintings," she suggested as she pointed out to a still life and a seascape left on the floor against the wall. "I can't stay here all afternoon long, talking about Paul," she then added teasingly.

CHAPTER 8

CLOTHILDE SAT UP on her bed. She remained immobile for a moment trying to put some order in her thoughts. Her gaze mechanically followed the play of sunlight along the curtain folds when she fully realized that no, it was not a dream. Yes, this was the day she would see Paul again. Yes, he was already here!

During the three weeks before his arrival, Clothilde had been tossed in a storm of emotions stirred by the most exciting suppositions or by the most self-persecuting dreads, all drawn from a thousand "*if*". And it had been such a long wait! How did she manage to confront each day efficiently? Now only a mass of spring air no larger than a mere two or three cubic kilometers separated her from him. He and Jean Luc had left Dreux Thursday afternoon to arrive at Grolejac late in the night.

When Clothilde awoke, it was a few minutes before half past seven on Friday morning. In spite of all her anxieties and of having been restless until the brink of dawn, she felt amazingly refreshed, even calm. She put on some clothes and went to see if Canon d'Or had been fed his breakfast. Yes, he was still eating. She covered his face with caresses accompanied by all sorts of affectionate epithets and then returned to her bedroom to shower and dress. She decided to wear white slacks and a long sleeve mustard-green top. She stopped in the living room to embrace Madeleine and Suzanne. They were enjoying a cup of coffee while deciding what work should be done around *la Brisante* before going to help Justine with the preparation of a dinner in honor of jean

Luc and Paul. Then Clothilde went to the dining room, and although she had no reason to hurry, she did not care to sit. She had just begun to take a few bites of toast when Elise arrived.

"So what are the plans for today?" Elise asked, as she hugged Clothilde after having greeted a bubbly good morning to Madeleine and Suzanne. She poured herself a cup of tea and helped Clothilde clean the breakfast table.

"Jean Luc should let us know any minute how he and Paul would like to spend the day. Shall we wait in the garden?" Clothilde proposed, and upon Elise's consent, they walked toward the front door.

"Oh, Elise, what a miracle!" Clothilde exclaimed as they sat on the wrought iron bench under the old cedar tree at the edge of the front lawn. "Is this true? Just the thought to see Paul one more time fills my soul with such immense joy! She heaved a deep sigh as if she had climbed a mountain and stopped a moment to look at the panorama. "This last year has been such a succession of uncertainties, of random happenings, which yet have been so decisive in my life, and now again here is another surprise, but what a wonderful surprise at last!"

Elise looked at Clothilde with an amused expression.

I believe that fate doesn't lead us aimlessly into undetermined situations. Fate takes no detours. Any circumstances that might seem to happen by chance or off course along our way are a necessary part of our journey. Collectively, they contribute to teach us the skills needed to help us reach our final destination. Clothilde too envelopped in her rapture, did not care a bit about what philosophical arguments Elise this time would procure for an analysis of Paul's return to France. From her point of view consistent with her indoctrination, it was Almighty God manifesting Himself in His bountiful kindness. Was he answering prayers, which had been secretly sealed in her heart? She glanced at Elise with affectionate indulgence when Emile came down the front steps of *la Brisante,* and then turned in their direction.

"Good day young ladies!" he greeted cheerfully.

"Good day, Grandpapa!" responded Clothilde.

"Good day, Grandpere Emile!" likewise rejoined Elise, who from the time she could put two syllables together, affectionately addressed Emile in that manner. (Likewise, Madeleine, was Grandmere Madeleine.)

Emile glimpsed around and above with a hint of mystery in his smile.

"You look in a happy mood. Is something joyful going on in the air? Well, it is a beautiful spring day, I must acknowledge."

Clothilde and Elise stood up at once.

"Very beautiful, Grandpapa!" Clothilde agreed while she and Elise hugged him. Emile was not endowed with an overdeveloped sixth sense, but he certainly could derive a conclusion from having observed a significant change in Clothilde since the news of Paul's imminent return to France. Furthermore, no doubt Madeleine had instructed him a little on the subject. He was ecstatic for his granddaughter.

He touched the rim of his straw hat with the tip of his right hand in a respectful gesture indicating he must take leave.

"Have a lovely time little ladies. I have an engagement at the town hall, if I do not see any of you when I return, please give my love to Jean Luc and Paul until I embrace them myself when we meet for dinner. So long!" He passed by them cheerfully and then walked toward his jeep.

Clothilde smiled fondly as she watched him leave. She grew attentive to the songs of the nightingales and thought they sounded particularly melodious this morning. She noticed also that the fruit trees breaking into bloom exuded the most intoxicating fragrance, and that the daffodils, the primroses and the violets had begun to strew the front garden with patches of incredibly cheerful colors.

"Yes, dear Grandpapa," she thought, "yes, you are right, it is a very beautiful day." She felt like dancing all over the meadows.

At last the phone rang. Suzanne answered and soon after beckoned Clothilde to come in. It was Jean Luc who phoned to propose an excursion. Since it was not quite yet nine o'clock A.M. he really would like to take Paul for a scenic drive along the Dordogne valley and introduce him to a more extensive area of the region than he had been able to achieve upon Paul's previous visit. Clothilde related the invitation to Elise. Without a minute hesitation they both accepted. However, Clothilde required a little bit more time before confirming their approval, for by courtesy they wanted to be sure it would be in full agreement with their respective family.

Fifteen minutes later, Clothilde informed Jean Luc that she and Elise would be ready to go whenever he wished.

"They will be here instantly," relayed Clothilde as she took a deep breath in an attempt to dissipate the tension, which constricted her heart. She hastened to fetch her purse left in the drawing room, then joined Madeleine, Elise and her mother who had already stepped outside to watch for Jean Luc's and Paul's arrival.

"Be calm ... Be calm ... Be calm!" she silently ordered herself. "Be calm, there is no reason to feel so nervous because ... because ... Oh, here they are!" she announced as a beam of brilliant light caused by the sunrays striking directly against the metal fender of Jean Luc's car, turned slowly in the orchard road. As they approached, she caught sight of Paul's handsome profile. Though she had known him so briefly and had not seen him for almost a year, she would have recognized his features among a million other faces. Oh, and he and Jean Luc were alone! Whatever the consequences she had feared, only that moment existed. She even felt at peace when taking part in the warm demonstrations of their joyful reunion. When Paul saw her, the void in his heart was filled anew with an ineffable joy that time and distance had not lessened. As he shared in the affectionate embraces it would have seemed so normal to hold Clothilde everlastingly in his arms.

CHAPTER 9

AFTER A SHORT but heartwarming visit with Madeleine and Suzanne, Jean Luc, Clothilde and their friends left to spend a few leisurely hours along the road bordering the shores of the Dordogne.

The air vibrated with springtime vitality. Nature was still garbed in the tender hues of the new blossoms, which the morning sun stroked softly with a pearly whisper, lest too bright a touch should wither their fragile glow.

Jean Luc insisted to be in command of the steering wheel. Next to him sat Paul. Clothilde and Elise occupied the back seats.

With much regret, they were forced to abandon the hope of taking a ride as far as the "Gouffre de Padirac," a timeless abyss plunging in the rocky flank of the earth, which ceaselessly attracts flocks upon flocks of visitors. Although it conceals a far deeper subterranean waterway inaccessible to the public, at the first few hundred yards inward, a navigable river offers the possibility to take an awe-inspiring tour of the Grotto. To glide upon the clear stream reflecting the emerald green foliage of the underground vegetation intertwined with the spectacular stalagmites and stalactites strung along the walls of the cave, is an unforgettable adventure.

However, as they soon realized that time would not permit such excursion, they agreed to linger along the Dordogne nearer Grolejac, where Paul could admire many other splendors epitomizing the chronicles of bygone epochs. He was enchanted by the impressive medieval castles, by the magnificent Romanesque architecture and sculpture of the churches and monasteries, by the elegant Renaissance chateaux and manors, all facing each other across the valley. With intense interest, he listened to Jean Luc, Clothilde or Elise who took turn acting as docent, so to speak. They eagerly gave him an historical synopsis of what they jealously claimed as a legacy bequeathed to them by ancestors they could proudly traced back to the stone age. Yes, their roots clung deep and impassioned into the soul of that old land.

They tarried at the Roque Gageac, a fortified village structured against the steep slopes of a cliff ending its drop along the main street bordering the riverbank. It has bravely endured the landslides occurring now and again in the course of the centuries. They lingered at Beynac and Castelnaud, built on a rock face as well. The vestiges of their feudal fortifications everlastingly stating their reciprocal enmity from the time of the hundred years war between France and England.

Before they returned home, they went back to La Roque Gageac and sat in a little café on the waterfront, to enjoy a light *aperitif.*

During those hours, what were Clothilde and Paul to do concerning their concealed feelings for one another? Soon this day would end. The next morning after an early brunch Paul would leave again, for Jean-Luc had to report for work very early on Sunday. Consequently, he would need to spend a good night rest at the Base.

"What would ensue from this visit?" Paul questioned sadly. "What could he do?" Although he knew by then that Clothilde was completely freed from any commitment to phillippe, he surely could not ask Emile for Clothilde's hand so unpredictably, let alone when not having the slightest evidence about the nature of her sentiments toward him. Everyone would think that he was seriously deranged. At that very instant though, he certainly could have eloped with her, and after having pronounced a quick *"I do"* in front of some magistrate and having received a priest's blessing, he would have gladly taken her to Santa Barbara to meet his mother. He covertly smiled at those ridiculous thoughts.

When they were back in Grolejac, after having taken leave of Clothilde and Elise, Jean Luc briefly took his eyes off the road to cast a sideways glance at Paul. He frowned and shook his head.

"Paul!" he called, "at first, I thought that perhaps I imagined things, but as my attention was again and again drawn to it, I became convinced that my observation was not mistaken."

Paul looked at Jean Luc with an intrigued expression.

"It's about my cousin," Jean Luc explained more clearly, "about Clothilde. Did you see how she looked at you? Although she apparently made an effort to remain discreet, she gave me the impression to be mesmerized by you. She seemed captivated by your every word, by your every gesture, by your every smile. She amazed me! I have never known her given to such a fascination. Have you noticed all this? Well my friend, excuse my candid conjecture but could it be that she has fallen in love with you?"

Paul caught unawares by Jean Luc's scrutiny and forthrightness, was seized by a pang of apprehension, but also by a certain relief at the thought to confront the emotions which for so long had been sealed in his heart like laden water in a lightless tank. He examined Jean Luc's profile as if he sought further assertion of what he had equally suspected himself, but of which he could not be certain. After a brief moment of reflection he yielded to the unmasked truth.

"You can be assured that if Clothilde's feelings toward me are as you have gathered, the sentiments are mutual. I have fallen in love with her the moment I first saw her, and ever since to reason it out of my mind has been beyond my power. It has remained a constant paradox impossible to fathom."

Jean Luc, astounded by his friend's disclosure, was stricken dumb. His chin drooped almost to the steering wheel. He stared at the road as if he had witnessed the parting of the red sea, then he briefly turned to Paul.

"What? Are you serious Paul? You …? But why on earth haven't you told me?"

"To admit it to someone," replied Paul with a thoughtful expression, "would have forced me to admit it to myself and therefore reject the feeble thread of denial to which has clung my sanity."

"But I am not just *"someone"* I am your friend!" Jean Luc protested.

"I appreciate your thoughtfulness, but what would have been your reaction? What would you have assumed, if as a result of your kind invitation in your home, I had told you like an impostor, that I was coveting another man's fiancee, who happened to be your cousin?"

Paul justified. He could not resist laughing at the ridicule of his own comment. "However," Paul went on, "as a result of the change in circumstances and prompted to a resolve, I had begun to consider that I should speak to you about it."

"I hope so," said Jean Luc as he flashed a glimpse toward Paul and smiled in acknowledgement that indeed his friend had valid reasons for not having confided in him yet.

By then they had reached the driveway of *la Madrigale*, which obliged them to discontinue the conversation.

CHAPTER 10

Meanwhile, back at *la Brisante*, Clothilde wondered where the day had fled. It would have seemed that she had left the house just a few minutes ago if the clock had not reminded her otherwise.

No one was home. Her grandparents and her mother were already at *la Madrigale*.

Elise had gone to freshen up for the evening. Before doing the same, Clothilde took time to visit Canon d'Or. She gave him a brief report of how her day was spent, and as he seemed to nod in approval while he chewed a carrot Clothilde had brought him, she prayed to be granted some time alone with Paul, before his departure. She inhaled a few deep breaths as a breeze carried the scent of hauthorn beginning to bloom on the hillock behind *la Brisante*.

Already the western horizon unfurled in pink and mauve folds over the far end of the dusky forest. It conveyed a certain gloom to her soul, as if her happiness was to dissolve into the fading daylight. She went to her bedroom and changed into a lilac-blue long sleeve dress of fine wool, for the night was still a little chilly. Moonstone earrings and necklace completed beautifully her understated elegance. She stood in front of the mirror, looked askance first at her right side than at her left side. Presumably satisfied with her appearance she walked to the window. Elise had just stopped her car at the edge of the front lawn. She blew the horn once and let her engine run while waiting for Clothilde. They had agreed to drive together from *la Brisante* to *la Madrigale*, and Elise had volunteered to be the chauffeur. Along the short distance, which separated the two houses, Clothilde briefly discussed her desire for a few moments of privacy with Paul.

"I sense he has something to tell me, and if we were alone with each other it might give him the occasion to express it," she claimed pensively. "If it is otherwise, if my intuition is mistaken, what is waiting for me in the days ahead?" she then questioned. "Until we meet once more, perhaps in a year from now, must my gladness be sustained by the anticipation that he might smile at me again? yet I would rather know, for I can't face to live in that limbo for another day."

She put her hand upon Elise's right forearm, and then in a reflex, removed it to smooth down her dress, which had been crinkled by her purse resting upon her lap.

"I am sorry Elise. I have regressed exactly where I don't wish to be. Please grant me your patience a little bit longer. I promise I will not allow this pathetic setback to persist too long. After Paul leaves Grolejac, I am determined to never, never again give it another thought."

Elise smiled kindly, feeling helpless to provide the answers Clothilde sought. She tried her best to be helpful.

"I wish I were a magic fairy having the power to put your mind at ease. However, don't drive yourself wild with anxiety by suppositions purely based on your fears. Sometimes it seems that fate considers favorably those who maintain a positive attitude even against all apparent odds, and chastises those who wallow in self defeating conjectures."

Clothilde looked at Elise thinking, her friend's mind was no doubt under the influence of an uncanny planet, but she could also be very sensible.

As they drew close to *la Madrigale*, bursts of laughter echoed from the front terrace where a group of guests had gathered to revel in this magnificent April evening while the setting sun sprinkled a midst of ethereal tints over the valley. When they approached the house, her heartbeat silenced all other sounds at the thought that no, she was not dreaming, that yes, Paul was actually there, barely a few meters from her. Then suddenly all her restiveness gave way to the sweetest exaltation. As they arrived among the guests, their appearance elicited the most delighted expressions in every one's eyes. Veronique and Suzanne seated opposite each other at a marble round table, casually chatted. Bernard,

Charles and Frederick were amid a very lively discussion. Father Vernier absent due to another obligation, was missed. Jean Luc close by, leaned pensively against the rim of the terrace, and now and then took a sip of his gin and tonic. Clothilde's gaze rested on Paul. Once more Emile had monopolized him in a conversation but he had anxiously waited for her. At the very moment she appeared, his whole world recovered a sense of balance. Arrested by his presence, she stood still for a moment almost expecting he would rush to embrace her. Their eyes met and they exchanged a smile. Afraid to blush from the onrush of emotions he arose in her, she lowered her head and hastily turned toward Charles who was hugging Elise in a jovial welcome. Feeling a little gauche she addressed a few words to everyone as she went inside the house where Madeleine and Melanie helped Justine set the dinner table.

Jean Luc had replied to her affectionate greeting without being much aware of it. Clothilde could not avoid noticing an unusual quietness about him. She hoped nothing serious troubled his mind; but she had to wait for a more pertinent time to question him about it. Had she known that Paul had given him a lot to reflect upon, and she certainly had no less contributed to it!

Jean Luc was still in a state of shock from the rapidity at which the attraction between Paul and Clothilde had developed. He deeply loved both and feared that such a sudden infatuation might eventually amount to naught and cause pain to either of them. "Was Clothilde ready to enter into a romantic relationship so soon after her separation from Phillippe? Did she look for a diversion, for vicarious excitement to fill the void that lingers in one's heart from missing a loved one? Could the nature of Paul's work and his handsome appearance attract much attention from the ladies, and therefore be the cause of a blasé sensibility, a certain propensity for shallow flirtations? Was he sincere when he told about his fond sentiments for Clothilde, or was he no more than a mundane man behind a social varnish?" Much apprehension cluttered his head. Then he reproved himself for having entertained such dreads about his dear friend and his beloved cousin.

"Ah," he at last yielded after further pondering. "Ah, they are not children any more. What shall be, needed to be. Time never lies, on its own term it shall disclose that which must come to pass."

His face took a dreamy expression as he recalled his grandfather telling him last summer: *"If I had another granddaughter I would absolutely insist that she and Paul fall in love with each other …"* Could these words from Emile, have been prophetic? I certainly would not mind at all to have Paul for a cousin in law," Jean Luc concluded still a bit giddy from amazement.

In the meantime, Madeleine and Emile knew exactly what sang in the heart of their granddaughter, they could equally perceive in Paul's eyes, the tender whispers of his love for her.

As Clothilde and Elise entered the hall of *la Madrigale,* they met with Justine coming out of the dining room.

"There you are young ladies!" She exclaimed cheerfully as she received Clothilde and Elise both at once in her arms. "Now my guest list has materialized to completion, I can serve dinner!"

Melanie and Madeleine instantly gathered around them and amid kisses asked about the excursion.

"Well, come along, shall we summon everyone to the table?" Justine proposed, and she gaily began to move toward the front door.

It was a pure delight to walk in the large dining room and behold the beautifully set table. Scintillating crystal glasses, shimmery silver candleholders and Limoges porcelain plates decorated with brilliant flowers were all elegantly arranged against a sparkling white tablecloth. At the center, a bouquet of blue irises and pink tulips exuded a crisp springtime fragrance, which lavishly permeated the air.

As soon as everyone was seated, upon Jean Luc's suggestion, a coupe of Champagne in each one's hand was lifted to hail Paul's move to France. An indefinable energy and joy stirred deep in everyone's heart.

Clothilde's spirit leaped in a surge of rapture when Paul most graciously thanked his hosts for their kindheartedness.

Oh, what a miracle! What a blessed miracle to see him there gathered with her family! Clothilde rejoiced. He could not resist from resting a smile upon her lovely face and be moved by her bedewed eyes.

However as the evening advanced, Paul painfully kept his love for Clothilde restrained by a calm dignity. Clothilde subdued her feelings for him, behind an affable appearance.

Although both sensed there was an attraction between them, for want of expression, each remained unsure if their sentiments toward one another were shared. It was upon this unresolved ambiguity that they bade each other good night.

CHAPTER 11

CLOTHILDE HEARD THE clock strike every
hour of the night. Unable to relax, her mind spun all the possible
trepidations she could imagine from fear of having to regress in a
renewal of her former torment? To slip back into the way of life she
had led since last summer, seemed like reentering a desolate house, and
dwell there surrounded by a bleak loneliness. Paul had unveiled new
soul-stirring horizons she yearned to reach with him. Oh, she barely
knew him and yet she would miss him so terribly!

At last, overcome by fatigue, before the chime had completed to
ring five o'clock in the morning she had succumbed to a light sleep. But
again, an all-consuming agitation mercilessly denied her reeling brain
enough time to repair. Shortly after, she awoke in utter panic as though
she would be late for a very important appointment. She deemed it was
caused by an unconscious anxiety to have overslept and be unprepared
to welcome Jean Luc and Paul for brunch. She heaved a sigh of relief
when checking the time on the alarm clock next to her on the night
stand, she saw that it was only a little past seven o'clock A.M., with
haste she threw over her coverlet and sprang out of bed. At the sound
of voices around the house, she opened her bedroom curtains and
caught sight of Suzanne and Madeleine talking on the front lawn while
they slightly bent over a flower patch. They were probably examining
if the newly sown seeds had begun to sprout. At the farthest limit of
the orchard, her grandfather was engaged in a conversation with a

neighbor. Already, farmers surrounded by animals, bustled in the fields and the meadows. Suzanne noticing her daughter, waved. Clothilde in response opened the window and after an affectionate exchange of greetings, Madeleine informed her that Canon d'Or had been looked after, not to worry about him. She then showered and as if she were in a haste, she dressed in white pants and a navy blue sweater not bothering too much about her hair, which she simply gathered in a ponytail. She didn't bother to stop in the dining room for breakfast, but grasped her purse containing her car keys, and walked outside. She was going to see Elise who, in spite of her most abstruse, arguments to explain life contingencies, could also convey the most positive encouragement by simply lending a kind ear to one's grievances. Clothilde wanted to spend sometime in her friend's company before she would say goodbye to Paul.

She went to kiss her mother and her grandmother.

"This sweater looks so pretty on you, where are you off to darling?" Suzanne asked.

"To Elise's; I won't be long."

"All right sweetheart. I don't think the boys will be here so soon. They will need their rest to be fit for the journey back to Dreux," Madeleine added indulgently.

Clothilde kissed both of them once more, hopped in her car and drove away.

Guilty for having neglected to give Canon d'Or his usual morning care, she stopped in front of the pasture, whereupon he hurried to meet her at the fence. After he had received her sincere apologies, and a profusion of caresses over the sides of his faces, he readily forgave her with a spirited neighing and then he returned into his stall to finish his hay. Half way down the orchard road, she beeped the horn to get Emile's attention and waved at him. When she arrived at the junction where she should have turned left toward Elise's, at the last minute, she impulsively changed her mind and without an after thought, she veered in the opposite direction toward the village church. "At this time, there should be no one there," she thought. She knew Father Vernier was officiating at Carsac, another parish nearby. "To pass a quiet moment of meditation favorable to inner peace would not be a bad idea after all," she conceded as she went on driving.

She parked her car in front of the North façade and entered the church through the door of the Holy Virgin's chapel. Here she kneeled and made a short prayer. She then moved to the pews on the right side of the nave, in the transept. Looking around she took a deep breath filled with the perfume exhaled by the lilies of the valley deposited in bouquets as votive offerings adorning the altar and the different statues of Saints. Again, she went down on her knees and prayed. After a short while, she silently sat, subdued her thoughts, and listened to the sounds that seeped through the thick ancient walls. In front of her, shafts of sunrays filtering through the stained glass windows studded the choir with emerald, sapphire and ruby gemlike inlays. Birds fluttering about the belfry, paid tribute to the new day, in a merry aubade.

She surrendered her soul to the mystical ambiance. Soon she was gently enwrapped in a shroud of spiritual serenity, and had the impression to have reached a blissful shore after a long journey upon a stormy sea.

While she entreated council to approach prudently those incredible events, which had happened recently in her life, she heard the West portal grating on its hinges as it was slowly opened then closed. Subsequently, footsteps resonated upon the medieval, tiled nave. On a reflex, she quickly turned her head to check who had come. In the semi darkness of the doorway she saw the profile of a tall man's silhouette extending a hand toward the blessed water in the font baptismal. Undisturbed, she simply relaxed intending to recapture her quietude when all at once an intuitive suspicion constricted her chest as if it were crushed by the jaws of a vise. Is it...? Could it be...? She looked again. No, she was not hallucinating. Oh God! Yes, it was Paul.

In spite of only a very short rest, Paul also quite agitated had felt compelled to rise early. Dressed casually in his favorite old, faded but very comfortable blue jeans and a brown sweater, which followed him everywhere, he stopped into the kitchen to greet Justine who had been up for awhile already. After he joined her for a cup of coffee, the temptation to take a morning walk in the magnificent countryside and try to unravel his muddled thoughts, won him over. Strolling randomly at his pleasure with no particular objective in mind, he soon found himself within the church precinct, which was not far from the Madrigale. He decided to dally inside a while. The tranquil beauty of its interior at this time of the day seemed so appeasing to his swirling thoughts. Since Clothilde's car had been left on the north side, whereas he had approached the church from the west façade, he deemed himself alone.

When Clothilde for the second time looked in his direction and without a doubt had recognized him, he had not yet noticed her presence. He was turned sideways again, looking at the delicate interlacing stonework of a triforium. She allowed herself a few seconds to regain possession of at least an outer calm and then moved away from her pew to step in the nave. Sensing a presence, he spontaneously cast a glance over his right shoulder, whereupon he faced her and immediately realized who she was. Caught unawares beyond all expectations, he gazed at her as if he were beholding a heavenly apparition.

"Clothilde!" he called, and pressed on toward her.

"Hello! Paul." she said gently, powerless to restrain the tears already shedding over her smile. She came forward, held out her hands to him, but he, without an instant hesitation gently drew her in his arms as though it was the most natural thing to do. She rested her brow against his chest. Softly he kissed the top of her head. They embraced like two lovers, like two dear friends restored to one another after an interminable estrangement. At first, spellbound by the awe-inspiring encounter, they both were unable to pronounce another word, but they did not need to speak; their heart now knew and understood perfectly what each yearned to say.

"Clothilde! I have so often dreamt of this moment, but never dared to envision it could become a reality," Paul finally uttered.

There was a silence.

"It seems like all my life I have searched for you and now I have found you," he then added holding her close while he softly stroked her hair.

What supreme joy pervaded Clothilde's soul! She had the impression of completing, a never-ending circle of time also spent in a desperate search for him. Finally they were brought together. Now, locked in his embrace, she felt whole. She wished they would never part from each other, ever.

She drew a long sigh.

"Oh, Paul!" she said, "I can't visualize my life on this earth without sharing it with you. I don't want this to end."

"It couldn't be otherwise," he said while holding her closer to him. He then put his right arm around her shoulders and led her outside.

They sat on the low wall near the church west entrance. Taking both of her hands in his, he looked at her tenderly.

"Clothilde," he began to ask, "will you …?"

"Yes, yes I will! Oh, yes Paul I will!" she answered ecstatically before she allowed him time to finish his question as though someone else had spoken through her. Shocked by her own unseemly bravado, she blushed then melted in sobs from an incommensurable happiness. She raised his hands to her lips, and showered them with kisses. He withdrew from her a little, cupped her chin with the tip of his fingers, lifted her head and looked at her with a smile suggesting he was pleasantly amused by the impetuosity of her sincere acceptance. He enfolded her in an embrace again.

"I love you," he said simply.

The sound of a car prompted them to assume a more casual demeanor. Good-humoredly, both laughed at the rather uncommon aspect of their situation when at the top of the hill appeared a green Aronde. It gradually slowed down, and then turned to stop in the church parking lot at a short distance from where they sat. Madame Vaudrin had come to clean the church. She carried an arrangement of white and yellow daffodils to place at the shrine of the Virgin Mary. She greeted them cordially. Clothilde was pleased that the good woman had recognized Paul and came to welcome him with as much fuss as if he were one of the villagers who had returned home from a journey.

"Why was it that on this special morning every single happening seemed to follow one another with such extraordinary ease? without any struggle on her part?" Clothilde thought, being ever so grateful to heaven; for indeed her prayers were answered.

However, it was now time for Paul to rejoin his hosts. As he escorted Clothilde to her car, both looked forward to meet once more at brunch, but felt sadden knowing they had to part again. Yet, a sweet parting it would be, for now they could freely fashion dreams upon their love.

Before Clothilde would venture into driving, she needed a few minutes to recover her equilibrium, for her whirling emotions made her head dizzy. She could not possibly focus her attention upon the hazards of a country road. She cried, she laughed, she sang, and at last unbridled all those feelings, which had been so agonizingly aborted for so long. She was spinning in rhapsodic joy unbounded, limitless, and absolute. Words were inadequate, much too ordinary to express her love, for it transcended the imperfections of the sentiments experienced by common mortals. Although she had no idea about composing the slightest piece of music, at that moment she could have easily written the most beautiful sonatas and concertos even symphonies to express the purity and exquisiteness of her joy. She had received a new spirit transfusion. She had reached the loftiest heights of happiness. Surely God had fashioned love on this planet to satisfy specifically her heart's desire!

As Paul began to walk the short distance back to *la Madrigale*, his feet did not feel the ground. He had acquired physical attributes that defied the law of gravity. He glided weightless. The colors of nature had grown more vivid, the sounds more melodious than barely an hour before. The entire cosmos had been reshaped into a radiant whole since he had found his beloved.

CHAPTER 12

After and indefinite amount of time, perhaps a quarter of an hour or so, Clothilde judged that she had regained a reasonable level of calmness and could now go on home. Well, first, since it was still early enough, she would hurry and bring the glad tidings to Elise who certainly was most deserving of being promptly told about it.

She had barely left the church precinct when in an instant from the peak of her euphoria she plunged into the depth of distress. Too tormented by the new situation she was now facing, she felt compelled to stop again in the nearest area offering a safe parking. It seemed that reality like a squad of army sergeants looming from nowhere, had abruptly blocked her path, admonishing her to think carefully about what her new commitment to Paul would implicate.

"What am I to do?" she questioned, stricken by the frightening thoughts painfully pounding on her mind. "What am I to do? Must I renounce everything I love to follow Paul? Must I tear myself away from my grandparents, my mother, Jean Luc, Elise, Canon d'Or, the land and the traditions I cherish, the museum, even Phillippe if only on his occasional visits? Oh, no!" she deplored, "I could not bear to leave all this to go and live in the Beauce, but I could not bear to give up Paul either. Oh! what am I to do? Why can't Paul be a part of what I treasure most without having to contend with so many obstacles? My family has suffered enough disappointments through the cancellation of my marriage to Phillippe, now should I go home and announce I must pack my suitcases because I plan to be soon moving away? Oh, how could I? How could I explain to Canon d'Or that I must sacrifice his happiness so I can reach mine? He would sorely miss me and fall ill with grief, or if he should come along with us, at his age the change would be too traumatic for his well being. How could I forsake my dear grandparents in their approaching old age and abandon my mother to it all?"

Clothilde overcome by a surge of piercing anguish took a sharp U-turn out of the parking area and sped back in direction of *la Madrigale*, praying she would still find Paul walking.

"I must talk to Paul," she decided. "Who better than Paul is qualified to understand my dilemma?" She found him strolling along on a path slightly set back from the road. He seemed calm, but deep in reflection. As soon as he caught sight of Clothilde, he was extremely surprised by her reappearance and he hastened to her car. Instantly and with an astonishing ease, she poured her heart to him, hoping God would intervene with a workable solution satisfactory to both of them. She couldn't have imagined that now He would ask of her to give up Paul or separate herself from all she so dearly loved.

Paul reassured her that having realized the emotional intricacy arising from their situation, he too had already given it his foremost thoughts because he had no wish either to build his happiness by causing pain to anyone. Clothilde smiled at the likeness of their thinking. He understood that other options agreeable to everyone would have to be considered, and asked Clothilde to please trust that he would not deceive her. She parted from him with complete faith in a workable resolution satisfactory to both of them and to their respective family. She thanked God for having intervened.

Immediately after Jean Luc and Paul had left for Dreux, Clothilde so giddily happy, informed her grandparents and her mother of the extraordinary happenings, which had developed between Paul and her in the space of only a couple of hours. Anyway, it would have been quite difficult to be overlooked. Already a change had been noticeable during the little time they spent together while having brunch at *la Brisante*. Moreover, how could one have ignored the daily phone calls that had begun to be exchanged between them after Paul's departure, and the transformation so manifestly visible in Clothilde's appearance? Her smile glowed with a new sparkle and her complexion had taken a radiant transparency that can only bloom under the magic of love. In her eyes, one could see the reflection of so many wonderful visions soaring in her soul. She even moved with a more spirited stride. After she had explained her fear of having to move away, and how Paul had acknowledged her legitimate concerns, Clothilde's family, bravely reminded her that a good wife should unreservedly follow her husband wherever necessity might urge him to go. However, what a relief it was when everyone was told that a compromise would be reached for the satisfaction of all involved. Once Paul had been reassured that in agreement with the precepts of etiquette, circumstances were perfectly appropriate to ask for Clothilde's hand, he formulated his wishes to marry her by a letter, which completely stole the heart of her grandparents and Suzanne. From this moment forward, not only Clothilde, but the entire village as well, seemed swept away in a whirl of euphoria. Jean Luc was in a state of unappeasable exultation at the thought of having Paul as his cousin and furthermore as a new affiliate of his "Diggers of the soil coterie." His parents were no less overjoyed and to the delight of all, Veronique was pleasantly affected by the uplifting influence this union imparted on those who were touched by it. She could never wish enough happiness to her dear Clothilde.

An engagement party was given at the end of October as soon as Paul and his mother had transitorily moved in the Beauce. A beautiful diamond ring was passed down from Isabelle's grandmother to Clothilde who looked lovely in her ivory white gown enhanced by a delicate sapphire necklace with matching earrings given to her by her mother. Suzanne had received it herself from Madeleine at her own engagement to Clothilde's father.

Although it had been in anticipation of different circumstances that Emile had promised to waltz his granddaughter breathless on the day of her betrothal, he gladly kept his word.

CHAPTER 13

CLOTHILDE AND PAUL were married at the end
of February, about eleven months after Paul's eventful visit to Grolejac
the previous spring.

Upon the insistence of Clothilde, the wedding was an elegant but
modest celebration. She wore a simple white satin gown with fitted
bodice. Her headdress made of satin also, molded beautifully the top
of her head. From a coronet garnished with lily of the valley, a veil of
Flemish lace flowed into a train held by four maids of honor all dressed
in lavender blue muslin dresses. Emile as the mayor performed the
civic requisite. Soon after, in the little church strewn with all kinds of
possible flowers pervading the air with the most exquisite fragrance, he
led his radiant granddaughter down the nave to Paul. Elise at the organ,
and a flutist played the "Andante un poco largo, from G. P. Teleman's
concerto in A Major."

Phillippe had obtained a special authorization to come home for the
occasion. When Clothilde walked toward the alter at her grandfather's
arm and she and Phillippe exchanged a glance, he prayed to have set
her free to a long life of happiness with Paul, and she prayed to have set
him free to a blessed life as a servant of Christ.

In an endeavor to put it into words, no literary feat could possibly
do justice to the simple but supreme beauty embodied in this soul-
stirring event.

On this special day, to Clothilde and to Isabelle, there was no finer looking young man than Paul was, as he stood there so handsome in his white tailcoat and pink carnation boutonniere. Next to him, Jean Luc, his best man, did not look second to any one either thought Elise. Lately, she had been contemplating that it was time to let him court her seriously. Soon, he would be discharged from his military duty. Then, she would be ready to pronounce the traditional "I do" standing by him in front of this very alter and make him the happiest human being in the world. She would feel very fortunate also to venture into the future with such wonderful man for a life companion. They both agreed that they had been in love with each other since the beginning of time. It would have been quite impossible to imagine either of them destined to be with anyone else.

Paul and Clothilde's nuptial union and vows were blessed in a Mass offered by Father Vernier while a choir accompanied by a guitarist, a violinist and the organ still played by Elise, sang extracts from Beethoven's Missa Solemnis in D major which seemed to lift the entire church to exalted heights only accessible within the celestial realm.

Paul's mother warmly received by Clothilde's family and friends naturally partook in the ceremonies and festivities. She was delirious from the joy caused by her son's happiness. Upon her arrival at Grolejac, she fell in love at first glimpse with her daughter in law to be, and easily befriended with Madeleine, Suzanne and indeed everyone else. Certainly all those unanticipated events caused many changes in the plans she had formulated concerning their move. As soon as Paul and Clothilde had announced their intention to get married, it was understood that where they would choose to live would have a significant bearing upon all involved in the newly extended family unit. Consequently, many conferences had been summoned by telephone, first from both sides of the Atlantic Ocean, then from the Beauce to Grolejac.

The relocation of Paul and Isabelle to France was now definitive. Proposing that Clothilde endure the immense sacrifice to part from family, friends, Canon d'Or and whatever more, to go and live with them on their estate, was inconceivable in spite of her profound love for Paul and her desire to be a dutiful wife. Paul and his mother being considerate for Clothilde's feelings and those of her loved ones, had a much better alternative. They readily offered to sell Isabelle's house and shop as well as Paul's condominium in Santa Barbara, which would represent a substantial capital for the acquisition of a property around

Grolejac. They also decided to lease again the farm in the Beauce. To the gladness of all, this option demanded no traumatic separation from any one, but only necessitated to give up some possessions for which there was no deep emotional attachment. Isabelle was delighted by this choice. The weather of the south west of France being warmer than in the Beauce and similar to the Santa Barbara climate as well as the beauty of the region suited her perfectly.

Jean Luc once back home would be amply busy with the management of *la Madrigale*, with very little time at his disposal for tending to Emile's land if the need responsibility should arise. Since Suzanne had no son, until then it had been upon Phillippe that this dependability had partly rested, and even more in provision for the day when Emile would be unable to carry on with such charge. Inasmuch as Paul had expressed his enthusiasm to become a landowner and devote part of his life to farming, why not transfer this role to him? Therefore, instead of investing the money available to Isabelle and Paul in a new farm as previously considered, it was concluded to expand the land already existing in Emile's estate, which proved to be a very satisfactory resolve. Emile was ecstatic.

A charming old house in the midst of beautiful far-reaching fields and woods was bought for Paul and Clothilde. Some of these ancient family domains were occasionally left behind by younger generations, who for one reason or the other had settled elsewhere. Paul and Clothilde were lucky to happen upon one of these. It had belonged to the village schoolmaster who with his wife had taught at the elementary school then attended by Suzanne more than forty years since. They had no children. Their heir was a nephew living in Paris. When he took possession of the property he had never bothered to exploit its potential. Consequently, part of the land had been rented; the rest of it had gone fallow. He had closed the house where now and then he and his family would come to spend a week or two in the summer, just long enough to sweep up the spider webs. It was a rather spread out, low house which consisted chiefly of four bedrooms, a dining room, a sitting room and a large kitchen, all distributed at the ground level. A loft provided a large room with windows overlooking the vast countryside. In the past, this space had been used as a library and study. Paul gladly would continue the tradition, for the area offered the ideal retreat and setting for the apportioned time he would dedicate to writing. This charming property was called *la Buissoniere*. It was a bit set back from the main section of the village, but not far from *la* **Brisante**. The location was perfect for Canon d'Or to frolic at liberty, for he was already very familiar with the area. There was plenty of green meadow to enclose a pasture with a comfortable stall. To move him with Clothilde was wise, considering his attachment to her and his expectation of the daily cajoleries she lavished upon him. However, Emile and the remainder of the family would ensure he was not given occasion to miss their affectionate attention.

A small but very lovely cottage was built near Paul and Clothilde's home to suit Isabelle's needs. It duplicated the guesthouse of her farm and consequently offered the same arrangements she had initially contemplated. Meanwhile she rented a small house. Isabelle rapidly and gracefully integrated in the life of the village.

As for Emile, he had tears of pride when at last Paul for the first time affectionately began to refer to him as Grandpapa. Although when addressing him or the other members of Clothilde's family, Paul continued to use the deferential *"vous"* instead of the more familiar *"tu."*

Clothilde equally applied the same etiquette with regard to Isabelle.

Clothilde impatient to settle in her cozy new house, had no particular desire to travel anywhere for a honeymoon. Paul did not argue against it, having sufficiently been on the move lately. Besides, where could there be a better spot on this earth than Grolejac to offer the perfect surrounding for their idyll? Therefore, by the onset of spring everything was well organized for them to be comfortably settled and to attend to the day-by-day necessities. There was already so much to do. The care of the domestic chores was a never-ending task. The museum at this stage still demanded a lot of attention. The land as if at rest, had allowed some respite for a while, but it was time to plow the fields again, for soon the new crop should be sowed. Moreover, all those ideas proliferating in Paul's mind demanded many hours of his concentration to be structured into the coherent treatises he wished to compile them. No doubt all those commitments busied them from sunrise to sundown and often far later in the night. Oh, but it felt so much as it ought to be!

CHAPTER 14

A NEW SEASON WAS moving toward the end of May. Paul and Clothilde had been married for well over a year already. They were so taken with being happy, that they hadn't realized so much time had passed them by.

Clothilde and Elise were spending a Monday afternoon in the museum, setting up a spring exposition of watercolors. After having hung a collection of brilliant aquarelles in the art gallery, they drew away from the walls to assess the display.

"It looks fine," nodded Elise. "A lovely show."

"I think so," agreed Clothilde. She glanced from one painting to the next while blinking her long dark eyelashes.

"We are very fortunate to have obtained the work of so many talented artists for one exhibit," pursued Elise. She gently but decisively laid her left hand on Clothilde's arm.

"Now, come along mother, let's go and have tea, you have been standing on your feet too long already."

Clothilde laughed.

"Yes nurse Elise."

"Come along," Elise motioned again as she hurried to draw water into the kettle.

Amiably, Clothilde followed. Arriving in the kitchen, she placed two cups, a sugar bowl, a small jug of milk and a jar of cookies on the table, then sat quietly while Elise prepared the tea.

"You seem deep in thought," Elise remarked in a carefree tone of voice.

"Me? Oh, I was just … Oh, for whatever reason I have dwelled in an awful lot of retrospections recently. Clothilde sighed. "You know, like old people do upon things of their past. I must be aging." She laughed.

From a pretty porcelain teapot, Elise poured steaming tea in Clothilde's cup.

"Any extraordinary incidents I might have missed along the way?" she asked with amused curiosity.

"I don't think so. How could you? It seems like we have never left each other's side from the very instant we were born," Clothilde said as she looked affectionately at her friend. "I have just pondered over time gone by in general, about when you and I were children, when we celebrated our first communion, our confirmation." She added sugar and milk to her tea and frowned at Elise reproachfully. "How I cried the first weeks we boarded in the convent and you called me a spoiled brat seriously deranged by separation neuroses. That was pitiless.

"It was. I am sorry. Please forgive me," Elise apologized with a meek expression, feigning to be deeply contrite.

"You were exonerated long ago," Clothilde reassured good-humoredly. She casually gazed outside through the open door. She smiled when her attention was caught by a calf who in a sudden gambol alarmed a flock of sparrows quietly pecking about the neighbors' meadow. She followed their flight as they soared above the frothy brook swelled up from the spring rain.

Clothilde changed abruptly to a sterner mood and looked back at Elise.

"In a strange way, Marie Joelle has been on my mind also," she continued. "Do you remember how she amused everyone with her taste for French fries dipped in strawberry jam? Well recently, I have felt strongly inclined to favor this kind of concoction. Needless to say, I find it rather peculiar."

Elise bit her lips to keep quiet. "Oh, my God!" she instantly wondered in amazement, as if she had just heard that one of the Revelations from Saint John the Divine might shortly come to pass. "Isn't it said that a departed soul who had some particular fondness for a certain food in a previous life, during the course of a rebirth may transfer it as a craving to the expectant mother? Could Marie Joelle …?

"I was thinking also about poor dear Phillippe," Clothilde went on, "How he has missed his sister and I am sure he still aches for her," She drew a deep breath as a light wind carried the scent of freshly mowed grass throughout the kitchen. "Ultimately, it might have swayed him to enter the orders. I hope he has found great comfort in his calling."

Elise tried to listen, although she felt distracted by her own preoccupations.

There was a silence.

"Oh, Elise!" resumed Clothilde, "who would have imagined when we were by the Dordogne, and I waited for Phillippe to return from Egypt, that almost three years later I would be standing here married to Paul and already expecting his child!"

Elise for a second gave the impression she felt compelled to express a thought but then decided to withhold it.

Clothilde waited for her to speak while she grew attentive to the calls of the cuckoo echoing across the woodland.

"Did you want to say … ?"

"No, no, go on," Elise interrupted as she shook her head brusquely, suggesting she was trying to dissimulate a certain earnestness.

"Indeed, some very special angel must have been assigned to remove any obstacle likely to prevent us from being together. Don't you think so Elise?" Clothilde questioned, awestruck again by the unraveling of events since the minute Paul had come into her life.

Elise's enigmatic smile, implied she had additional explanations regarding those changes, however extraordinary they might seem. From her point of view, the circumstances unfolding in Clothilde's life, or in any one's life for that matter, were not a sequence of happenings liable to be altered by chance. They were the logical result of her soul seeking such experiences for the purpose to work out some unresolved issues from a former life and consistent with the fulfillment of her destiny progress toward a higher level of evolution. However, Elise knew that under the circumstances, it was better to refrain from any discourse on such subject so unacceptable to Clothilde. Moreover, she certainly did not wish to aggravate the uneasiness Veronique had unwittingly provoked about a month ago, a few days before Clothilde found out she was with child. Early in the morning, Veronique phoned Clothilde asking her to stop by as soon as possible. She urgently needed to tell her about a dream she had just experienced.

"I am sorry to bother you so, darling," she apologized when she nervously received Clothilde in her arms and led her to the living room, "but I must share with you what happened to me last night while it is still vivid in my mind. I had a dream. *It was after one of our summer storms. Paul and you were walking along the bank of the Dordogne, when you came face to face with a little girl seated amid the reeds that grow along the beaches. When she saw you, she rose and rushed in Paul's arms. At that point, her gay laughter suddenly awoke me.* I was then overcome by a feeling of immense elation. Oh dear me!" exclaimed Veronique as she broke into sobs, "she looked like my Marie Joelle!"

Clothilde immobilized by shock, stared at Veronique. She had no recollection of having told her about that dream.

"How do you know about this?' she finally asked.

"What?" Veronique questioned with a baffled expression.

"How do you know about that dream?" Clothilde asked again emphatically.

"I told you, I just dreamt it last night," Veronique replied growing rather confused.

"But I had the same dream myself a while ago," Clothilde pointed out, as if Veronique had stolen it from her.

"Oh, really …? You did?" Veronique inquired completely at a loss.

"Have I told you about it? I must have," Clothilde resumed. "How in the world would I have disclosed this dream to Veronique?" she then wondered. "Could I have been so careless as to commit such stupidity, possibly when I was disturbed by all what went on at that time? But why is it that Veronique doesn't remember either if I told her? Well, she probably was too upset on account of Phillippe to attach much importance to what I was saying, but it still left an imprint on her memory."

Upon that supposition, Clothilde felt she had drawn a logical explanation from this perplexing incident.

"My dear Veronique, I am sure I have spoken to you all about that dream and your subconscious simply reenacted it, because its content made a profound impression on your mind. This really should not cause you to be upset."

"Well I suppose you did then and I have forgotten, which doesn't surprise me," Veronique conceded, but not without some reservation though, for she had grown to assume that those reoccurring manifestations of Marie Joelle, were not created by her fantasies. She felt that there was something revelatory, something trustworthy in it. However for lack of proof to validate her beliefs, she stood alone against the rationale of others and she had learned to become more pliant to their contradictory arguments.

"But all the same, the pink dress she wore was the exact replica of Marie Joelle's favorite dress when she was around that age," Veronique added, justifying as it were, that she had a good reason to be concerned.

Clothilde looked at her tenderly.

"Well, you know how we associate many images in our dreams even if they are unrelated."

"I am aware of that darling, but I can't help to get emotional when anything refers to my Marie Joelle and I needed to share it with you since you are included." Veronique finally tried to point out almost apologetic for the disturbance she had caused.

Clothilde gently stroked Veronique's hand.

"Of course. I understand. I am glad you shared it with me," she said while she realized with puzzlement that she had not given too much thought to that dream for sometime, until recently when it seemed to have surfaced anew.

She imparted this intriguing episode to Paul. He advised her that Veronique's faulty recollection was probably the result of some oversight occasioned by so much stress in her life.

To spare her friend from further upset, Elise outwardly agreed with Paul. For again, under the circumstances, she surely could not disclose her notion that such dreams might herald the rebirth of a beloved soul among the loved ones who had been left behind on this earth.

In the midst of those baffling developments, Elise gradually and steadily sought deeper and deeper into their possible meaning. She had long rejected that the pledge of return from Marie Joelle, could only be fabricated by Veronique's imagination. Until then she had thought it wise to hold back from voicing her assumptions, lest her interference should be untimely. She chose to remain silent because she did not want to upset anyone with her too "unconventional conjectures," particularly

Veronique who was in an extremely vulnerable state of mind, and now, Clothilde as well. Oh, but how she wished she could have shared with them all those wonderful and yes, perhaps even insane ideas contemplating the return of Marie Joelle. If proven to be only chimeras of short duration, well, wouldn't they be worth the disappointment?

Thank goodness Clothilde's uneasiness was soon eclipsed by the heavenly tidings of motherhood, which allowed no time to think about strange food combination and dreams that did not make a bit of sense. There was so much to rejoice and so much to do in preparation for the blessed event.

PART IV

CHAPTER 1

"SHE HAS HER mother's beautiful brown eyes," would say one.

"But the shape of them bears a definite resemblance to Paul's," voiced another.

"Her skin is flawless, like satin, and of such transparency, she has inherited her grand mother Isabelle's beautiful complexion," stated someone else.

"Oh look at her pretty little hands! Look at her long fingers! She shall take after her grandmother Suzanne and be a gifted pianist," was stated further.

"Have you noticed how a bright spark in her facial expression already reveals an alert mind? No doubt she has been endowed with her father's keen intelligence," was quickly called to attention as well.

"The little darling smiles so readily and doesn't cry much for a baby so young, she will have her grandfather Emile's jovial disposition," was observed also.

"I could tirelessly listen to her prattle, it sounds so musical, she will sing divinely like her grandmother Madeleine," was not overlooked either.

It was even pointed out, good-humoredly of course, that at times, a suggestion of a few charming mannerisms particular to Veronique appeared in the baby's ways of communicating.

In other words, this child had it all from being fashioned so marvelously after some of everyone's most desirable attributes.

They were talking about Clothilde and Paul's little girl. As they stood by her pretty cradle adorned with folds of muslin gathered around it like a floating pink mist, she lay adorably clothed in the delightful dresses and bonnets Madeleine had knitted for her.

As a gracious gesture from Clothilde, she was named Anais in honor of Isabelle's late grandmother whom both Isabelle and Paul adored.

Anais was born during the last week of January. Ever since she had begun her life journey on this earth, she shined like a little star shedding a heavenly glow upon the heart of her family. She elicited many smiles also in the eyes of mothers who nostalgically looked at her while they remembered the days when they too bent beatifically over the crib of their own newborns. Naturally Veronique was among them, although for her not only fond reminiscences but great sorrow as well lingered into her soul. However, despite the weight of her affliction, from the moment she beheld Anais, she felt irresistibly drawn to her. The love that grief had smothered deep within her seemed to be kindled anew and warmed her heart with the most tender emotions. Assuredly, Anais was Clothilde's daughter, yet she felt compelled to love her as if she were her own. From dawn to night and from night to dawn, why was she so consumed by someone else's child? Having been entrusted as her Godmother she could only attribute this excess of attachment to the ties binding a Godmother to her Godchild. Moreover, how could she remain indifferent to the surprising amount of affection Anais displayed toward her? At a few months old, when Anais saw Veronique, invariably she would extend both arms in her direction and babble the syllables "ma ma ma." If the baby cried she would instantly stop at the sound of Veronique's voice. When she began to crawl and later walk, if Veronique was near by she would hasten to her while bubbling with joy. No wonder the dear lady was so taken with this precious little girl.

Subsequently, although it was less pronounced, Anais behaved in the same fashion when in the presence of Frederick and Phillippe upon his most recent visit.

No doubt, everyone was quite amazed and could only conjecture that all this was due to that mysterious magnetism that sometimes draws a certain soul towards another. Only Elise stood alert to what might be transpiring from this unusual attraction between Veronique and Anais. However, through good discernment, she persevered to withhold any comments concerning her own interpretation.

Due to the fondness by which she and Clothilde were bonded, Veronique was as much welcome in the role of aunt, than exclusively in the assigned function of Godmother. Therefore, after a certain amount of time had elapsed, any demonstrations of endearment between Veronique and Anais were integrated and wholeheartedly accepted as just another expression of love within Paul and Clothilde's family circle.

As time went by, no other extraordinary or even slightly unusual incidents susceptible to cause concern occurred during the first three years short of three months, of the baby's life.

From the responses to her immediate surrounding, indeed one could sense Anais was an intelligent child. Her bright, alert eyes denoted a precocious mind. Even at such young age, she seemed capable to process selectively certain impressions she received as if she sought to correlate the awareness of her budding selfhood and the outside world.

"How had they survived more than a quarter of a century estranged from each other and without her?" Paul and Clothilde wondered as they marveled at the Divine Providence that brought them together and the heavenly miracle of parenthood. Their imagination could not stretch any further to envision the possibility that a happiness greater then their own, could be reached upon this planet. Enraptured by their love, together they raised their little girl while each attended to the demands of daily responsibilities. Indeed, their life was simple, but felicitous beyond measure.

CHAPTER 2

As THE MONTH of October was ending, one night after dinner, Paul had retired in the quietness of the study to ponder for a while upon the next thoughts he wished to express concisely through his pen. Before closing the shutters of the drawing room window, Clothilde cast a last glance over the iced fishpond reflecting the frosty automn moonlight. She then sat in the armchair close to the fireplace. For a brief moment, she watched the flame dancing up the hearth, and then looked through a catalog she had recently received and would use later to chronologically document slides on the architecture of the Perigord. She was waiting for Paul. Both had planned to enjoy a cozy evening together with their daughter. The baby now three months away from her third birthday, had been amusing herself with toys spread out around the colorful Persian rug. After a short while, she interrupted her games and as she often did, climbed upon the piano stool to strike randomly a few notes on the keyboard. But on that particular evening when the brief pounding improvisations she typically liked to perform came to a close, her little right hand began to gently play what Clothilde could have sworn was part of the *Pastourelle,* the ancient folk song so special to Marie Joelle. Before Clothilde transfixed by puzzlement had the opportunity to listen further, Anais was already back on the floor, occupied with one of her dolls.

"Where did you learn that pretty music you just played on the piano, darling?" asked Clothilde thinking how absurd her question probably was.

"I don't know," the little girl mumbled absentmindedly.

Clothilde grew silent and gazed at Anais who was beginning to show signs of drowsiness.

"How ridiculous of me!" she conceded, shaking her head as one would when exasperated by someone else's stupidity. "How would a little girl not even three years old yet know of a song she has never been taught to play and obviously has never heard either? Clearly it was mere imagining from my part." She shook her head again, rose and gathered up Anais in her arms to put her to bed. She stayed by her side lulling her to sleep under the magic of the most delightful fairy tales. Soon Anais had fallen into a deep slumber with a smile on her lips. Most likely, she was already dreaming of some frolicsome adventure amid silvery elves, unicorns and pink butterflies in green meadows strewn with dainty flowers, all out of the stories she had just been told. Clothilde returned to the drawing room where soon after, Paul joined her.

The rest of the evening was spent without any other disturbances.

Even though Clothilde was essentially reconciled to the idea that she had experienced a strange moment of mental evasion caused by only God knew what, she could not rid herself from a feeling of uneasiness.

As the hours drew deeper into the night, she listened to every sound while lying down next to Paul who rested like a pure heart is only allowed to repose. Soothed by his calm breathing, she at last yielded also to a tranquil sleep.

When she awoke, the daylight filtered dimly through the patterns of the Valenciennes lace, which trimmed the curtains. The wall clock in the dining room had just chimed seven o'clock in the morning. Paul was no longer at her side. Mindful not to disturb her, he had gone out early to take care of a few winter tasks required by the land. She at once hastened to Anais' bedside. The little girl was asleep. Clothilde watched her adoringly for a moment and slipped into the hall as silently as a shadow. Vigilant to any noise, which might stir from the nursery, she went into the kitchen, poured herself a cup of freshly brewed coffee from the percolator Paul had left on for her, and stepped out on the back patio to wish Canon d'Or a fun-loving day. Quickly, she ventured to make sure that the inside of his stall was maintained at a comfortable temperature and then she adjusted his winter coat that at slipped a little to one side. Canon d'Or still busy with the rest of his breakfast Paul had given him, looked at Clothilde with a twig of alfalfa hanging out of his mouth. He neighed a couple of times then buried his head back in his trough at the bottom of which could yet be found a few scattered grains of delicious oat. Clothilde drew a deep breath as a crisp breeze swept over the barren garden except for the shivering blades of newly sprung grass asserting that nature was always in a state of renewal. She glimpsed over the countryside bathed in a translucent wintry glow, then hurried back inside, pleasantly motivated by all what she wanted to do in the course of this new day. The house seemed quiet, but naturally she had in mind to check again on Anais before pouring herself another hot cup of coffee, and then snuggle in a chair to go through the pages of a magazine on gardening, that had been left on the table. She had not yet crossed the kitchen door to enter into the house, when suddenly she withheld her breath, stiffened like an Egyptian stone statue, tilted her head and strained her left ear toward the drawing room to better discern what she was hearing. With an extraordinary effort to maintain a certain self-control, as noiseless as a ghost, she stealthily went down the hall until she reached the living room entrance and could steal a quick peek at Anais. She then stepped back and breathless she listened.

No, she was not imagining it. Yes, it was real and clear. Yes, her daughter sat at the piano accompanying herself as she gently sang the ancient *Pastourelle* Clothilde believed to have heard the previous evening. And if yet Anais spoke the french language in the infantile jargon, which fitted her age, the most distinct, the most perfect patois of the region flowed from her lips. Clothilde nearly collapsed while she leaned for support against the door jam. Once Anais had ended her incredible recital, Clothilde allowed herself a moment to regain some self-possession and approached her daughter.

"Good morning darling," she greeted with an overly cheerful voice prompted by the need to conceal her bewilderment. "Sweetheart, when did you learn ... who has taught you such a lovely song?"

"Manouche would sing it to me when I was bigger," Anais simply answered as she yawned lazily and came down from the stool.

"Manouche ... ? When you were bigger ... ?

Clothilde questioned as her legs almost gave way under her. She picked up her daughter and instantly sank in the chair near by. She overlooked the lack of logic in Anais's explanation. Under normal circumstances she would have corrected it instantly, but at that moment, she had other more pressing concerns on her mind.

"Manouche!" thereupon she exclaimed utterly baffled. "What are you talking about? Manouche was Tante Veronique's grandmother. She is gone to Heaven since very long ago, well before you were born!"

"Yes, I know," agreed Anais in a grown up tone of voice which seemed to mean, "but Maman why do you act so surprised?"

Indeed yes, her mother had valid reasons to be surprised.

"How did my child obtain the knowledge of all this?" wondered Clothilde, who had grown speechless while enfolding Anais close to her bosom.

CHAPTER 3

FOR AT LEAST five minutes, Clothilde remained in a state of shock. She clang to her daughter and motionless stared at the floor. At last, Anais showing signs of impatience plainly stating that she wished to be freed from her mother's embrace, drew Clothilde out of her stupor.

"Oh, sweetheart, forgive me!" Clothilde apologized, realizing she had detained Anais inconsiderately too long. She got up and stood the little girl on the floor.

"Come along, let's have breakfast, just you and I. Papa has already left to work on the farm," she said in a feigned carefree manner. Hand in hand, they both walked to the kitchen. Clothilde driven by the urgent need to seek counsel with Paul, used every single minute to ready herself and Anais; for this time without the least doubt, she had witnessed a strange phenomenon.

Although she looked for Paul everywhere about the fields, she was unable to find him. She assumed he had gone on some errand; consequently she gave up her search and instead of returning home drove on to *la Brisante*. There she found her grandmother alone who at that moment was energetically polishing the ancient bronze gong fixed on the entrance door. Emile had gone to the town hall, and Suzanne was at the public school.

Upon Clothilde's arrival, Madeleine instantly ceased her work, took off the rubber gloves she wore and with a bright smile hurried down the few steps of the front porch. Anais rushed in her open arms and after a profusion of kisses and cheerful giggles, Madeleine examined Clothilde more closely before they began to walk toward the house.

"You seem anxious and look a little pale, do you feel quite well dear?"

"I am fine Grandmaman," Clothilde answered with a finger in front of her pursed lips to convey that she did not wish to elaborate on that matter in front of Anais who conveniently at that moment watched a flight of wild geese passing above them. Madeleine understood. Hopeful that nothing serious troubled Clothilde, she took her hand and beckoned Anais.

"Now we shall have tea and since maman told me you have been a very, very good girl, you may have some of the apple tarts Grandmaman Suzanne has baked specially for you.

They enjoyed tea in the kitchen near a large window, which opened on the back patio where Anais had soon gone to play with her imaginary friends she liked to invite along when spending time at *the Brisante*.

"Please do tell me what bothers you?" Madeleine inquired, when she and Clothilde were able to talk freely.

At once, Clothilde related all about Anais having mysteriously learnt the old *Pastourelle* Marie joelle used to sing, through a channel that defied the presumed laws by which the human brain acquires knowledge.

"Oh, my!" burst out Madeleine after she had listened to Clothilde while partly holding each breath. She then shook her head from side to side indicating perplexity.

"I don't know what to think, except that Anais obviously must have heard the song from someone."

"From whom, Grandmaman?" Clothilde questioned with exasperation in her voice, "from whom? certainly not from any of us, and certainly not from Veronique; the poor lady would not survive the emotional distress caused by the memory of it. Moreover, how could she possibly know about Manouche? And how can she so fluently recite the lyric in such perfect patois when she is yet incapable to build and articulate correctly one complete sentence in French?"

Meanwhile, Anais happily entertained herself outside by the back door. For a moment Madeleine's gaze followed the dainty gestures the child mimicked so well to imitate those of adults.

"She acts so mature for her age," Madeleine observed. For a moment she questioned if perhaps Anais had received the gift of a spiritualistic medium, and Manouche sang the *Pastourelle* through her to convey some kind of message. But she soon rejected the idea. It didn't quite sound right. She then thoughtfully turned to Clothilde.

"Indeed, all this makes one wonder."

Neither Clothilde nor Madeleine were able to find an answer to ease their baffled mind. for

Upon leaving *la Brisante*, Clothilde did not pursue her search for Paul. She and Elise had a busy agenda planned at the museum the afternoon, Isabelle would be arriving soon to baby sit Anais, therefore she directly went back to *la Buissoniere* to take care of the most immediate necessities before leaving. She was washing her daughter's hands and face, which had been besmeared by the stewed apples she had for desert when she heard a car stop in front of the house. She reckoned it was Isabelle, but to her pleasant surprise, Paul appeared, having decided to come home for lunch as he occasionally did when spending the day outdoors. After Anais had been allowed to greet her father, she was asked to go and play in the nursery, "so Maman and Papa could discuss grown up matters of no interest to little girls."

Paul took a quick lunch, sat in the drawing room to enjoy a cup of coffee and listened to Clothilde fretfully describing Anais' eventful activities. Of course he was soon led to deduct that even if the child had received some details about Marie Joelle's life, it certainly would not explain how she obtained her extraordinary knowledge of the song in its original dialect, and her ability to play it spontaneously on the piano. Paul then exposed very basically to Clothilde, a certain phenomenon by which apparently, memories collected by an ancestor can be transferred through genes to some of his or her descendants. But since it could be attested by Clothilde that Anais and Marie Joelle even remotely, were not descendants from the same bloodline such supposition was also eliminated.

"A certain theory could perhaps validate a case of paranormal manifestation. It expounds that the very sensitive brain of a child can draw some knowledge from the recollections of others, by simply being receptive to their thoughts. A form of psychic perception so to speak, although it is quite debatable," Paul finally concluded as the sole offhand explanation he could give at the moment for Anais' truly mystifying abilities.

"You mean, our daughter would then be a ... a clairvoyant?" Clothilde panic-stricken, at once inquired, thinking about the quaintness that surrounded Amelie, the seer mentioned by Madeleine.

"No, I am speaking of a certain telepathic susceptibility supposedly possible in very young children, but which eventually disappears as they grow older," he reassured with a smile not wanting to alarm Clothilde even more. But he went back to work with a puzzled mind, unsure of what to think about this truly astonishing account of Anais' accomplishment. From then on, he watched her closely in case she should repeat a similar behavior.

To Clothilde, all this explaining sounded like the obscure jargon of an occult science. However since she could not prove otherwise, and since it had been formulated by Paul, she was disposed to accept the probability of thoughts transference, which hopefully would be temporary. As soon as Paul had left the house to spend a few more hours outside, Clothilde immediately phoned her grandmother. She was eager to inform her about what she had gathered from Paul.

"Oh!" Madeleine uttered in wonderment, after having asked Clothilde to repeat a few times what she at last had come to understand. "Oh, it is absolutely amazing! Life conceals so many mysteries to be yet fathomed!"

When Elise was told about Anais' staggering recollection, she did not react by being so presumptuous as to openly challenge whatever Paul would suggest regarding some probable causes behind it. All the same, she was compelled to sense that it was the manifestation of "something else, something much more awe inspiring than Anais being endowed with a memory unrelated to her own experience

CHAPTER 4

ONCE AGAIN, LIFE settled down at *la Buissoniere*. Anais' genes were on their best behavior, thus allowing everyone's daily activities to resume normally. As a result, Clothilde was able to enjoy a very productive life. Body and soul she gave herself wholly to her yet new roles of wife, mother and very efficient curator of a quite successful museum. However, Elise very subtly but quite attentively was watching for any signs that might reinforce her speculations on what had provoked Anais' knowledge of the *Pastourelle*.

The beginning of summer gave occasion to an irrepressible exhilaration that seized the entire village. Indeed, there was a good reason to be overjoyed, for Phillippe at last was a seminarian graduate in Divinity and ready to be a pastor of souls. As wished by his family, by Clothilde and by everyone else, including all the inhabitants of Grolejac, on the first Sunday of July, the holy orders were conferred upon him in the village medieval church. Naturally, his uncle Aristide and his aunt Celine didn't disregard to partake in this very special event.

It was an unforgettable moment for all those who witnessed the sacrament.

When Phillippe lay prostrate to be ordained, everyone joined to pray aloud the litany of the Saints. The bishop of the diocese had come to Grolejac to administer specially the rites of consecration.

Once Phillippe had been anointed and the Eucharist had been

celebrated, the ceremony was extolled to a glorious finale when Madeleine and Father Vernier sang in a superb duo the "Ave Maria" by C. H. Gounod.

Veronique and Frederick in a state of Euphoria were transported to dimensions which they thought must be very seldom reached by common mortals.

Clothilde's eyes were never tearless and when Phillippe gazed at her, his soul embraced hers with the most profound love.

But alas, those very special moments were too brief.

Only two days after his ordination, Phillippe was summoned to Brittany where he had already received charge of a parish.

During his sojourn of a week at Grolejac, Anais showed a particularly strong attraction toward him, almost a fascination. His departure inexplicably affected her with a sadness unusually pronounced for a child so young and quite at odd with the circumstances. However, knowing that Anais was of a very sensitive, affectionate nature dispelled any cause for great worry except to make sure she was vigilantly consoled. Accordingly, her grief soon gave way to a more cheerful mood, and again life returned to a normal routine while summer went by.

At the onset of Automn, Anais then about a little over three and a half years old entered a strange rebellious stage. She would express strange complains such as feeling too small or not liking to be treated like a baby. At times, she would respond angrily to the least refusal of her wishes, which seemed to prompt her into sporadic explosions of temper tantrums difficult to subdue. On occasions, she would display a certain irritability without having been provoked or conversely she would slip into periods of an even-tempered disposition during which she would be often found gazing into space with a smile as if pleasantly daydreaming. Now and then also, she would curiously stare at someone, and make remarks concerning a change, which had happened a certain amount of time before she was born. For instance one day in that manner she asked Elise "why did you cut your hair? Elise had worn her hair long but had it cut short quite a while before Anais' birth.

Meanwhile, she had developed besides, the new fancy to often call her parents by their first name.

"Clothilde, may I have a cookie?" Or, "Clothilde, come see!" she would voice to draw her mother's attention and so forth.

Consequently, she behaved likewise toward her father.

"Ah, here is Paul!" she would inform her doll, upon hearing her father come home.

With insistence she was reminded that children address their parents respectively by "Maman" and "Papa," but all in vain.

One morning, while a torrential rain pelted against the windowpanes, Clothilde had decided to spend the day indoors at *la Buissoniere*. It was the perfect weather that would allow compensating for the neglect the household had suffered because of the seasonal demands required by the museum, which after summer had ended, was open only three afternoons a week. It was not quite nine o'clock yet, therefore relatively early. Paul had retired in the study where plenty of work waited for him as well. Clothilde having already cleaned and put away the breakfast dishes, assisted by Anais of course, had in mind to dust and polish the dining room furniture. Then she would restore to its original glitter the pretty glassware displayed in a delicately chiseled rosewood buffet, which had belonged to Madeleine's great grandmother. With Anais along behind her, Clothilde went in the pantry to gather glass cleaner, buffing cloth and furniture polish. Before Anais could enter the little room, Clothilde pushed the door ajar to fetch a feather duster, which hung on the back of it.

"Clothilde!" cried out Anais, while anxiously shaking the doorknob, "I want in! I want in!"

Cothilde sighed, stepped out and not knowing what to say any more, stared at her daughter.

"Anais!" she at last admonished, clearly out of patience, "Papa and I have reminded you time and time again and once more only a short while ago at breakfast, that children do not address their parents by their first name, have you already forgotten?"

"No," replied Anais.

"Then, why do you persist in doing so?" Clothilde questioned, baffled by the child's undaunted composure.

"I don't know!" hastened to say Anais. She saucily bypassed her mother to enter the pantry and reached for a bottle filled with water that was used to spray the houseplants.

"Put this back darling, we have no need for it at this moment," requested Clothilde with outer calm, though rather exasperated by Anais' conduct. Anais sent forth a spurt of water over the kitchen hutch next to her, clearly under the impulse of a spiteful intent.

"Anais, no!" urged Clothilde, grasping the bottle. "No! One does not spray water on furniture!"

Thereupon, the little girl capriciously stomped her right foot, threw the water bottle on the floor and ran away from Clothilde.

"You are not my mother anyway. You can't tell me what to do, you are not my mother!"

"Stop that nonsense, and come back here immediately," demanded Clothilde going after Anais across the kitchen.

She took hold of the girl's hand and led her to an armchair in front of the hearth where they sat. Clothilde lifted Anais' face to search into her eyes.

"What is the matter darling? Please do tell Maman what annoys you. All Mamans wish to help their little daughters with the occasional upsets of growing up."

"But you are not my mother," Anais repeated with a chilling aplomb.

"Well sweetheart, who then is your mother? We all must have a mother in order to be born."

"I won't tell," defied Anais.

For an instant, Clothilde out of desperation, almost screamed for Paul to hurry down and rescue her from this madness; but she restrained herself even though she felt rather inefficient. To disturb him from his work would have been most inconsiderate, and what was the matter with her, was she incapable to discipline her own daughter?

"Papa told me Tante Veronique is my mother," Anais consented to disclose, while maintaining a vexed expression.

Baffled, Clothilde frowned and grinned all at once.

"Tante Veronique? Papa told you Tante Veronique is your mother?"

Anais nodded a few times.

Papa told me she is my "Godmother." He told me that a Marraine is a "Godmother" That means she is my real mother because she comes from God, only real things come from God."

Clothilde broke into a sudden laughter at the little girl's uncommon logic.

"Oh, my darling! Listen sweetheart," she thereupon endeavored to explain drawing Anais close to her.

"Papa was simply teaching you, as part of the English lessons he gives you every day, that "Godmother" is the English translation of the french word "marraine." A Marraine or Godmother like Tante Veronique is appointed to oversee the welfare of a child, would the real maman for some reason or another be unavailable. The same applies to a "God father" which means parrrain in French. Uncle Jean Luc is your Godfather, therefore your Parrain, but he is not your Papa. Do you understand?"

"Oh!" uttered Anais as though coming out of a trance and not quite knowing what to think.

"Clothilde, I am sorry," she then apologized in a meek voice. Like a candid cherub, she raised her eyes to gaze at her mother's while she seemed trying to read forgiveness in them.

Clothilde renewed her embrace and silently held Anais close to her for a while.

"There is something clearly abnormal with my daughter," she concluded as tears glistened on her eyelashes.

CHAPTER 5

Paul was not too disturbed concerning Anais' conduct. He smiled understandingly, not believing that there was anything markedly abnormal about it for a little girl of that age with such a precocious intelligence and gifted with such a fertile imagination. However, due to his sensitive position as her father, he was quite aware that his opinion could not be immune to any bias and since the incident of the *Pastourelle,* he had not neglected to be watchful of Anais' activities, taking note of the slightest oddities in her comportment and never disregarding even the least of her caprices.

Again, Elise had a different view on those issues, but could she middle in Paul and Clothilde's life? Could she interfere in the way they were parenting their daughter?

Once more, life at *la Buissoniere* entered a period of tranquility but it was meant to be of short duration. In the beginning of March of the following year, a rekindling of the child's peculiarities finally culminated to their most extraordinary manifestations.

One evening, after dinner, Clothilde, Anais, Elise and a mutual friend Rachel with her nearly five-year-old daughter Bernice had gathered on the back patio at *la Buissoniere,* delighting Canon d'Or with their company. At this time of the year, the days had grown a little longer and the weather already invited to outdoors pleasure. Late in the afternoon, a light rain had briefly splattered the ground, and then had suddenly ceased. In the sky, the sun's rays dancing upon the raindrops had formed a grandiose rainbow, which Anais wanted to catch and twist into a pretty jumping rope. A mild breeze carried the fresh chlorophyll scents from the moist grass. In the pasture, the gentle bleating of sheep mingled with the merry twittering of tiny birds hopping around in the bushes. A pink glimmer that gradually seeped through a violet mist over the distant hills announced the twilight.

Anais and Bernice at first amused themselves by making cartwheels around the lawn or improvised other games. Finally, they decided to calm down and play "mothers" while strolling with their dolls in cute baby carriages. Occasionally, Clothilde and her friends smiled tenderly and interrupted their conversations to overhear the girls' delightful chatter. At one of such moments, Anais leaned toward Bernice's doll.

"Bernice dear, what's the name of your beautiful baby girl?" she inquired with an expression of great admiration.

"Olivia," Bernice replied, affecting the bearing of a proud mother, "and Anais, what is your baby's name?"

"My baby is a boy, I call him Phillippe, because once in real life, I had a brother I loved very much and his name was Phillippe. I was told he said Mass when he was little because he wanted to be Pope," Anais mentioned, very matter-of-fact like.

"Oh, how lovely!" acquiesced Bernice with feigned enthusiasm. "But Anais, I didn't know you had a brother in real life," she added acting surprised.

"It was a very long time ago. Oh, and you can call me Marie Joelle. Everybody calls me Anais, but my real name is Marie Joelle," Anais insisted affecting a prim and over-confident stance.

"All right," Bernice assented good-naturedly, though she gazed at Anais as if a bit puzzled by her little friend's somewhat far-fetched imagination, not quite sure if Anais was playing or if she was serious.

Clothilde, Elise and Rachel looked at each other speechless. However, Elise no less than awe struck and breathless, managed to restrain a certain triumphant expression. "Dear God!" she mused contemplatively, "my presentiments might gradually prove to be well founded!"

"Anais!" Clothilde was able to barely articulate, "come here at once!"

Anais ran to her mother and inquisitively stopped in front of her, wondering why she had been summoned so abruptly. Clothilde looked at her utterly dazed.

"Darling, what did you just tell Bernice?"

Anais turned toward her playmate as if she sought help to recall what exactly she had told her.

"What did you say your name is?" Clothilde impatiently questioned further.

Anais, then, capable to rely on her own memory, looked at her mother assertively.

"Marie Joelle."

When Elise parted from everyone, she could not go home and find rest. Unable to contain her exultation, she hurried to *la Madrigale* to confide in Jean Luc that Anais had finally given enough reasons for one to strongly suppose that she might be Marie Joelle reincarnated. He had always lent a compliant ear when Elise would discourse on the rebirth of souls. Not that he believed in it himself, but sometimes, he found the subject quite fascinating. However, Jean Luc on that particular evening, readily found that Elise made as much sense as any other implications concerning the enigma surrounding Anais.

Because of such momentous development, Veronique was beside herself.

"Oh! Imagine!" she would exclaim in wonderment. Oh! Imagine, may be my Marie Joelle has come back! Haven't I told you I was not dreaming up things when I heard her say, *"don't cry mother, I shall return?"*

From that very moment, Anais remained unswerving with her claim. For Clothilde, for those close to her, for the neighbors, for the inhabitants of Grolejac and for many others far beyond, a profound and irrevocable change took place. Would she answer to "Anais" was only because she considered it like a second name to which she had grown accustomed. This quasi-double identity at times, gave the impression to cause her a certain disorientation, which naturally was worrisome.

CHAPTER 6

IMMEDIATELY, A FAMILY meeting in the intention to contrive some rational insight into Anais' uncanny behavior was summoned to take place at the Brisante. Veronique and Charles naturally were asked to participate, Father Vernier was present as well. Whereupon Clothilde, because of her Catholic upbringing and of a certain susceptibility to superstitions, voiced her terrifying fear that Anais might be possessed. Could the devil have implanted the ghost of Marie Joelle in her daughter? Thank goodness, Father Vernier assured her that Anais manifested no indication that could justify such dread and rejected all request for exorcism.

Anais was the object of intense scrutiny. The entire spectrum of possible mental illnesses was cast upon her such as Schizophrenia, split personality, multiple personalities and what more. Even a brain tumor was considered.

Paul having had the opportunity to observe his daughter closely with enough certainty, could refute the suspicion of those psychological disorders or tumor. Moreover, the identification with Marie Joelle, the memory of the *Pastourelle*, the fluency of the dialect would not be symptomatic of any such conditions and though he could even think of a hundred other abnormalities in addition to those already mentioned, none would fit either. However, would he have had even the slightest opinion about a diagnostic, by virtue of his scientific training and professional ethic, he would not have ventured into any rash, unverified conclusions. But truly he had to concede he was as baffled as anyone else was, and specified the necessity that he should entrust Anais to the most proficient specialists in that field.

When the conference ended, they all looked at each other more confused than ever. The only person who felt less troubled was Elise, for what she had already perceived seemed to become more and more elucidated by Anais herself, and quite eloquently. However, she surely didn't wish to cause Clothilde more anxiety than what she was already coping with. Besides, as if she didn't wish to adulterate a sacred anticipation by exposing its content to the uninitiated or to the skeptical, she protectively kept her outlook on the situation to herself. She had faith that through so much disclosure and cooperation from Anais, in good time the truth should surface to be ultimately recognized, and she was so won over by what that truth might be!

Paul not wanting to waste any more time upon sterile inferences, forthwith, requested an appointment with Doctor Caudoing, the traditional family physician, to determine the condition of Anais' physical health. In this area, it was concluded there was a total absence of disease. The child was growing beautifully. In the course of this examination, the doctor again took notice of a perplexing mark on Anais' knee. It looked like some persistent scar, which had appeared at birth without anyone ever knowing what had caused it.

"I am still wondering what has happened here?" The intrigued doctor questioned.

Until then, Anais because of her very young age had been unable to deliver her own explanation for it. However, at that particular time, she pointed to her knee.

"You mean this?" she asked somewhat nonchalantly.

"Yes, this?" specified the kind doctor.

"Oh, I fell from my mother's bicycle and cut myself on a piece of glass."

"You did?" pursued the doctor much surprised at Anais' unexpected answer. "But dear child, you don't ride a grown up bicycle yet, do you?"

"Oh no, not now," replied Anais, "but when I used to before."

Doctor Caudoing amused by the child quite resourceful imagination, smiled at her and taking into account the purpose of the consultation, pertinently recorded this peculiar conversation in her chart.

A psychiatric evaluation was next conducted. Here also, the result was wonderfully sound, with clear indication of a very precocious intelligence, as Madeleine and Paul had already perceived. Indeed, all this was very encouraging, but then why did Anais continue to switch intermittently into an estranged persona? Why did she show unpredictable and extreme reactions to certain stimuli, which in comparison affected everyone else more moderately, if any at all. For instance, why did she so nervously avoid walking near the deepest water of the fishpond? Or why did she bemoan to her psychologist, Doctor Lonjac, in a voice that sounded older than her own did? "I feel so, so lonely, I have no friends who care to hear me when I say I am Marie Joelle, except Papa who at times lets me talk about it, but I don't think he really believes me. Aunt Elise seems more interested, it is probably because she wants to be nice to me. Maman thinks I am strange. I wish I was not so small, when I was grown up they listened to me more." undeniably there was some defect in her ability to gather facts chronologically.

Meanwhile Paul had been in conference discussing his daughter's condition, with two of his professional colleagues in the United States, Doctor Thorpane and Doctor Saloric, both Children psychiatrists. In their practice, through hypnotism, they induced a regression reaching far beyond the patient's present lifetime, into supposedly past lives. They reported astonishing revelations from their young patients who, through this technique not only had supposedly reenacted prior lives but also had been relieved from disorders recalcitrant to other more conventional methods. Even children no older than Anais had successfully responded to this procedure. Although Paul was familiar with such undertakings, up to then he had remained loyal to means that were more conventional. But under the circumstances, his friend's new approach was becoming very appealing.

Moreover, Doctor Saloric was dedicating a good part of his work to additional investigations concerning children who manifested behaviors implicating a rebirth from a person who was no longer of this earth at the time of their own birth. The outcome from inquiries conducted to verify the authenticity of their stories, were sometimes staggering. Given that he and Doctor Thorpane worked as a team and spoke french fairly well, they readily volunteered their assistance to Paul by offering to meet with him in Grolejac. Indeed, they could not think of a better arrangement to observe and test Anais, than in her habitual environment while causing the least disturbance to her daily pattern of activities.

When Doctor Lonjac informed Paul, he had never dealt with a case as bewildering as Anais and told of her complains, Paul at last considered to summon his friends for help.

Needless to mention, the whole concept threw Clothilde in a severe trauma at the thought that her husband could accept such an idea. "This was stepping into the heathen's world," she protested. Paul stood firm against her objections. Clothilde, finally too spent from arguing, finally yielded to his wishes. The rest of the family not so enthusiastic either about having Anais put through such an unconventional examination, being also exhausted from weariness, was ultimately persuaded as well. Thereupon everyone reached an agreement that after all, different initiatives despite how desperate or inconclusive they might prove to be, were well worth the risk to be introduced in the objective to not overlook a single chance for answers.

Elise overjoyed by the resolution, was eagerly prepared to give her unconditional cooperation.

Upon Paul's request, Doctor Thorpane and Doctor Saloric with great anticipation confirmed their readiness to assist. Accordingly, preparations were made for them to arrive at the beginning of April and stay in Grolejac for a month at least or longer if necessary.

As soon as that decision was taken, not understanding why, a feeling of order and relief began to prevail.

CHAPTER 7

To CREATE A propitious ambiance and eliminate any inhibition, which strangers could cause in Anais' comportment, Doctor Thorpane and Doctor Saloric were presented to her as friends of the family who like many others, sometimes came to spend their vacation in Grolejac. One could have thought that the child subconsciously was determined to plead her case. For, immediately after their arrival she manifested signs consistent with the concepts of reincarnation with inconceivable abundance, either spontaneously or randomly by provocation intended to awaken memories.

When introduced to Doctor Thorpane and Doctor Saloric, it was preplanned that Clothilde and Paul would refer to Anais as simply "their daughter." They deliberately allowed further inquiry about her name, and in so doing, give her the opportunity to identify herself according to her own sense of who she believed to be.

"What is your name?" Doctor Thorpane asked amiably.

"Marie Joelle," answered Anais, with perfect confidence, "but they call me Anais," she added looking up at her parents.

The next afternoon, Anais was taken to a house on a hill at the west part of Grolejac, where Marie Joelle had grown with her parents and Phillippe. The property had been sold after Marie Joelle's fatal accident and since then had never been visited again.

As they reached the front of the house, they intentionally drove slower while they closely watched for Anais' response. From their experience with past life recollections surely if Anais was Marie Joelle, she should express some sort of reaction.

"Stop! Stop!" she cried out when the front facade appeared to her from amid a semi circle of trees at the end of the driveway.

"What is it, darling?" inquired Doctor Thorpane who immediately guessed what was happening and thereupon wished to stimulate a further response.

"My house! My house! Stop! I want to see my house!" Anais insisted. "Clothilde! remember when I used to live here?" she then called to attention as she most candidly turned to her mother.

Discretely, everyone exchanged a furtive glance, which could not dissimulate wonderment.

The new owners naturally having been advised of this experimental visit graciously received the group. Anais had barely entered the hallway when she began to rush directly in direction of Marie Joelle's former bedroom.

"Mine! My other bedroom! Oh!" She exclaimed with awe as if she had found a long lost object from her childhood, which suddenly evoked the most tender memories. She entered the room and looked around; giving the impression of being surprised as she noticed the changes. She stepped back into the hall; wandered about a little, then stood in front of a door which she timidly pushed ajar. She pointed to the inside with a frown, apparently uncertain that her remembrance was accurate.

"Phillippe's bedroom?" she questioned.

"Yes sweetheart, once this was Phillippe's bedroom," gently reassured Clothilde who at this point was fully subjugated by the disclosure she witnessed. With repressed tears, she picked up Anais and held her in a close embrace, while sensing she was not alone having difficulty to master her emotions.

"Fanfan?" Anais called on an impulse. Her gaze searched the house then the front garden as they walked outside.

Fanfan was Marie Joelle's beloved Brittany Spaniel.

"Fanfan is gone to heaven long ago, darling," Clothilde explained, kissing her daughter forehead.

"Oh, yes Fanfan is in Heaven," Anais echoed, as though she suddenly realized it. She insisted to be put down and thereupon dashed downhill in direction of an old elm tree which leaned over a rivulet. There, next to its writhed trunk, was a large white rock under which Fanfan had been laid to rest a short while before Marie Joelle's departure from this world. Anais stopped next to it.

"Fanfan?" again she questioned, apparently seized by some kind of intense confusion. Aware that an increase of emotional burden weighed upon the child and her entire family, it was therefore decided that all tests be ceased for the remaining of the day.

When Veronique was informed about Anais's familiarity with their old house and her recollection of Fanfan, she broke into irrepressible sobs mixed with laughter at the thought that perhaps her Marie Joelle indeed had returned. She was given some medical attention to calm her agitation.

The next morning, as the investigation was resumed, another persuasive incident was witnessed while everyone took a walk along the bank of the Dordogne.

The frothy water of the river was still high and muddy from the flood caused by the winter rain. The beaches mottled by greenish lichen creeping over the white pebbles, were slowly expanding. As the group began to stroll along the shores, Anais grew restless. It could have been occasioned by the baleful appearance of the river. But upon moving onward, she showed a significant level of mounting distress. When they reached the area in front of the *Chambre* where she had never been taken before and where Marie Joelle had drowned, Anais abruptly broke into a fit of uncontainable panic. She pulled at Paul's clothes; begged to be held; screamed.

"No! No! Papa, no! No more! she pleaded. Then she fainted. She was soon revived and her father gently carried her back to the car. Clothilde watched her little girl being thus huddled in Paul's arms as he walked along the Dordogne. At once the dream she had about the child she and Paul had found amid the reeds by the river, came back to her mind. She thought Anais looked like her.

"Didn't Elise tell her long ago, that sometimes when a loved one is ready to reincarnate, dreams such as these sometimes occur to announce his or her imminent rebirth on this earth?"

"Oh! So much is happening! So very much!" Clothilde mused. "Is it possible? Is it really possible that Marie Joelle has returned to us as my daughter?" she now herself wondered. "Is it possible that God includes also the soul of His creatures in the universal principle of constant renewal and rebirth? Oh, Elise, my dear friend, my sister! How unfair I have been to rebuke your utterances." She went to put her arms around Elise's shoulders. They both tacitly understood each other's thoughts.

As the evaluation continued after a day of respite, Anais was purposely set apart and was asked very matter-of-factly.

"What is your mother's name? I have completely forgotten, feigned Dr. Saloric."

"Veronique," she answered without the slightest hesitation, "but do not tell Clothilde because she thinks she is my mother."

Thereupon, there was an element of inexplicable discrepancy as a result of a similar question concerning her father to which her reply was "Paul"

It was verified and proven that indeed, upon learning to ride her mother's bicycle, Marie Joelle had fallen and had cut her right knee. However, a flaw transpired when Anais, tested concerning her scar, failed to distinguish which, between two old bicycles still existing in Veronique's garage, was ridden by Marie Joelle at the time of the fall.

A relevant explanation was given about wounds, which often show up again when the entity reincarnates too soon subsequently to the life during which the injuries have taken place. However Anais not having related to the bicycle was a very acceptable gap of memory, which did not negate her identity assertions. The child's brain had been subjected to a lot of stress within the recent days and understandably was likely to fall short of accurate perceptions at times.

Once more when Anais was shown a picture of Marie joelle, she didn't associate in any way with it. There again it was pointed out that this incongruity did not disprove all other inferences, for Anais was still at an age when it would have been quite difficult to construct accurate memories from a photographic representation of supposedly herself in a past life. Yet the little girl amazed everyone by her effortless identification of people she was acquainted with for the first time, but who Marie Joelle had known.

One of her most staggering reactions was, when Phillippe came home for a weekend, after an absence of six months. Upon seeing him, she spontaneously exclaimed in an adult like manner:

"Oh, Phillippe, my dear brother, how good it is to see you!"

Was she simply echoing Jean Luc who always called Phillippe his brother or had she really recognized a brother?

CHAPTER 8

If CONSIDERED FROM the viewpoint of one who believed in rebirth, it was encouraging to observe at length that indeed Anais demonstrated many signs implicating a reincarnation from a previous life. However, in quest of further determinants, which might prove to be consistent or perhaps inconsistent with the previous tests, hypnotism was then considered, from which astonishing results emerged.

Invariably and repeatedly at the onset of each session, Anais at once regressed beyond the time of her birth and went through a noticeable change as she gradually slipped into Marie Joelle's identity. She then spoke like Marie Joelle, while accurately relating certain descriptions of her life as such, never swerving from the accounts she repeatedly stated.

She revealed how "*she had left this world.*" To use her own terms.

"*It was in the afternoon, at the end of August,*" she correctly recounted. "*She and two friends were in a canoe rowing upstream on the Dordogne, when a thunderstorm broke. Consequently they turned around to hurry back home, but in no time the lightning and thunder had moved over their head while a torrential rain ripped the sky open. An uprooted tree struck by a shaft of lightning, then hauled away by the strong currents, blocked their way. They became entangled in its roots and branches, and were themselves taken adrift. They crashed below the Chambre, where the canoe, caught*

in a whirlpool, capsized. Having lost complete control, they were fatally
swallowed by a powerful water vortex."

Anais explained, "So long she remained conscious of still being fastened
to the earth, she felt terrified; helpless. But after a seemingly short transition
of absolute nothingness, she entered an enchanting immensity strewn with
jade green trees, flowers of unimaginable colors and crystalline brooks
meandering in luxuriant meadows. People garbed in white, pink and
azure robes wandered amid peaceful animals. All was bathed in a golden
light and a sweet scent that gave the impression to be glorious music as
well. Then great Grandpapa Justin, great Grandmaman Manouche and
Fanfan appeared. Manouche and great Grandpapa, both brimming with
happiness, extended their arms to Anais. Fanfan jubilantly followed, her
barking communicated her immeasurable joy and affection as clearly as if
she had expressed herself in words. They all embraced, and then they sat
under a fragrant tree in pink blossoms glittering like Rhine stones. "Oh! it
was so beautiful! so very beautiful!" Anais stressed. "After an indefinite
amount of time, great Grandpapa Justin, who was now a guide, led her
away into the vastness for an educational journey while meeting with many
counselors. Overall, they taught on the merits of love as being the rightful
foundation for a rewarding life. Following her return, she joined Manouche
and fanfan in assisting the lonely souls having no one to welcome them upon
their arrival in the beyond.

However, Marie Joelle knew that soon she would duly return to
earth, where certain issues in the process of being resolved, required her
participation. She wanted great Grandpapa Justin, Manouche and Fanfan
to come along with her. She was told they were not ready yet, but not to be
sad, for their love shall bring them together over and over again."

Regardless of the hypnotist's perseverance to probe deeper into
Anais's psyche, Anais never gave more than those information about
her visit in the hereafter, as if all other memories had been erased, or
if for some mysterious reasons she wished to keep them concealed.
Accordingly, when she clearly persisted in remaining mute under
further questioning, she was guided back to the present reality having
no recollection of what she had revealed.

Following Anais' regression, it seemed mandatory to examine
Veronique through the same process in quest of similarities in their
disclosures. However at that time Veronique being too distressed by

Anais' saga, was in no condition to take part in any kind of test. Therefore, her cooperation was postponed until later on.

In the meantime, Paul, fascinated by his colleagues' hypnotic technique and by their uncanny ability to venture so directly into the mind of someone as complex as Anais, readily persuaded Clothilde to undergo such experiment along with him. He was curious to find out if their stories would be alike and would lay bare the reasons why they had been so spontaneously and so irresistibly attracted to one another. He hoped it might also explain those extraordinary deja-vus he had experienced upon his initial visit at *la Brisante*. Consequently, as he and Clothilde without difficulty regressed into what assumedly was their most recent past life, finally it all appeared to make sense. They unknowingly exposed an identical narration about their relationship as well as about the karmic triumvirate they formed with Phillippe. Both communicated that in that previous life, Clothilde was married to Paul {then residing in France} but fell infatuated with Phillippe who at that time was an ordained catholic priest. Clothilde left Paul to elope with him. As a result he was defrocked and excommunicated from the church. After sometime, Clothilde tormented by remorse, left Phillippe and entered the convent to take the veil. Phillippe, though somewhat contrite also, was never motivated to do penitence. Instead of moving on to nobler purposes, he went from one romantic liaison to another in an attempt to escape his haunted conscience and to console himself, unmindful about a child he conceived in the course of those transient attachments.

Paul, heart broken, never married again. From then on, he led an exemplary life channeling is grief into work as a doctor also.

For one who believed in reincarnation, it was quite self explanatory that consistent with the fundamental principles of such theory, the three of them were brought together again in this present existence, to interplay in roles predetermined by the law of fair retribution and return. They were also given the opportunity to rise above their past wrongdoings as a test to grow spiritually. Now driven by as sense of need for atonement, Phillippe was compelled to surrender his love for Clothilde and embrace anew the holy vows he had so irresponsibly forfeited. He knew subconsciously that it was the best for both of them, in spite of all appearances. Clothilde subjected to abandonment was coerced in a situation to expiate for having forsaken Paul. Given that she had admitted to have become way too begot, prejudiced, sanctimonious and self righteous when being a nun, obviously she was expected to do away with such reprehensible attitude and practice more indulgence, particularly in judgment of religious creeds different than hers. In other words, she needed to become a better Christian. Therefore, to be taught a more pliant acceptance of other's spiritual tenets, could it be the reason why she was exposed to Elise and Anais?

It seemed clear, that neither distance nor any other circumstances prevented Paul to fulfill his destiny and reap his restitution. Therefore, as a result of having grown instead of having regressed, he was reunited with his beloved. Moreover, if viewed from this set of circumstances, it could have been easy to gather that the deja-vus in question were nothing other than elusive reminiscences of visits he paid at *la Brisante*, when he courted Clothilde. She resided there also in their former earthly life.

Veronique having recovered a certain calm, and now almost anxious to learn why she had been deserving of such a sad lot in that present existence, at last was ready to comply. Doctor Thorpane was pleasantly surprised, when without any difficulty she responded to hypnotism and almost immediately entered into age regression. As if her burden had become too heavy to bear, she openly acknowledged in a whirlwind of poignant sadness, sobs and remorse, that she had aborted a child in a recent past life. Next, quite unexpectedly, something very strange happened. Her emotional distress suddenly stopped as if she had been relieved by her confession, and after a short pause, she drifted into a state much like a mediumistic semi-consciousness. Then bypassing the guidance and questions of Doctor Thorpane, she moved forward to channel insightfully a flow of information relating to the current researches in progress. She stated that she and Marie Joelle, for very specific reasons, had steadily been involved with each other in the course of many former passages in this world. In addition, she explained that Marie Joelle had been introduced in the sequence of those recent events, to play simultaneously the twofold role of a teacher and a chastised apprentice. For, she brought to light that Marie Joelle had been removed from her to awaken the recognition that life is sacred at any stage after the time of conception and had been taken away from Phillippe to remind him that we must not fail to care dutifully for our offspring as he had neglected to fulfill. A desertion that had ricochet on him, by loosing a sister in this life. However, it surfaced too, that conversely Marie Joelle in her last earthly existence had committed suicide. For that reason, she was put through the test of having to learn that to take one's life is as iniquitous as taking the life of another. Therefore, the multi-functions of her drowning.

The justification for Marie Joelle's rebirth as Clothide's child remained unspecified. However, given that Veronique since long ago had become barren, whatever the reason was for them coming together once more, apparently did not require the renewal of their former mother and daughter relationship.

When Veronique came out of her trance, she had no recollection of what she had told and was baffled by her disclosures.

CHAPTER 9

WHEN DOCTOR THORPANE and Doctor Saloric, left Grolejac, reincarnation had become the topic of the day. It was discussed in social gatherings; around tables at mealtime; in the fields; in the supermarkets; around churches after mass; in local buses; in trains and in airplanes up in the air.

For those who wanted to believe, yes, Anais was the reincarnation of Marie Joelle.

For those who where not sure, perhaps Anais was Marie Joelle, perhaps she was not. Who knew? Nonetheless, it surely was intriguing.

For those who did not accept such possibility, all this was either a nonsense fabricated by deranged minds or some kind of sham motivated by the devil. But that was the opinion of only a slight few.

Madeleine, Emile and Suzanne were disposed to be convinced that their great grand daughter and granddaughter was not crazy. She new who she was better than anyone else could determine it for her. "And really," they would debate, "if you came to think of it, why couldn't reincarnation be a reality like certain other facts of life? Why couldn't it be as valid as all these theories of religious dogmas scientifically unproven by evidences but assumed to hold a truth upon which entire civilizations have invested an unshakable faith?"

"We human being give many interpretations to God's Divine plans, but at the end it all leads to His many mansions," Father Vernier would answer them.

"Moreover," would deliberate Madeleine, "There exist many truths still impenetrable by our limited human vision."

"Certainly so," Father Vernier would further agree.

Phillippe, even so freshly indoctrinated in the traditions of the Catholic Church, to which he intended to remain rigorously faithful, didn't want to close the door against additional enlightenment into the questions aroused by Anais. While profoundly meditating over the scriptures for spiritual guidance he caught himself secretly praying for forgiveness if he really had abandoned his child. Soon he felt compelled to get deeply involved in the care of children raised in orphanages.

Jean Luc, now happily married to Elise, had been won over by his wife's outlook.

Veronique believed that her Marie Joelle was back. She thought Anais gave enough credible justifications to persuade her of it. In addition, why was it that since Anais's birth she had ceased to receive messages from Marie Joelle? Was it due to pure coincidence? She wished her beloved daughter had returned looking exactly as she did before passing away. She understood though, that changes are to be expected during the life process. Oh, but didn't Anais sound exactly like Marie joelle when she sang the *Pastourelle*?

Frederick vacillated between certainty and doubts while a deep paternal and filial bond developed between him and Anais.

Isabelle thought it gave one a lot to reflect upon. She regretted not having at least one concrete proof to lean on. Just one. Perhaps in time it would be discovered. She trusted her son would not recoil from exploring deeper into the enigma.

It was tempting to conclude that yes indeed, overall Anais had sufficiently demonstrated to be a nearly perfect example of reincarnation. How could it be otherwise? Alas, one had to concede that, not all doubts could be eliminated in order to scientifically confirm such rebirth.

Naturally, Paul was aware of the conjectures surrounding the results of the experiments. On the other hand, how could he succumb to complete disbelief when he listened and looked at his beloved daughter so passionately and convincingly committed to uphold her claims? Indeed, he had fascinating new horizons to explore. He was prepared to admit, "that, after all, the boundaries defined by his understanding were not necessarily the terminus beyond which no other realities could exist." He was now wholly conquered by the desire to investigate thoroughly the phenomenon of past lives recollections, and from there to pursue more captivating inquiries into the yet unknown. Quite an adventure! He might have to hire extra help to toil the farm, for the hours spent in his study would require to be stretched further than previously anticipated.

Clothilde also would need to put aside some time from her busy schedule, to educate herself in view to reach a better understanding concerning her daughter's odyssey.

Elise listened to everyone's comments, simply filled with awe by events she considered a great privilege to witness.

One person who had absolutely no doubts whatsoever about Marie Joelle being reborn, was Anais. As would be expected, she would eventually dedicate her life to investigate thoroughly all aspects of our existence by exploring as far as she could reach into the metaphysical dimensions accessible to human intelligence. She also would give lectures about her own beautiful, exciting experience.

With the crucial contributions of her father and Elise, as well as the support of Father Vernier, her entire family and ultimately Phillippe, Anais-Marie Joelle would in due time open a clinic. There, with Paul she would conduct tireless studies hoping to one day prove with incontestable testimonies that reincarnation can be a reality befitting perfectly all of God's glorious designs.

* This "Pastourelle" is among the SONGS OF THE AUVERGNE sung by Anna Moffo accompanied by The American Symphony Orchestra, in a recording orchestrated by Canteloube.